A MID-LIFE CRISIS THRILLER...

18 MILES FROM TOWN

JASON HENDERSON

CASTLE BRIDGE MEDIA
DENVER, COLORADO, USA

CASTLE BRIDGE MEDIA

Denver, Colorado

Cover Photo by MaxMaximovPhotography/Shutterstock

and Lucie Morel/Unsplash

18 MILES FROM TOWN

© 2021 Jason Henderson

All rights reserved.

ISBN: 978-1-7364726-6-8

Chapter 1

HUGE FLAKES OF SNOW FALL on the sloping back yard of my house in the south of Denver. The tragedy that hangs in the air doesn't reach through the curtain of snow. It has missed me and brought my children around, although they treat my birthday almost like a wake. We play at being merry in way that carries an undercurrent of questioning.

Heat lamps on the covered deck cast a slightly red light over the chairs, making it warm enough that all you really need is a jacket. My daughter Katie sets down a glass of wine in front of me on the stone-tile deck table. She doesn't care for wine and sits back with a Shiner Bock in a wooden chair with big outdoor cushions. Her short ash-blond hair reminds me so much of my late wife that it's as painful as it is wonderful.

Nearby, her older brother Stephen, who has dark hair in a ponytail—something I did myself until I started losing my hair at about thirty—takes a pull on his own Shiner. Stephen wears slacks and a leather jacket, meaning he either was working on Saturday before dinner or he's going somewhere.

"Why are you dressed up? It's not for my birthday."

"I have another party," he says. "Downtown."

"It's like nine o'clock already," I say. For me it's the end of the evening; at fifty I can't imagine going back out after nine.

My daughter rolls her eyes and Stephen does too. I feel sluggish—my birthday dinner, at a zany Mexican place that has been around since I was a child, has left me full and content. But of course they'd be going out. Each of them has a home to get to, which will leave the house quiet. The exact moment of new quietness always hits me harder than I like to admit, and for a split second I anticipate and dread it.

"Anyway, *I* thought they were great," Katie says. "Everybody I knew watched *Fearless,* but I was the only one whose dad wrote the books."

"I have news for you, I don't think anyone remembers there even were *Fearless* books."

"Wait, hang on." Stephen turns to his sister. "Are they still in your room?" When Katie shrugs, he sets down his bottle of beer and disappears from the deck. I look out down the slope at the back fence as the patio door slides open and closed. The wish for a cigarette slips across the back of my mind like a ghost.

The patio door slides again, and Stephen returns with a small stack of paperback books. My children lean close together, reading the titles and showing them to me.

For a moment they look like their former selves, twelve and ten or even ten and eight. Which sounds about right for when I wrote those books.

Fearless Goes to New Orleans by Max Ortega.

I chuckle despite myself.

"*Fearless*, see," I explain, as though they haven't heard this before. "They wanted the title of the show in the story even if it didn't make sense. Because a show doesn't actually *go* anywhere. But I wasn't alone—they really did have books like *Happy Days Goes to Japan*."

That world is long dead, I realize. Not long ago, drugstores and grocery stores were stuffed full of briskly-selling paperbacks. A lot of them were tie-ins—books that use or *tie in* to the world and characters of a famous brand—which I often wrote. You also had the best-sellers and countless niche books; your westerns and fantasies and die-cut horror books. And everyone bought books when they were out and about, because at night, it was *the only thing anyone had to do.* Because after the prime-time television shows went off, people were bored by the cheap programming that followed. Maybe they stuck around for the Tonight Show. And then United States Air Force jets flew in a strange, forgotten public service announcement that played the national anthem. And then: no more TV. At which point, rich and poor, black and white, people *read books*. And if they liked TV, why, there were always books about the Fonz or the wild and wooly surgeons of *MASH*. Or in the 90s, about *Fearless*.

"Why did they call you *Max Ortega,* anyway?" Katie asks, turning another of the paperbacks towards me. It says *A Fearless Halloween*. By Max Ortega, of course.

I sip my wine and look out through the curtain of snow as it falls gently, catching the light. "I don't know," I mumble.

But of course I know.

First off, the publisher *wanted* me to use a pen name. Nothing wrong with "Michael Dotson" per se, but I didn't own *Fearless*—White Pinnacle Pictures did. If a famous writer were doing a tie-in book, maybe the owners would want that guy's name on it, but in the 90s I was an unknown. Having me write under a pen name that they owned—and in this case, Max Ortega was all theirs—would allow them to fire me and have someone else take over the books under the Max name if needed.

Second, *I* wanted a pen name. I was going to write more books, Michael Dotson books.

I had a good time with them, though. I wrote each one in six weeks, and lived a sort of *bon-vivant* author's life. I even visited the kids' schools a couple of times to talk about book writing.

And then… I really can't remember. I remember proposing a few books along the way, plots that I barely recall at all now. One proposal after another. Eventually my agent got bored of getting rejected for me and by then I was working at Verizon in product management. And the kids were growing, and one thing led to another, and I wasn't writing books anymore, not even stuff like the *Fearless* books. After a while it became one of those things I would haul out at parties for a laugh.

Right now I take the books from Katie as she sits back, lost in her own thoughts. I look at the paperbacks, flip through them. Words flying past, whole sentences floating towards me, from moment to moment—sometimes I get the slightest inkling of my own voice. I can even remember coming up with certain phrases.

My wife, rest her soul, never read the *Fearless* Books. That sounds harsh to admit, like I'm saying she didn't like my writing, but I think she found them painful. Here was a kind of book that there was no reason for us to have in the house. Why would a couple of adults need a bunch of slim paperbacks about a globe-trotting, adventurer high school student? The fact that I had written them didn't really matter.

But the truth is, a book is a book. Whether you're rewriting *The Castle of Otranto* in the world of stock car racing, or writing about the romantic adventures of teenagers, a book in the end is words on paper: it'll have a beginning and a middle and an end. It'll have a protagonist and antagonist and usually a contagonist getting in the way and making things difficult for the hero.

Looking back, I can think of half a dozen, maybe even a full dozen books that I wrote proposals for. There were beginnings and middles and ends in an outline, and two or three sample chapters to show what the book would be like. At least a dozen stories begun, and none of them finished. It is so easy to give up.

That's what people don't tell you: it's surprisingly simple to just stop worrying about your dreams. To justify to yourself that watching reruns of *Wings* is a plenty good way to spend your evening. But I know that's too harsh as well. Once you have kids, your life moves *you,* the way a few inches of water in a flooded road can start to move a truck, in the opposite direction of your dreams. So you spend time at work meetings and school meetings and church services, in choir rehearsals and performances. And why shouldn't you? And the only one to speak for your dreams is you, and eventually even you float away from them.

My daughter re-orders the books in her hand and looks up, her gray eyes twinkling. "So who owns these things?"

"I suppose that White Pinnacle Studios does," I say, "just like they own the Max Ortega name."

She takes a sip of her beer and looks out at the snow. "You know, you could write another one, couldn't you?"

"You mean like fanfic?" *Fanfic* or *fanfiction* is this thing where fans of a particular series or a set of characters will create new stories—by just writing them, no permission or anything. They usually post these stories online for other people to read, not for money. Typically the *not for money* part is what keeps them from getting sued. I have read some and a lot of them are well done, and it is not lost on me that what I used to do for money was essentially fanfic.

"I guess," she says. "But couldn't you just write more of them and change the names of the characters? I mean how original an idea is a story about a set of teenagers in high school?"

I shift in my seat uncomfortably, like I'm being put on the spot. "Where'd you get this idea that I want to write a new *Fearless* book?"

"Well," she says. "Is there something that you *do* want to write?"

I think about this. Words filling a page. It doesn't seem as impossible as it did just a week ago. "I actually don't know," I say. "I haven't thought about trying to create something new in a long time."

My son smooths his pants leg. His every movement is so professional that sometimes I ask, how can this be the same creature who tore through this house for all those years? It's a genuine wonder. "How long do you have, Dad?"

Then he looks like he said something wrong, and for a moment he is a child again, covering. "I mean, how long until you have to be back?" I know what he's thinking. And I am not dying, but there has been enough death.

"Gotcha," I say. "Three weeks. They should have the headquarters ready again in three weeks, and I'm expected to be back then."

He shakes his head, his eyes glistening. "That's incredibly lucky. When you think about it."

"Yeah," Katie agrees. "You have a chance to do whatever you want."

Lucky.

When you think about it.

I guess I am. But there's no way any of us should be saying that out loud. What happened was anything but.

Chapter 2

YOU COULD DIVIDE EVERYONE IN the company into the people who never looked at the pictures, the people who looked, and the people who said that they would never look but did.

For years I held—and still hold—a unique position at Blaze Satellite Television. I started out as a product manager, but over the years sort of morphed into a general-purpose unlicensed lawyer. I had a law degree and a license, although my license was not current to Colorado, the state where Blaze was located. This allowed the company to use me as a lawyer, but also as a kind of businessperson.

This was a strangely useful trick. When Blaze had a meeting where it would be useful to have someone trained in contracts and law, but where both sides had promised to have only businesspeople and no lawyers present, I could be there. I could switch on the lawyer part of my mind, but we could say, *there are no lawyers here*, because I didn't count. And then when the meeting was over, they would ask me the law questions.

The job suited me just fine.

In June of last year, a woman who worked at the company started a very interesting blog. I call it a *blog*, but actually it was an Instagram feed, really just a series of images with captions on it. As a newly old person, these distinctions don't interest me. The blog was anonymous, and it was delicious and salacious.

The unknown woman used the blog at first to post shadowy images that no one could identify. Actually I had no way of even knowing a *woman* was posting, except that they had a lyrical way about the captions that somehow read as female.

They didn't show anything particularly racy.

Image:

A door frame, a window, a belt hanging on a doorknob, a pair of shoes by a bed.

The captions were full of an almost 1950s-level guilt and *badness*. At the company, slowly but surely, it became clear that the person was writing about their own guilt for sleeping with a married man. We *knew* it was someone at the company, because the poster occasionally showed images of recognizable spots in the headquarters, of hallways, the atrium, certain corners or desks.

The HQ of Blaze Satellite houses nearly three thousand people, and when something exciting gets in its system, all of the bodies and brains in a campus of two large, four-story buildings granite and glass will catch an idea, fixate, and breathe their new obsession in unison.

Caption:

When you hang up the phone with her, I get a tangle of guilt that sizzles, and the hair stands up on the back of my neck, and I can't stand it and I want more.

In all of the time that I've been at the company—roughly fifteen years, having come here because I wanted to leave Texas for somewhere with mountains—I have never seen anything capture the imagination of our headquarters the way this one Instagram feed did. It became a favorite game to try to guess *who was this woman who was writing these confessions?*

And who was her paramour?

The first question was the only important one for a long time. A month of posts. Sometimes she showed her own feet, usually in oddly old-fashioned short socks, on a hotel room carpet.

Guilt, bedposts, all strangely chaste and strangely scintillating. It was like someone in our midst had invented a weird new kind of porn with no porn in it, and everyone wanted to know whose guilt was driving it.

But after the first month, the second question became a central focus for everyone who looked, because the poster—*she*—started making little comments that indicated that the wife *also* worked in the company.

Caption:

I went by her desk today and I love that she has no clue.

That really began to whittle it down. It was like the writer—Short Socks, I called her—was begging to be revealed, playing a dangerous game with people's lives.

Image:

A shot of a woman's thigh as she lies on a hotel room bed—framed perfectly so that all that is visible is a strip of flesh, and past it, a large window looking out the mountains. A self-portrait.

As I said, none of this would count as pornography even in the 1920s. Yet the halls of Blaze Satellite crackled with a gossipy, electric charge of curiosity and eroticism.

Safe to say no one outside Blaze read the blog, and inside, you could not escape it. As I walked through the cafeteria at breakfast and lunch, I heard it on people's lips and saw snatches of it on people's phones. *Who, who, who.*

But after that first month and a few days, I figured out who the guy was, because I knew him.

This was not Hercule Poirot-level work. There were only about five couples in the company, and one of them was made up of Glenn Latour and his wife. Glenn was a director in product management, a little older than me, fitter, better clothes, overall a similar-slightly-better life. Better at playing the corporate game—I had spent the first decade in TV still trying to launch a writing career, which carved vast chunks out of my ability to advance. So on the third floor where we worked, I occupied a large cube, while Glenn had an office that looked out on the atrium.

At first, I didn't think it was Glenn. His wife Renee worked upstairs in Business Development, and they were considered a power couple. Holding hands, joking. Mirthful, even. I hadn't seen them treat one another with anything but respect, and I had never seen Glenn flirting with anyone else.

So there was no reason to assume the paramour to be Glenn. And if Glenn were having an affair—and I have to admit, I had no idea where a director, who had to come into HQ even on Saturdays, would find the time—

it would not be obvious who it would be with. Glenn had plenty of people reporting directly to him, both male and female, many of them young, but the truth was there was nothing in the photographs or the commentary to suggest that the poster was young at all.

In fact it struck me as damn unlikely they were young. I have two kids in their twenties, and while they have grown up in a world where guilt about sex is not prized; they have a generational loathing of cheating. Their generation loves frankness, honesty. This Instagram poster's toxic brew of fear and guilt and her clear desire to get caught didn't strike me as a particularly youthful expression, it seemed more the product of someone my own age, in their 40s or 50s. And a tiny glimpse of thigh didn't give away age. Neither did the short socks.

But I began to suspect Glenn at lunch one day. We were picking at overpriced salads and I brought up the feed on my phone. I'm not above gossip, and I was one of the ones who looked. Not that I had anyone else to gossip with—aside from a few of us lifers, Blaze is a forever-young company. I tipped my phone towards him.

Image:

A man's wedding band on the granite counter of a hotel bathroom.

Caption:

She has no fucking clue how many times I have held this ring in my mouth.

Glenn looked ill. "I don't ever look at that," he said. And changed the subject. Like I'd pulled out a Penthouse at a minister's house.

And that was when I knew. But I didn't pursue it, because honestly, why would I? I don't give advice unless someone asks for it.

I don't know if Short Socks made the mistake that she made on purpose or if she finally just got careless, but she did make a mistake. On the 18th of January, she posted the following caption:

I am addicted to the fear in your voice when I stick my hand down your pants and you tell me it's time for your 8:30 round-up.

Was I looking at Instagram that morning? Absolutely I was, because by this point everybody in the building was following these posts like they were Ernie Pyle giving us the latest on the Battle of the Bulge.

11

This time the image was a repeat, a man's shoes with the cuffs of his pants slightly wrinkled, as though the pants were being lowered. You have to admit that Short Socks had a flair.

Your 8:30 round-up.

I read that in my cubicle and nearby heard Glenn audibly gasp in his office. I heard Glenn moving, and he appeared from his office, visible above the walls of my cube. He glanced my way for a moment, ashen. He walked briskly towards the exit to the hallway outside our section, which runs around the Atrium.

I got up from my cubicle and went over to the window, and after a moment I saw Glenn emerge from the front of the building. He always parked his car close to the front, and I saw him reach the car, pacing around it for a moment. Then he got in and drove away.

Stories about the fact that it was Glenn shot through the corporate body instantly. Because there was only one meeting called the 8:30 roundup, and in it were Glenn, a number of other directors, and Glenn's wife, Renee.

A few minutes after Glenn left, Renee did too, in her own car, which she always parked near to Glenn's.

I texted Glenn about an hour and a half later a message that was so short that it could be interpreted as either playing dumb or playing smart.

YOU DOING OKAY?

I didn't see Glenn again until he returned the following day with the gun.

Chapter 3

THE EVENING AFTER GLENN STORMED out, I was on my back porch, enjoying the warm lamps and the snow, which was beginning to fill the hill all the way to the back fence. Glenn texted me as I held my mug of coffee in one hand and my phone in the other, scrolling through the political articles on Slate.

I ONLY POSTED THAT BECAUSE OF WHAT THEY WERE SAYING BUT ANYWAY IT'S TRUE.

I set down my coffee and rolled my eyes. My first thought was of the absurdity that Glenn, a fifty-four-year-old man, was apparently not just posting something emotional on social media, but already texting me in apologia.

I had no idea what he was talking about.

By *posting* he had to mean Facebook, where us oldsters hang out. I opened up the Facebook app on my phone and went to Glenn's page. There was one post at the top, a pic of the inside of his car, looking out at his driveway.

SOME PEOPLE DON'T KNOW WHAT THEY'RE ASKING FOR.

I looked at the phone and grimaced. Even then, after a nasty day that tore at people's lives, my first thought was: *Isn't that a little dramatic?*

No. Remember to be a friend.

When my wife died ten years ago, Glenn showed me the way to do that. It's not easy for men to communicate, not men my age. But he would ask how I was. He would put his hand on my shoulder. In a time when I didn't want to, he encouraged me to express myself.

His wife did, too. Renee and Glenn invited me into their home many times, and I even accepted on occasion, though I never quite felt comfortable there.

For one thing, I felt so exposed. Like every sentence from my hosts had an unspoken addendum, here, try this cognac especially now that you lost your wife; this raspberry vinaigrette is wonderful, try it, now that your wife has left you to mourn.

You look unfeeling when you don't respond. But it wasn't that I was unfeeling. I was feeling *everything*. And it would all run through my head, and every sentence would include the question they asked, *how is work going,* and the unspoken addendum *now that she's passed.* Then I was playing through the answers and thinking of how I wasn't the one who was dead, that I was lucky and hadn't *had* to deal with a painful cancer, that I felt so much worse for my son and daughter, both in college. That they were being too nice, that their home was nice, and they were missing the lovely evening they would have without me. And after all those thoughts jumbled through, I wouldn't respond at all. Because by then they'd be on to a new question.

But friends, they get it.

U OKAY? I texted.

Glenn responded with screenshots. Without commentary, just screenshots.

A text from Renee.

THIS IS THE LAST TIME YOU EMBARRASS ME. YOU'RE FINISHED.

And on Instagram. Comment. After comment.

Pig.

You can sue him, Maeve. I would sue him. This from one of the friends of the Instagram Poster.

So, Maeve is Short Socks' name, I thought. I remembered a Maeve in HR. Not older, like I thought. Maeve was in her twenties, and I guess a rather dramatic old soul.

That was where my mind was, at this point it all seemed like a kerfuffle, a horrible drama, but—and this gets me every time—it's not *cancer.* But it was blowing up.

I DON'T GET IT, I texted. WHAT HAPPENED???

I watched the little dots fill in as Glenn thought of an answer, then die. Then fill in, then die.

I set the phone down on the railing and lit a cigar that I had brought out and had been putting off lighting. Puffed.

The phone rang. It was Glenn.

"Hello?"

"What happened… is that I broke up with her." On the other end, Glenn's voice sounded dull. Like he was having to force the words out, the way a kid does when nothing has gone their way, and everything has turned against them. Everyone in that word-dredging mode sounded like a surly nine-year-old, but I know of no one who hasn't sounded that way from time to time.

As he talked, I looked across the deck at the sparkling night sky and the mountains distant in the night. I could see tiny car lights traveling through the mountain passes. People getting a jump on the weekend, off to ski. I came out here to Colorado just for this. I wondered where Glenn was. But that wasn't the first thing I wanted to ask.

"I don't understand any of this," I slurred around the cigar. "I knew that she was writing that Instagram, but—I don't get it, were you already broken up?"

"Did you know it was about me?" He sounded weary rather than angry.

"I mean… I thought it might be," I said. I put the cigar in the ashtray in front of me. "But it was just a guess… to be honest I don't think anybody else thought it was you."

Glenn took a moment to respond, and then he started again in a distant sort of drone. "You showed it to me once. I found out about that Instagram when I heard some people talking about it during the Consumer Comments meeting."

Consumer Comments was a weekly meeting that ostensibly had been created to go over consumer-posted reviews for Blaze Satellite that had been put up over the course of the week. But in fact, it was really a gossip-fest for a bunch of mostly-twenty-something employees to get together and talk about whatever was going on in marketing, and whatever was going on in the company. I had been to a couple of meetings and it didn't surprise me that the talk would turn to the mysterious Instagram poster. I remembered now that Maeve had been in some of those.

I shifted in my seat, pulling my jacket a little bit closer. Glenn had stopped talking, so I prompted him along, thinking of the note from his wife. "So… so you find out about the Instagram feed, and what happens?"

"Understand at first I wasn't even sure it was about me. It was so vague, you know? But it made me sick. Like, when you showed it to me, it made me sick."

"I remember," I say.

"And I caught up with her in the break room on five."

"Maeve."

"Yeah."

We let the name lay there for a moment and then he continues. "I asked her what it was all about. You know. Because I suspected. And she didn't even hide it. She said that she was just having fun with it and that nobody could tell who it was."

I could picture this conversation in my head, as she smiles and maybe even plays with his collar.

"But, come on, you read that thing," Glenn said.

I knew what he meant. It had been carefully written so that anybody reading it couldn't help but want to start to put the clues together. Then Glenn said what I had been thinking. "It was like she wanted to get caught."

"So…"

"Yeah, so," Glenn said, sounding exasperated, like he couldn't believe how things had worked out, "I told her this was getting to be too much. And that maybe it wasn't such a good idea anymore. I mean, come on, Renee has been pretty good, you know? And I don't know, I began to feel..." He stopped, looking for a word, and then finally dredged the word up. "Ashamed."

Then he added thickly, "It doesn't matter anymore."

"Where are you?" I was thinking I knew how this would go. I was going to have a roommate.

"It doesn't matter," he said again.

The line went dead, and I stared at my phone for a moment before hitting the green button to call him back. But it went to voicemail and the second time that I tried a few minutes later, it said: *We are sorry, but this voice mailbox is full.*

•   •   •

The next morning I headed to the office early, because although it had not snowed in several days, there was still ice on the roads. You have to leave early when there's ice, downshift at every intersection, take it slow and be responsible. Downshift because brakes don't really work. Every time I come to an intersection I think about teaching Katie and Stephen how to drive. How to get there by taking it easy.

Blaze Satellite is a strange place to work in winter, because while most companies have rules in place that say that on days when it snows, maybe you can come in later, or maybe you can work from home, the rule at Blaze has been the opposite for decades. On days when it's snowy or icy, even at the headquarters, you're expected to be in early and be through the security door with your badge on time. Even a minute late will trigger an email from HR, and you will have to explain yourself.

It's a holdover from the 1980s, when the largest number of Blaze employees were field reps who needed to be in service trucks and out on the roads, fixing damaged satellite dishes and other equipment. And sometime a long time ago, the chairman decided that everybody in the headquarters— desk jockeys and lawyers—needed to be under the same strict rules as those guys who had to risk their lives in the trucks. A completely fair system in a way, but it meant that on days with ice, those of us who had managed to be there for years knew to leave early and get there on time.

On time meant nine am, so I was out early and through the turnstiles of the main HQ Security entrance at 8:45. I climbed up three stories and was at my cubicle by five to nine. It wasn't until I sat and turned on my computer that I glanced over the top of my cube at Glenn's office and saw that it was still dark.

I heard some of the younger employees in the cubicle farm whispering to one another.

I heard that she kicked him out.

17

I heard that he's fired.

I wondered if any of that was true, whether Renee in fact had already kicked Glenn out. It was completely plausible, or at least plausible that she might have told him to go stay somewhere else, reminding me that he had not answered when I asked him where he was.

Probably he would have gotten a hotel. Maybe he was looking at a much longer commute, though, because I knew Glenn and Renee had another house in the mountains. But that wasn't likely, because he would have had to go out there and then drive a couple of hours back.

I texted Glenn again:

CHECKING IN, YOU DOING BETTER?

Kicked out, plausible. But *fired,* that I couldn't see. It just didn't seem likely that the company would fire somebody overnight for what seemed like a completely personal and rather stupid fuckup and a lot of drama.

My cubicle was located towards the end of the cubicle farm on the third floor, one or two cubes away from an enormous glass wall that looked out on the parking lot. For a moment I was tempted to get up and go look outside and see if I could spot Glen's car to see if he had made it in already, and just hadn't made it up to his office. But I didn't, because as with everything, it really wasn't any of my business.

My phone buzzed. It was a text from Glenn.

HIDE.

Then I *did* get up and go look out.

That should have made me panic all in itself, and yet I consistently pushed danger signals to the edges of my mind. It was the kind of dissociation we all learned to practice, so that we all wound up as adults who could see a gorilla walk across a basketball court and ignore it, render it invisible. I crept to the window with something more like curiosity.

Glenn's car wasn't in the parking lot, but it *was* here. It was parked illegally along the curb in front of the large walk towards the entrance. Glenn's hazard lights were flashing, and then I put the whole story together in my head.

I went back to my cube.

He didn't intend to be here long. So it was true, Glenn was fired, and he was going to go in and maybe sign a paper or maybe just get some things and turn around and drive away.

All these thoughts because I was in denial.

Hide?

I had a vision of my wife, snapping her fingers at me from across the breakfast table, *get your head in the game.*

Glenn's office was still dark. People were chattering up and down the third floor about the weather and about the stupid corporate rules, and a few of them about the ballad of Glenn and Renee.

In the distance I heard couple of flat *pops* like balloons popping in the distance, like someone slapping a chalkboard.

It almost didn't register at all. And then from somewhere out in the atrium of the building, I heard someone scream.

My hand was on my mouse, and I actually still clicked the little icon to open up my web browser. Like a normal day. We fight for that normal day. My brain brought the scream forward as I heard two more: *pop pop.*

Gasps echoed up and down the cubicle farm and I stood up, just like everybody else up and down the rows. A whole collection of heads stuck up out of their cubes. In that instant it reminded me of an old cartoon, maybe a *Dilbert* cartoon, likening all of us to groundhogs sticking their heads out of holes. I heard somebody yell *Shit!*

An alarm began to sound, the fire alarm, a slow, long, klaxon with a pre-recorded voice extremely loud, THERE IS A FIRE IN THE BUILDING PLEASE MAKE YOUR WAY TO AN EXIT.

A fire alarm. Since time immemorial, the fire alarm is the warning of choice for whatever pandemonium God has wrought, from terrorist attacks to vengeful husbands.

But in the background, I heard the *pop pop* and I was nowhere near an exit and that was no fire. I was at the end of a cubicle farm next to enormous glass wall. The only way out was to go down the row of cubicles and to the atrium, the nexus of countless stairways and halls leading to the other floors. People began to scream.

They tell us—because we have a half-hour training about this—to do three things in the case of an active shooter. The first is to try to escape. That was a phenomenon discovered years ago that most people who get hurt in an emergency do so because they freeze. Freezing is the one thing not to do. You need to move and escape.

In an active shooter situation, if you can't escape, the next thing is to hide.

There's one more. If hiding doesn't work, you have to fight.

Glenn had put on his hazard lights, entered the building, and somewhere in there, texted me to advise me to hide.

Pop pop.

Chapter 4

I BECAME AWARE OF MY own skin. Fire ran in rivulets from my fingertips to my shoulders. The feel of hot coals at the small of my back. My teeth hot and stinging, my skin loose and prickly.

Pop, pop.

I heard the sound again, and I turned around, away from all the heads that had popped up in the cubicle farm and ran. With no thought at all, I ran straight for the glass window behind my cubicle. I'd had this cubicle for years, a sort of accidental, eventual reward for sticking around. I had a decent view of the parking lot. The way to escape—and no escape at all. It was very far from any kind of entrance. I thought briefly of using something to bust the glass and jump three stories to the snow below. But Bruce Willis I am not. For one this, there was nothing with which to break the glass—I doubted an office chair would do it. And with my luck I would miss the snow and land on a sidewalk. I willed myself to forget the window.

I turned around and looked down the cubicle farm and saw people literally moving in every direction. Amber Mikkelson, one of the millennials, a woman with shoulder length, brown hair, was running into one of the little offices that ran aside the cubicle farm. I snapped at her with my fingers, hissing, "Amber, Amber, Amber." She spun around inside the office.

Just then, I was aware that it was in fact Glenn's office that she had run into. I called, "What are you doing?"

"I'm hiding."

"You need to get out of here." Because of the training module. The first thing that you should do is run, but she had jumped past that to the second thing, hiding. Overachievers, always skipping lessons. She was spinning in place inside Glenn's little office, wringing her hands.

On the other side of her was a glass window that looked out onto a walkway and the atrium. I was aware of screaming sounds coming from the atrium, people running towards the security desk in the front of the building. And off toward the big staircases, more *pops*, meaning that Glenn was somewhere towards the back of the building, at the system of staircases that ran up and down the building.

I pictured him, wandering amidst a pair of majestic fountains, with something in his hand that went *pop*.

I said to Amber, sounding like a dad, "Come on, we got to *go, go, go, go*."

Amber pressed her hand against her face and then ran out of Glenn's office and along the cubicle farm. I lost sight of her as she left and disappeared out to the walkways.

I followed, running along the cubicle farm until I bunched up with ten or so other workers, and we poured out of our section and into the walkway along the third floor of the atrium.

As I banged against somebody else, a large young man moving through a doorway, I thought of Tweedledum and Tweedledee: *after you, no no, after you,* and I was suddenly struck by how seldom you physically touch anybody that you work with.

I was alone for a moment on the walkway and looking down on the atrium, awash in shiny dark brick and plants. And people, running from the back towards the security desks at the front. I could even hear the burbling of the fountains somewhere amidst the screams.

Quickest way to the exit was left, towards the staircase just a few floors above the security desk. I have no memory of running, but I was, pushing through into the stairwell, suddenly alone as I made my way down.

After a moment I found myself in the bottom of the stairwell, next to a metal door with a panic bar. And I knew that opening it up would take me into the atrium right in front of the security desk, right by the turnstiles that I had just come through a few hours before. I pictured it all in my head. *Step out, turn to your left, walk through the turnstiles, and then run for the glass doors. Out to the parking lot, wave at Glenn's illegally parked car, and away.*

As I put my hand on the metal of the door, I heard shouting—countless voices right outside the stairwell door. I didn't look out, but I could hear. The turnstiles were backed up with people.

I instantly shook with revulsion. I could see myself getting into that crowd, pushing forward towards the turnstiles. And just then it would happen.

The gunman—Glenn, it's Glenn—would find us, riddle the whole crowd with bullets as we pressed together. Just as I was thinking how rarely we touched one another, we would be pressed back against one another, bleeding against one another, and we would die and suffocate. We would fall into a heap against the turnstiles.

Just about a door and twelve feet from the turnstiles, I made up my mind to go in a different direction.

The cafeteria.

The cafeteria where Glenn pretended not to have looked at the Instagram was on the other side of an elevator bay at the far end of the atrium—in a connector between the two large buildings of the headquarters. If you went through the cafeteria, when you came out the other side, you would be at another huge, tiled entrance with another set of turnstiles and another security desk. Getting there would mean passing the fountains where last I'd heard the *pop pops*. If he was still there. But it was a better way out.

I ran back up the stairs to the second floor and burst out into the walkway, not sprinting but jogging, because my sprinting days are long over.

Office and meeting room doors zipped past my vision and I tripped, thinking madly that I'd stumbled over a person. But as I looked down, I saw that somebody had taken off their shoes. Instantly I thought of a woman running in pantyhose, though of course, I'm not even sure if people wear pantyhose anymore.

Within a few more yards, I did have to jump over somebody who was dead.

His khakis were soaked in blood and I couldn't bear to look.

Pop, pop, pop.

This time the shots were coming from the offices on the other side of the

23

atrium. It was impossible to tell which floor. He could be on this floor, could come out to the walkway across the atrium and pick me off like a tin turkey at a carnival.

I reached the end of the walkway at the main atrium staircase.

This wasn't good. It wasn't an enclosed stairwell like the one by security, but a wide, open, brick showpiece of a staircase that departments took Christmas card pictures on. Stepping onto it, bounding down, I was exposed. If the gunman—Glenn, it's Glenn—were standing anywhere in the atrium, he would be able to shoot me. Exposure was an icy wind trying to freeze me—*just keep moving, just keep moving.*

I reached the bottom floor and tripped over a young man whose head squished like a melon under my shoe and I sprawled out over the floor of the elevator bay.

My whole body shaking, I found my feet, my fingers oily with blood, and I ran screaming. Past a set of Coke machines and candy machines and paper towel dispensers. And then I was in the cafeteria.

The cafeteria ran longways north and south between the buildings, with an enormous, long glass wall on the West side, where I could see the mountains, with sandwich shops and candy dispensers and pizza makers on the left, the East side. I saw three people dead at one lunch table, printed-out PowerPoint presentations strewn over their bodies and seeping blood. I kept running straight through the cafeteria even though directly to my right in the enormous glass wall was a security door that would open up to the outside, out to an enormous snowy field. I looked at it and for some reason did not run through it.

There was no gunman or even a frightening dead person lying in front of that door. There was nothing preventing me from using the door, but I ran past it, nonetheless.

The truth is the company discouraged us from using it because employees were required to badge in and badge out of the building to show how many hours we had spent in the office. And if we didn't spend enough, human resources would send us angry emails.

And so over time it was as though that door did not exist. It was only later that I thought about how I could have simply gone out that door.

Instead, I ran the length of the cafeteria until I reached the hallway at the end. My mind was fixed on the other building's security desk.

Past more bodies. Screams. I didn't hear pops anymore, but I knew Glenn must have reached the turnstiles I had avoided and would be laying waste.

All because some people don't know what they're asking for.

I didn't stop until I was at another panic bar, another door, and on the other side, another set of turnstiles and security desk, another exit.

I froze at the panic bar. The stairwell I stood in was quiet and safe. And that was one of the times when I most felt fooled by my own emotions because I *felt safe*. I just stood there with my hands on the metal of the door, feeling the coolness against my fingertips.

Somewhere deep in my mind, consciousness was clawing its way out. *Not safe*.

I pushed the panic bar and opened up the door.

I saw the turnstiles and the security desk. The security guard was slumped over his desk. In front of me was Amber, standing in front of the turnstile, just at the corner of the security desk, with her hands raised. Frozen, Amber had a look of stunned horror on her face.

I thought, why didn't you go through the turnstile?

I followed her eyes. I turned right and saw Glenn standing just about a yard and a half away from me. And he was pointing his gun at Amber. It was a long gun of the kind that I've never used, but that I've seen on TV a lot. Every gun I have ever used was boring, the kind you have behind a farm door, a boring kitchen blender of a gun for shooting snakes and scaring coyotes. This thing was like a Transformer. It had a large magazine, so that he could fit in a lot of extra bullets. I've never really cared one way or the other about guns very much. These guns always looked pretty exciting to me, but not enough that I was willing to spend about a thousand dollars on one. The kind I knew from my grandparents' farm, the kitchen blender kind, cost about a hundred and fifty bucks.

I jerked backed, slamming my shoulder against the wall next to the door that I had just come in. And Glenn glanced at me.

In the movies, people always say something really smart. I've always winced at all of that, when they use phrases *like give me the gun, Harry*, or *put the gun down, Reggie, it's not worth it.*

Reggie, give me the gun. TJ Hooker puts out his hand and tells the person in a psychotic break that they should just give TJ the gun. After which he'll be taken into custody to get "the help he needs."

I didn't say any of those things.

What was the help Glenn needed? *I* had no idea. This is the reality; never in my wildest dreams did I imagine that Glenn would come back to the office with a gun. And when he did, I was not at all prepared to deal with it.

It was as though what was happening to me was happening to someone else, some writer in a *Vox* article, and I was just clicking through, observing. Like the guy in *The Man in the Gray Flannel Suit* said*: it will be interesting to see what happens.* Except that the guy in that book was talking about the risk of jumping out of an airplane. And I had taken that attitude with my entire life.

Finally, I said: *"Don't."*

He pulled the trigger on the terrible weapon. Amber's collarbone bloomed with a geyser of blood flying all around her as she whipped back. Her body jerked and blood splattered, and panic took me over once again.

It didn't matter if it was Glenn or anybody else. I ran, not because it was what they said in the training module, but because I was terrified. I ran straight through the turnstile and out the front exit.

As I got out onto the front walk, I was struck by the flickering of police lights and police officers running towards the entrance. I heard shooting. I didn't even stop running but kept on through the parking lot and towards a parking garage in the distance, until I found myself standing in the dark, in the cool of the garage.

I learned an hour later that the moment the police had come in, it was over.

At the headquarters of Blaze Satellite Television, Glenn Latour murdered fifteen people before turning the gun on himself.

They closed the offices for three weeks. Three weeks paid leave while they cleaned up the mess. Some people don't know what they're asking for.

Chapter 5

A COUPLE OF DAYS AFTER the post-shooting birthday gathering with my kids, I'm at a bookstore in Littleton, Colorado, not far from the house. Littleton is one of the most famous cities in the state-- mainly for a shooting that took place over twenty years ago. The mass shooting at Columbine High School was a benchmark in our culture. Many people remember Columbine as the *first* school shooting, although of course it wasn't: school shootings go back to the 1800s in this country.

I didn't move to Littleton for any reason involving violence—I moved here because my wife and I wanted to be in Colorado, somewhere close to where we could ski. But we weren't rich, and we needed jobs, so a bedroom community outside Denver was just the thing.

It's strange to visit a bookstore if you're a writer. If you've ever published a book, walking into a bookstore is an odd mixture of joy and sadness— sadness if your writing career isn't where you'd like it to be, but joy because there are books there. Even if you didn't write them. Even today, in this era when the Air Force jets no longer fly and there is no more end-of-the-night for TV. I glory at the fact that somehow, there are still books.

I'm very partial to the used bookstore on Broadway called Fahrenheit's, which is crammed to the gills with old vintage paperbacks. *They* would have copies of my *Fearless* books, and even the three titles in my other series, the one I owned, the *Dream Tasker* books. But today I'm looking for something new. And so I'm going to Barnes and Noble, the big box store. And it's at these big box stores that those emotions most come up, because I love seeing books and I love seeing *new* books, and I will always buy more books than I can ever find time to read.

But at the same time, a writer walking through the bookstore asks, why am I not here? Why are my books not on the shelf? Because I stopped, because watching reruns of Wings seemed just as good?

And as a matter of course, I go over to the media tie-in section where half my books *would* be. Even though I haven't had a book come out in two decades. And I still look for my own name, if only to kick myself that it's not there. Even though I have not tried to *write* a book in at least fifteen years. I wander over to the remainder tables. These were always a favorite of mine. When I was a boy in the early 1980s, my grandfather used to bring me into the B Dalton in the mall near his place in Texas. This was in a time when every mall had at least *two* bookstores, usually, at least in my part of the country: a B Dalton and a Waldenbooks. People were literally so eager to buy books that they could buy them at one entrance, wander across the mall, and buy some more. And of course, I understand that people can read eBooks and buy them from Amazon, but there's definitely something missing. Or maybe I'm just getting old.

I wander through the section on writing and notice Strunk & Wagnall's *Elements of Style,* a very slim book that gives wonderful advice on the basics of writing. The advice is often contradictory and is laughably outdated, but it stays an extremely popular book. I pick it up for a moment, remembering using it myself and remembering recommending it to people who would come into the bookstore that I worked at when I was in law school.

And it hits me just like that.

I have three weeks off work.

I bet I could write a book in that time.

The thought comes to me, not in a thunderclap, but more like a fever that has been threatening to come on. Like something I know that I've been thinking and haven't wanted to think out loud. But now that it's there, a *new* idea comes to me.

An idea that seems dramatic and total and complete, right in the moment that I think it. When I was in college in Dallas, Texas, I took Spring Break and drove to Oklahoma to the farm owned by my grandmother. And I spent the entire week working on what would become my first book. The book that I sold, before I did the tie-in work. The only one of three that ever appeared under the name Mike Dotson. In my mind, I see a montage of myself, pacing around the living room of the ranch house and scrawling ideas on paper. And then sitting down furiously to type it all up on a sort of early portable writing computer, a Brother WP75 Word Processor.

I could do that again. And I know exactly who I need to call first.

I'm standing in front of the books on writing and research and I take out my phone and dial my grandmother.

My grandmother is ninety-three years old, and she answers the phone on the third ring. Her voice is somewhat creaky, but she is eager to talk.

"Hello?"

"Hi grandma," I say.

"What are you up to?" She sounds concerned because I know she's heard about the shooting from my mother in Texas. Behind her, I don't hear any TV on or anything. It's one of those things I'd often find when I would call old people when I was young; I would always hear the TV running in the background. But with my grandmother, there was never any noise. I know she likes to watch TV. But the house is never very loud.

"I'm fine. Stephen and Katie were over for my birthday." We chat for a moment and she tells me about my mom who still is just two towns away, and about my brother and sister who also live nearby. I am the only one who left Texas.

"I wanted to ask you a question," I say, giving some reality to the montage in my mind. "I have three weeks off. And I was thinking of going to the farm to try to get some writing done."

"Get some writing done?" she repeats. It must sound odd. But it's the phrase I've always used, *get writing done*, like even *I'm* not sure how it happens.

"Well, yeah, I have three weeks off." I'm repeating myself. "And I figured if I went to the farm, you know, it would take me about twelve hours to drive there."

"It would be pretty cold," she says. "Middle of February."

29

This has to be true. When I went there on Spring Break in the 90s, it was still freezing. But I tell myself that was a cold March. "Well, I mean, are you planning on using it?"

She seems to think for a minute. "No, I don't think anybody's going to use it for a few weeks. Your brother and I are planning to go. We'll need to go up in a bit just to make sure that everything's okay." She takes another pause. "Of course you can do that. If you're going up—or down as the case may be."

"Down," I agree. It would indeed be down, to get from Denver to the farm, which is about 40 miles south of Tulsa, Oklahoma. I will need to travel east across Kansas. And then down through Oklahoma. As I said, twelve hours if you drive fast.

"Do you still have a key?"

"Yeah," I say. I'm pretty sure that I do, and I hope so because otherwise she'll have to mail the key to me, and I feel a need to move, to do this *now* before the time wastes away and I don't take the chance.

"You'll need to make sure that the water is turned off when you leave," she says emphatically. "And I mean that—when you leave, make sure and turn the water off." She's not talking about leaving a faucet running—she means the water into the house. This is a big deal to her, and it should be, because otherwise the pipes are likely to burst from freezing after I'm gone.

"Okay. I can do that."

"I'll put some instructions together for you," she says. "Your brother does it all the time."

"That sounds great."

"What are you trying to write? You're trying to write another book?"

My grandmother always enjoyed the fact that I wrote books— she put together a shadow box for me when I was in my twenties, with the first books that I had written underneath pictures of myself at the farm. The *Dream Tasker* books, the Mike Dotson books, the first and, as it turned out, the last.

Already my mind is churning with things I will need to get done. I look down at my phone and notice that there's a text waiting for me. And I almost gasp.

The text is from Shane Dornich, who I guess is still my literary agent, but to whom I have not spoken in twenty years.

HEY, GIVE ME A CALL IF YOU GET THE CHANCE. BOOK QUESTION.

Book question?

Decades past my own career expiration date, my heart races, because no writer in the world does not jump at any question with the word *book* in it.

My grandmother is talking to me and I realize that I've stopped paying attention. "Well, when did you want to go?" I hear her ask.

"I guess soon," I say, wandering through the stacks.

What could my *literary agent* want?

I stop by the newspapers because something has caught my eye: MURDER AT BLAZE TV.

There's an article about the shooting—a long one; I've seen a few short items that ran the day of. On the front of the Denver *Post*, right below the headline, is a photograph of me.

I don't remember it being taken. In the photo, I am running like an overweight Olympian, leaping over a curb, as police lights flicker behind me. It names me:

MIKE DOTSON, AUTHOR OF THE *FEARLESS* BOOK SERIES IN THE 1990S, RUNS FOR COVER.

"Uh…." I don't want to mention this photo to her, though I can't help thinking it's a cool shot. I'm also instantly, in my mind, adding the words *and Dream Tasker!* "I think this coming Saturday."

"Well, gosh, I'm sure that's fine. You should give your brother a call because he may have some instructions for you on how to get the place open."

I imagine the farm. The one-hundred-sixty-acre former ranch and soybean farm is eighteen miles from the nearest town. And the ranch house, called that to distinguish it from the old "farmhouse" that now lies in ruin, is in reasonable shape, but there are plenty of creaky problems about it. The farm is a strange hodgepodge of houses, abandoned and not, and old barns and other buildings. The whole place is gnarled with trees and overgrown blackberry bushes that I have personally picked from to make cobbler. And I presume there are cattle, because I know for a fact that other farmers in the area rent my grandmother's pastures, both for growing crops and for grazing cattle.

It's more or less settled with my grandmother. We exchange goodbyes, and she makes me promise again to make sure and not leave the water turned on. One thing I've always loved about my grandmother is she is not much in the way of small talk and doesn't really like to hang on the phone. I tell her I love her. And then I hang up.

The next person I call is my agent.

When I was a kid, the idea of having an agent was the kind of thing that I only read about in books and saw in movies. Those images, more than I dare admit, are what drove me to become a writer. My mother and I watched *Return to Peyton Place* when I was very small, because she was into both the TV show and the movie series. In that film, young novelist Allison stays up all night and orders in Chinese with her editor. And although the important part of the story is that she falls in love with her editor, what really intrigued me was that over the course of an entire evening, she rewrites an entire book. I was hooked at that moment. In fact, ever since, I've always loved any element in a movie where a writer deals with their agent or editor. Of course, nothing in the movies or the books is really like what a relationship with an agent is like, because a real relationship with an agent is a lot like a relationship with your lawyer or your vet.

The phone rings twice, and then my agent picks up. "This is Shane."

"Hey, this is Mike Dotson," I say.

"Hey, buddy!" he practically shouts. We spend a couple of minutes talking, but I don't remember at all what we talk about because it's pure blather. There's really no way to get around the fact that we have not seen fit to speak to one another in two decades.

The last time we spoke, he was so distant that it was like speaking to someone who was suing you, but instead what was happening was a very slow, unspoken semi-firing. It had nothing to do with him and everything to do with me, though it's a story so stupid I can barely stand to remember. A story of a young, dumb writer saying no to an edit on a tie-in book that nobody cared about.

Finally I say, "So... I don't understand, what came up?"

"Craziest thing," he says. "I heard from Bale Books. And they were curious about the *Dream Tasker* series."

I shake my head in amazement. "I'm shocked anybody remembers *Dream Tasker*." The Denver *Post* certainly didn't. They managed to cross-reference my own name with the pseudonym under which I wrote my tie-ins, but my own actual name must have come up dry.

"Well," he says, "I don't know if you heard, but Jerry Bale retired a few months back and they're handing control over to Vicki Mitchell." Jerry Bale was the publisher of Bale Books, which eventually became an imprint of Penguin. I can still remember getting his call on a Saturday afternoon to offer to publish my first book. For him it was just another work call, and for me the thrill was so great I was vibrating out of my sneakers. I can still see the white paint on the cinder blocks of my North Texas University dorm room. I realize now that as thrilled as I felt, I had no idea at the time just how lucky I was to have an editor in my life.

I am shocked that Jerry is retiring only now, thirty years later. And let's be real, I'm a little shocked he's not dead.

As for Jerry Bale's replacement, I know her too. Somewhere in my digital footprint are countless editing notes sent by email to and from Vicki when she was an Associate Editor at Bale. To hear she's being promoted is like hearing my own daughter is—and then I realize I'm in a time warp of memory. I'm thinking of Vicki as in her mid-twenties, but myself as what I am, and so suddenly she's a child.

"Anyway," Shane says, "they're thinking of publishing follow-ups to a number of the series that Jerry championed back when he was running Bale."

"So what are we saying?" I ask. "Do they want a proposal?"

"Yeah. My understanding is they would like to see a proposal and then maybe they would publish the book. And maybe if we played it right, we could get three."

"Three new *Dream Tasker* books? Just like that?"

*I don't sell a book for twenty years. And all of a sudden, you're talking about three? A*t the same time, I'm aware that this is the kind of conversation that when I was a kid, I would fantasize about having. But I've had all of these experiences before, and it's lost some of its specialness for me.

I say, "Well, actually, I'm headed to the farm for about a week. And my whole plan was to work on a book." My heart sinks a little bit inside, because

I'm thinking I wasn't planning on working on something old, I was going to work on something *new*. But the reality is I have no idea what I'm going to work on. My plan was to spend the entire twelve driving hours figuring out what was going to be the Magnum Opus that would fill up my time. I do know exactly *how* I'm going to use the time at the farm. I intend to divide it up into periods: morning, noon, and night, like shifts.

"Why don't you see what you can get together?"

"Absolutely," I say. "It's good to hear from you."

After I hang up, I look at the newspaper and the picture of myself again. And for a moment, I think of carrying it home and showing it later to Stephen and Katie. And then I realize that that's not something that they would enjoy.

Ever since my wife's death, my kids have been very protective of me. And I know enough now about how other people think that I know that they would not appreciate this, even though it is solid proof of two things: that I have survived, and that someone at the paper has bothered to look up the books that I had written.

I put the newspaper back.

Instead I pick up a copy of Stephen King's *On Writing*, a book that at one time I actually used as a text when I taught an undergraduate course in Austin, Texas. I also pick up a thick, cheap collection of public domain ghost stories. Just as I'm checking out at the front, something in my head tells me that I should play a game. Before I leave for my trip, I will flip through the collection and point my finger at any story, a story that will be the genesis for whatever novel I'm going to write.

As I'm carrying the giant Barnes and Noble bag, which is much too big for the books, out to my car, my phone buzzes again. I get into my little Matrix crossover SUV and turn the key, hoping the call won't go to voicemail yet. Just as the Bluetooth speaker connects, I hear my brother.

"Hey," he says. The deep voice fills me with warmth. My little brother, like me, is a giant guy of decidedly gentle disposition. Nicholas is six years younger than I am and lives in Texas, not far from my grandmother. "Grandma says you're going to use the farm."

"Yes, totally," I say.

"You want me to come and get it set up for you?" he asks. I laugh, backing the car out of its spot. It is dead cold. But as often as the case, I find the cold to be invigorating. As he talks, I'm careful looking behind me because I have a dreadful fear of running over things with my SUV.

I realize that I haven't responded to his question. "No no, it's no big deal. I'm planning on maybe getting a book written."

"Okay," he says, as if this didn't answer his question at all. "Well, do you know how to turn on the water?"

I say I could probably do it, but he starts to describe everything about the water again.

"It's really important that you get it turned off, too. And if any of the pipes are busted, you'll probably have to turn it off to begin with."

That does not sound like a fun idea. I think if I get to that ranch house and I don't have running water, I'm not sure how I'll be able to make it a week. I would essentially be camping. But one thing at a time.

"I can send you instructions," he says, "on how to get the house set up and how to get the water turned on."

"Sure, okay," I say.

"Because—"

"Nick, I get it."

"And be sure and get everything locked up."

I tell him that I absolutely will, but if he wants to send me the instructions, I will be sure to use them. When I get home, the sun is still out and there are about three inches of snow in the driveway, and Katie's car is in front.

I drive over the snow and into the garage, and when I get out I immediately grab a snow shovel, because it's always better to sweep a couple of inches out of the way than to wait for it to pile up.

Katie apparently heard me come into the garage because she comes outside after me, picking up an extra shovel along the way.

She talks to me as we shovel. It's heavy work, but I'm careful. And she looks at me sometimes askance as though, even though I'm only fifty, she thinks that I'm liable to have a heart attack shoveling the snow.

As we're shoveling, my phone buzzes again.

I look down at the screen and it says DENVER POST.

I look at Katie and she glances at me as she heaves a shovelful. The driveway is beginning to line with snow, forming miniature cliffs down the length.

"Who is it?" Katie asks.

I shake my head as though it's all just so silly, but the truth is, it's kind of exciting the way the phone is ringing. And instantly, because I am me, I feel guilty that my reaction after mass death is something close to joy because of all the attention.

I step towards the sidewalk, letting my shovel rest. I'm not wearing snow boots, which isn't a problem except that the wind has picked up, and it's cold against my dress socks. Because there is no water in the air, the way the weather feels is completely dependent on the sun and the wind. If the wind blows, you shiver. If the clouds come out, you start to freeze.

"This is Mike," I say, the same way I'd answer if it were anyone but my own family.

I hear a rustle at a desk and a woman clears her throat. I can picture the Denver *Post* headquarters; if I walked half a block west from where I'm standing and turned to look North, I'd be able to see skyscrapers that surround the 19th-century stone building in which the paper sits. Because I am a writer, the first thing I think of when I consider the paper is, *did they ever review anything I wrote?* And to my knowledge, they did not. So in the *Dungeons & Dragons* game that is life, they are neutral.

"Hi Mr. Dotson," responds a youngish, low, female voice. "This is Sally Rohmer at the Denver *Post?* I wondered if you could tell me how you're doing since the shooting."

I admire this question. I admire that she didn't start with, *I was wondering if I could ask you some questions.* Because it would have wasted time during which I might hang up, and it would have given me permission to waste her time with a *no.* I have done a fair amount of freelance journalism between law school and now, and I never plummeted into interviews as well as this young reporter has. Of course I pity her because she's interviewing *random worker at shooting*, but it's a start.

"Doing fine," I say. "A little cold. We're out sweeping the snow." This is an inane answer, but what am I supposed to say?

"You're holding up okay?"

"About as well as can be expected," I say. Now I realize I sound like my own father, who was interviewed on the night he lost a house to a Texas tornado. There is really nothing to say. *Yes, it's a wreck, I guess.* We are both now *men in disasters.*

"So did you know Glenn Latour, the shooter?"

I pause. I could lie here, but really, what would be the point. "Yeah. I knew him. We worked together for about seven years."

As she decides what her next question is, I hold the phone to my face and feel cold wind crack my cheeks. I close my eyes and I am inside the stairwell and Glenn is outside, and he is about to decide whether or not he will shoot me or let me leave. It will not play like much of a choice. Because we are friends, Glenn will just let me go. But it doesn't have to go that way—nothing that day has to play as expected—and the moment in the stairwell aches with terrifying fate.

"Do you blame the company for the security lapses that allowed Mr. Latour to go on his rampage?"

So much in that question: *lapses,* not *any lapses.* And *rampage,* which I guess is right. I know what she'd like to hear—anything dramatic. But I don't have any desire to get a talking to from HR, and I suspect that it wouldn't make much difference. I blame Glenn.

"I haven't really thought about it," I say. "It was just a sad thing. I'm glad to be home." At this my daughter, who is listening, frowns with sympathy.

"Mm." The reporter answers. "What's your plan now?"

"Oh," I say. "I'm taking some time off. I have a farm. I think I'm gonna write a book."

My daughter kind of whipsaws her head like this sounds preposterous, and I turn away from her, looking at the street.

"Yes, you were a novelist in the nineties, is that right?" The reporter says *the nineties* the way I used to say *the sixties.* As though a year can drift far enough downriver that it's not quite real, even though we are touching the river and the river is touching that year. It's still there. But if you don't remember it, that way is dark and magical.

"Yep," I say.

"Well, good luck," she says. And she's gone.

As I listen to the click, I realize how off my game I am. I should have loaded her up with titles, with my website, my twitter handle, my Instagram. But I didn't think of it, and now, as I realize I'm thinking about promotion during a *tragedy* after a *rampage*, I realize I'm lucky I forgot, because I would have sounded like an ass.

When I put my phone away, I turn back towards the house. Katie is leaning on her snow shovel. "You have a farm and you're going to go write a book?"

"I meant grandma's farm," I say.

"Well, yeah," she says. "I don't know how many farms we're supposed to have. But you're really going? In February?"

I tell her it has been the subject of many calls today. For a moment, I think she's going to ask if she can come, and actually that would be okay, but I know in my heart that it would completely change my plan. Because the kind of marathon writing I plan doesn't lend itself to easy suppers and conversation. If I'm going to do it right, to fill the whole three weeks' days with solid work, I'm going to need to be alone.

That's the funniest part. Even though there are multiple rooms in my own house, I'm going to travel twelve hours to be completely alone somewhere else. And I'm going to dedicate myself to this work. I'm going to go and try to write a book in three weeks.

"Maybe it will be terrible," I say. "But I'm going to try and get a whole book done."

Katie scrapes the snow with the shovel, tossing an enormous clump of snow aside. Her response is so perfect it could heal bones. "I absolutely think you should do that."

Chapter 6

ON THE MORNING I LEAVE Littleton, it is freezing with a very light snow. For a moment I contemplate asking my son if I can borrow his larger vehicle, but then I settle on the beat-up old Toyota Matrix crossover SUV.

There's something special about leaving for a long car drive at five or five-thirty in the morning. It's very cold when I start, and I put a hot cup of coffee into the cup holder. I have my phone and it's hooked up to Bluetooth so that I can listen to a couple of books that I've downloaded from the library. And by a couple I mean, a lot of books. I have also bought a pack of cigarettes. Although I've told myself that I'm not going to smoke. Not yet. Probably.

I was married for nearly thirty years, and my wife hated my smoking. And one of the things that has been my greatest shame is that in the decade since she died, I have occasionally gone back to smoking, though I usually limit this to a cigar in the evening. But one thing that is very true is that I've always associated smoking with writing. And so on this trip, I know that it is very likely that when I get to the farm, I will smoke cigarettes. But for the last few days I haven't been smoking and I'm not craving it.

Out onto the freeway and headed east towards Kansas. This is the part of the drive that is going to be the most predictable, because once you're east of Denver, what you will be faced with is essentially an uninterrupted series of fields going on for many, many hours.

I've been going to the farm for as long as I've been alive. When I was a child growing up in North Texas, my grandparents used to take me up there, especially in the summers where I would go for two months or more. And whenever I think of what life was like before, all of the things that take up my time before Twitter and before reading every article on Vox, or seeing what's on the Washington *Post* this morning, just by opening up my phone— when I think of what was *life* before, I think of those summers at the farm. I would go with my grandparents, leaving my parents in Dallas, and we would drive the four or five hours up to the farm. Usually our last stop was in town, Hollow Hill, where I would buy something to read. The comic books (which my grandmother called *funny books)* and paperback novels that I bought would keep me company, laying on the couch at the farm underneath a window AC unit that made constant noise.

The interesting thing was at that time, I could completely *absorb* myself in a book or in the comic. Today for me to do that, to be that absorbed, I have to take my phone and put it on airplane mode. Or I have to put the phone across the room, or lock it up. Or I have to turn on some kind of app that is built to help people turn off the constant entertainment of the outside world. It is nearly impossible to immerse myself the way that I once did. Today I find it difficult to do any one task for more than a minute or two without looking at my phone, and I know I'm not alone. No matter how immersed I am, it's as though there's a tiny alarm clock that says, *it's been three-and-a-half minutes, have you checked out the headlines on Salon?*

But back then, immersion came as a way of life. I could go outside at the farm, stepping down the front steps, sit in the grass and I could watch *ants*. That could take hours if there weren't any chores to do. I could walk about the farm from what we called the ranch house to the farmhouse, which was actually just an older house that was still in use by my great-grandmother until I was in college. I could wander around the various barns, the only thing in my ears the sound of cattle and wind.

These sounds are so familiar to me that I can remember the difference between the sound of wind in a barn full of equipment versus a barn that is empty. I can hear the whip of the wind, and I know what part of the farm I am in. I am driving now, newly fifty years old, and I'm hoping that by putting myself back in that sound of wind, that somehow, I will be able to write a novel.

Other people might complain about having to drive twelve hours. But actually this is one of the things that I am most excited about, especially because I have brought books to listen to. Even though once upon a time I wrote novels, I play lecture after lecture on how to write.

I listen to *On Writing* by Stephen King. And what King says, put simply, is that the secret to writing is *reading*: "If you don't have time to read, you don't have time to write." He also preaches against outlining. He believes in starting at the beginning of the story, not even where something gets exciting, but just start at the beginning and then you just go. And if you feel like you know where the plot is going to go, you kind of follow it, but generally you don't write it all down in advance. He says the one time that he did try to plot out a novel was the time that he felt that he was least successful. That's Stephen King.

I notice a couple things, such as that King doesn't grapple with that inability to immerse, which is making reading so difficult for me and for everyone. And how would he grapple with it? How will we solve it? National Airplane Mode hour?

On the other hand, you have the *Writer's Journey* by Christopher Vogler, which posits exactly the opposite of King's no-plan-is-the-best-plan philosophy. As he drones on and I drive, Vogler says that all stories, if they are to be successful, must be organized into not just the old three-act structure, but the three-act structure broken down into segments of a story, all of these apparently based on the teachings of Joseph Campbell. Sections include the "crossing of the first threshold," "tests, allies and enemies," and somewhere along there, the meeting of a mentor.

As Vogler describes all of this in the *Writer's Journey* audiobook, I can see myself drawing the line on a whiteboard and dividing my idea up into those sections. The problem is that I don't actually know what it is exactly that I want to write about. My agent has given me some idea that he would like a sequel to the *Dream Tasker* books that I wrote back in the day. I try to think of plots and listen to another audiobook.

The next book I listen to—*Romancing the Beat: Story Structure for Romance Novels* by Gwen Hayes, offers yet another outlining format. This time it's completely built around relationships. The story begins with people fundamentally missing something. And the story carries on with them rejecting and finally accepting the parts that would make them whole. I find this fascinating, but for the life of me, I cannot imagine how exactly one would use this to plan a story. I can, however, see how it would be useful in completing a story that was already underway. Maybe. I'm a sponge now, ready to take in even the advice that won't be put to any use.

I listen to seven hours' worth of lectures from different knowledgeable people on how to put a novel together.

But of course I *know* how.

The truth is, thirty years ago, I knew exactly how to write a novel, and the way to write a novel was simply to *write the novel*. I remember being twenty-five years old and deciding to write a book about a man who discovers he can send dreams telling other people what to do. And I knew basically how I would begin the story. I remember getting up every day and hammering out *four thousand words*. And in my mind, I could remember the tug of when I was moving into the next section of the book, and when a chapter would end and when one would begin. And all of it just *happened*, as if by nature. It is amazing to me that as I think of it now, I don't remember how to do any of that.

One thing that I do remember is what it's like to actually begin to write. Or rather I remember how strange the moment is, and how memory collapses altogether right there. I can remember being at the monitor and thinking, *well now is the time to get some writing done.* At these moments, I've been fiddling around and not doing anything. And all the while I feel like a small ship drifting in space, near the edge of a black hole, right near the event horizon. And then comes that moment when you're not getting the writing done, and suddenly you *are*, and you don't even notice it happen. Suddenly you're over the event horizon, *shoomp*, and you're *in*. And I remember looking up, bewildered and having written, exactly as though I'd fallen into a black hole and come out again.

The whole of writing is an effort to maneuver myself back to the event horizon.

Six hours into my journey I reach Salina, Kansas, where I stop and use the restroom and fill up with gas and pick up provisions; an enormous coffee and some Good Old Raisins and Peanuts. Then I am back in the car, this time shooting southward towards Oklahoma, less rural now, through more suburbs and towns. Then down into Oklahoma, the cities closer together now. By two in the afternoon, I can feel myself getting closer to the farm.

I can feel its changes, like I'm seeing flimsy maps laid atop one another. I see the weather pond that was there in my youth, which is gone now because that's where the house I'm going to use sits. I can feel the pull of a late-60s Ford Ranger pickup, parked finally next to a tree and never moved—except once, by me—now overgrown with weeds, essentially one with nature. I know that it is waiting for me.

I reach Oklahoma City and then drive about fifty miles to the west of that to reach Tulsa. I stop to buy more coffee and shoot southward again, finally joining Interstate Highway 75 and entering Hollow Hill. As I reach the edge of town, there is a casino on my left—not an enormous casino, but a place made up of two or three very large buildings and a hotel. After this is a community college, and then I'm passing through the main highway with the usual fast-food restaurants, Taco Bell, Subway, Walmart, McDonald's. Hollow Hill is the County Seat of Hollow Hill County, and as such it makes sense that it has all of these new businesses on the main highway. But I am moving pastward. I reach Highway 56, which is the old main street of the town, and turn onto it, leaving the modern era behind.

As I move down Main Street, I may as well be back in 1982 or '72 or even '52. Everything from the streetlamps strung across the road to the glass storefronts are frozen in the past—the only difference being that half the stores are now closed. A few places thrive: besides a 7-11 at the end of Main, I see a few open cafes, a few antique stores and bars, even an INTERNET CAFÉ, something I thought went out in the 90s. When I turn off onto another road, I pull into a gas station with a large convenience store. I use the bathroom again, buy another enormous coffee, and stock up for the week in the freezer section, buying tortillas and buffalo chicken strips (too spicy to be good for me, but I can't stop), cheese and lunch meat, and several twelve packs of Diet Dr Pepper. Everything that I will need.

As I leave the convenience store, I am leaving town, traveling through roads that pass up and down hills into the countryside, almost as though I'm moving into a picture book. Artists in children's books love to show country houses in the center of long undulating waves of hills, and so it is. On this plane, you can see hills and valleys for miles and miles around. I pass signs for feed stores and for cattle trades. Finally I reach the turn-off road for Dentonville Road. I feel my heart palpitate. Eighteen miles from the gas station, the road turns to dirt, and I reach the gate of my grandmother's farm.

Chapter 7

ALTHOUGH I'VE BEEN AWAY FOR many years, I know my grandmother's one-hundred-sixty-acre farm like the back of my hand.

The first gate you could take is the entrance to the old house. This gate is rarely used, although it is wide and steel, and perfect for going in and out of at any time. If you unlock this gate and drive through, you'll be on the old main driveway.

The old farmhouse faces east and is sided with wood laths, one story with a covered back porch that is enclosed for winter warmth, and a covered front porch that is open.

Nobody ever uses the front porch for the entrance because it enters straight into the living room. Instead, everybody enters from the side, which is the entrance that goes in and enters through the kitchen. This is what once would have been known as the servants' entrance, even if the house never had servants. As long as I can remember, it is the way that everybody entered the farmhouse. On that side entrance, there is a cement walkway and a steel blade for cleaning off your boots. You enter the enclosed back porch where there are sinks and places to store foodstuffs, and then go up into the kitchen. Through the kitchen into a small dining room, and a living room, and several bedrooms off of that. It is the quintessential small and humble farmhouse.

Traveling up the main drive past the farmhouse, you reach a garden that has not been touched in some time. Past that a set of several barns, including a small tractor barn on the right, where to this day there sits a 1938 Farm-All tractor that has not been driven since my great grandfather's time (although there are pictures of a tiny me on this tractor while it was still running). On the left, a large barn with grain stores, and several large rooms inside the barn, a chute for inoculating cattle, and a variety of troughs.

In a way, the place is like a compound, the way people use the word to describe insane cultists or the Bushes and Kennedys, land and buildings and resources all for the use of one family save one key aspect: every building but the ranch house is overgrown and rotting in place.

If you go left around that barn, you'll enter the south road, which travels along the southern edge of the farm and goes all the way back to the creek that forms the western boundary. There are fields after fields after fields and numerous ponds. Throughout my childhood, when I came to stay with my grandmother, I would often get a walking stick and a jug of water and head off towards the back creek. There's no memory so peaceful in my mind as that of walking along the creek, which is full of sounds of babbling water and bugs and distant cattle, walking towards the ponds and down into the creek bed.

There are dangerous brown water moccasins. When you are by yourself and walking through a clearing shaded by pecan trees in heat closing on a hundred degrees, the heat has a voice. Frogs deafen, and in the right years there are cicadas everywhere.

If, instead of going left and heading down the south road towards the creek, you were to go right, you would curve past a large clump of pecan trees and blackberry bushes and reach a combine harvester—an enormous, red hulk—that has sat in one place for all my adult life, becoming one with the vegetation.

Traveling farther, you will meet up with a high ridge just wide enough to drive on. It is the path to the ranch house, which was built in the 1980s. This is where everyone in the family goes to stay when they visit the farm. Most people who visit go on holidays, especially Thanksgiving or Fourth of July. On the Fourth of July, my brother is liable to show up with hundreds of dollars of store-bought fireworks, plus homemade contraptions for firing off mortar rockets. The ranch house is two stories, with a wide front porch, and a dangerous, uncovered, unrailed back deck with narrow metal steps.

By the time my son and daughter were teenagers, even if the whole family came to visit the farm, we typically did not actually stay in the house, because there was simply not enough room. We would get a hotel in Hollow Hill, and then drive to the farm every morning, spending time with the family.

I feel very close to this land, and yet I cannot pretend to be a product of it. I am a suburban person. I spent many months on this farm from the 1970s to my time in college, but I was always a guest of my grandparents. I have ridden horses in the fields, and on tractors with my great-grandfather and grandfather as they plowed. I have snapped metric tons of beans and I have shucked tidal waves of corn.

But I've never done any of these things as a *necessity* for my family. I'm aware of the heat under the pecan trees, but I have always been able to escape it. The farm, for me, has always been a coat that I can take off the rack and put on, but always by choice. I do not have a deep understanding of what it is like for those who lived primarily in this rural environment. But at least I understand that I do not understand.

But today, as I embrace my new age, the farm means one thing. Above all else, it is secluded. It is the perfect place to write a book.

Chapter 8

THE FIRST THING THAT I have to do when I arrive at the gate is turn on the water.

This is harder than it sounds because Grandma keeps the water off during winter months. So restoring it is a multistep process that she and my brother have explained to me many times, both in person and in written and emailed notes.

First, you have to get the water from the road to the house. I need a special tool for that, a long sort of fork that is strong enough to turn the iron valve where the pipe running under the road meets the pipe that runs to the house.

I pull off the road and get out by the wide, metal gate, leaving the car running. Cold wind slices against me. The ground is sludgy and near frozen. I find my padlock key and feel the sting of the cold on my fingers as I unlock the padlock on the gate, I let it swing open. Next, I have to hunt for a manhole next to the post inside the gate. After rummaging in a lot of wet weeds, I find the manhole, which isn't closed with a real, iron manhole cover—thank God—but plastic.

I pull the cover up and fish around in the dark hole beneath it until I find the valve. This is the moment when those who fear snakes should be most nervous. I finally feel the valve and I use the big tool to turn it… and there it is, I can hear the water as it starts to run underground, racing toward the house.

Now, as though ushered in by the water, it starts to rain, frozen droplets pelting my skin and making a ratcheting songlike sound against the top of the Toyota Matrix. I drive the little crossover SUV up onto a slippery car-wide ridge that runs around about a third of a mile to another gate near the ranch house. My heart does another flip when I see the house with its peeling red paint and the dimming shadow of the truck-one-with-tree, but I don't have time for memories; I have to turn the water on to the house itself.

The water valve outside the house is in a buried box under an old refrigerator door, itself underneath the bare, rail-less deck at the back of the house. It hasn't rained much up until now, I guess, because the box that holds the valve thankfully isn't flooded, but now the rain is coming down frozen and it makes my hands ache to turn the valve.

This valve isn't as hard to turn as the one out on the road, but unfortunately this valve turns all the way around, making it difficult to know if you've opened it properly. If I turn it enough, the water starts to run, but if I turn it too far, the water will cut off again.

I spend about twenty minutes turning the valve, and then slowly, slowly climbing the metal steps to the deck, into the back of the house—which I have yet to really take in—to check on the water in the back bathroom, to see if it's coming out of the faucet. Then back down under the porch to move the valve a little way. Then back up the metal steps, which are getting so slick with new ice that I have to take each step square with my boots, straight up and down. I hold on to the rail along the metal steps. It is absurdly dangerous, but it's just a matter of time.

Time.

That is the thing I am looking forward to the most.

Finally I have the water running.

This done, I drive the beat-up Matrix around to the front and park near the porch steps. I set to carrying bags and the groceries that I bought at the gas station. I have to unhook a barbed wire fence across the steps, there to keep the cows from climbing up onto the porch.

The wide steps are sturdy enough, but as my brother warned me, they collect algae on the right side. I find myself alternating between walking gingerly down the slippery side, or quickly down the dry side. I get everything in the refrigerator.

I put on a pot of coffee because there's a coffee maker and filters and coffee grounds. I turn on a space heater. I set my computer on the dining table. I have a whole house to choose from, complete with a kitchen dining area, a living area, a master bedroom, plus a built-out attic or second floor. Although it is old, this house is much more modern than the decrepit farmhouse near the entrance—this house is spacious, but has less spaces.

The polished wood dining table is best for work. I get my computer set up, moving everything else out of the way, sliding aside ceramic roosters and napkin holders. I pour myself a cup of coffee and sit down in a recliner a few yards away in the living area.

Time. That's what I have now.

I look at my cell phone. It has almost half a bar of signal and I have a text waiting.

MAKE IT IN OKAY?

DID YOU GET THE WATER TURNED ON?

My brother. Apparently, he and my grandmother think I am going to forget.

It occurs to me that they aren't so much against my using the farm as they are simply cautious. The beat-up old house needs to be treated gingerly, or I might break it. What this says about their idea of my clumsiness, I don't really want to think very much about.

I take out my phone and open an email my grandmother sent me over the weekend. I take off my glasses and clean the smudge off of them with my shirt and read my grandmother's note.

MIKE, HOPE YOU HAVE A GOOD TIME AND GET SOME WORK DONE.

USE THE WATER TOOL TO TURN ON THE WATER AT THE STREET.

USE YOUR HAND TO TURN ON THE WATER AT THE HOUSE.

BEFORE YOU LEAVE, TURN OFF WATER AND DRAIN ALL PIPES.

FLUSH ALL COMMODES, TAKE OUT ALL TRASH, UNPLUG ALL THE HEATERS.

IF THE PIPES BURST, TURN OFF THE WATER TO THE HOUSE AND USE THE GIANT BUCKET TO BRING IN WATER FROM THE TAP OUT BACK TO RUN THE COMMODES

LOCK ALL DOORS.

USE THE MICROWAVE NEXT TO THE SINK, NOT THE ONE TO THE STOVE THAT ONE WILL BLOW A BREAKER.

THE BREAKER IS IN THE LAUNDRY ROOM NEXT TO THE BACK DOOR

HAVE FUN. WE LOVE YOU!!!

I pick up the phone and I text my brother back. I MADE IT OKAY.

But there are no bars. My service has gone out.

I get up and walk through the kitchen to the laundry room, checking for reception along the way. I have a couple more bars now, and I send a text to my kids.

MADE IT OKAY, LOVE YOU.

That will be enough.

I set the phone down on the washing machine by the back door and I leave it. I don't want to use it anyway. I have a story to create. And the beauty of it is that I have nothing but time to do it.

It's still cold in the house. The thermometer on the space heater says the temperature in the room is forty-eight degrees.

For a moment I contemplate what it will be like if I can't get the temperature up over 48. Right now I feel like I'll take it in stride, like the cold will be part of the adventure. And then, once I'm done and I suffer through a week of high-forties weather inside a house, I'll have a book and a story about how it got done. Oh, how I will tell people I suffered!

I keep my jacket on and I go to the table. I open my backpack and pull out my writing tools that aren't my computer: several spiral notebooks and a stack of yellow pads and pens and pens and pens. I set all of these down. Most of the notebooks to the left and a single spiral pad in front of me.

Then I get up and I pour myself another cup of coffee.

I sit down again and on the left side of the paper, following the blue line that flows from the top of the yellow pad to the bottom, I put a *I* one at the top, a *II* about a third of the way down, and a *III* about a third from the bottom. I'm going to outline tonight. Then the writing will start tomorrow, in sections, just like when I was out of law school and studying for the bar, three hours in the morning, three hours after lunch, another session at night. If I can do that for four days, by then I should have a rough draft. And then I will start reading it. I have it in my head that I can create the whole novel in this first week. I make myself comfortable, sip my coffee, and I begin to scrawl.

Chapter 9

HAVING LISTENED TO ALL OF the writer's advice books, I've still come down on the side of *hell yes, I will outline*. Outlining is something that I find vital for a lot of reasons, but above all it's a way of easing yourself into the work. You're laying down a plan for what the whole book is going to be about. Since I'm not going to need the computer, I decided that I'd rather not spend this time at the dining table where I'm going to be typing for the next several days. Instead, I pick up the yellow pad and the pen, and I begin to wander the house. I poke my head out the front door, looking at the front porch.

It wouldn't be a bad place to do the outlining. The front porch has a wooden railing, which definitely cannot be trusted to be leaned on, and a number of old rusted farm implements. But this isn't my deck in the dry air of Colorado, where a heat lamp can turn the winter into spring. It won't be pleasant to be outside, especially since the freezing rain is still coming down on the front steps. The rain is making *tick tick* sounds against the wood.

I go back inside, looking at the living room section. I remember that when I studied for the bar exam here twenty-five years ago, I moved the dining table into the living room to spread out my papers, and I would memorize things and pace back and forth and even write out long mnemonic devices for the various rules of law. And I would pin those to the wall.

Many of the items in the room have not changed in decades. In a tin for holding magazines, which no one in the family that visits the farm reads very much, there are farming and general interest publications. I stop and bend down, knowing that the outline is the only thing that I have to do tonight, and I can afford to be a little luxuriating. I find a *TV Guide* that advertises the new shows of the fall for September of 1986.

I used to love the *TV Guide* that previews the shows of new fall. For a moment, I pick it up and flip through it. From what I can glean, 1986 was a big year for shows that were supposed to be just like *Moonlighting*. Most of the shows previewed didn't last. I am fascinated by success, but I am just as fascinated by failure.

I put back down the *TV Guide* and go to the couch, which sits in front of a wide, short, polished wood coffee table.

You should start right now. Just sit down and start. You remember how to do this, right, Mike?

But sitting here is not going to be ideal for writing on a pad. I'm too tall to be comfortable sitting on the edge of the couch and leaning over.

Plus it's *cold.*

There's gotta be some way to get heat in here. I wander the ground floor looking for a space heater. Then I remember that there is a desk upstairs in the attic, in one of the bedrooms. I step around to the kitchen and then onto the stairs, which has a curtain that you can pass through. I walk up the stairs and find an old door painted in flat beige paint.

The door pushes open roughly across the stiff old carpet. In front of me is a queen-sized bed with night tables on both sides. I flip on the light and it lights up several lamps throughout the attic. Because of the walled-off staircase section, the attic is essentially divided into two small bedrooms, separated by a hallway with a few shelves on the wall. And something that has always fascinated me: a calendar of very mildly humorous religious cartoons that my grandmother put up. It is turned to March of 1986, which is not a particularly important month. It is simply the last time that somebody turned to this calendar for information. It's fascinating to me because I know that not only do my family members come here at least every fourth of July, my brother and my grandmother come to see about this farm at least every other month, and yet nobody ever bothers to move this calendar.

I touch it briefly and consider changing the calendar from March to

April, by pulling out the pin and flipping the calendar date and pinning it again. But somehow, I feel as though it's possible that this calendar being held exactly where it is important to the universe and switching it over to April 1986 may cause world-ending floods. So I leave it where it is with a little image of a preacher, visiting somebody at their door and a punchline that I forget as soon as I read it. It may as well say, *we think preachers are funny, but we like them.* Through the hallway is the second bedroom with a twin bed, a night table, a lamp and a desk and a chair.

There is a space heater up here as well. And although it is not as cold in this space of quilts and low ceilings, it is still about fifty degrees. I turn on the space heater and pull out the chair and I set the yellow pad on the desk. This is perfect.

I, II, and III.

Those are the acts of the book. When my agent said that he wanted a new *Dream Tasker* trilogy, I think I know exactly what he meant. *Dream Tasker* was a series of fantasy adventures about Jupiter Chris, a young man who can control people through dreams. In each book he would usually uncover a vast criminal undertaking and take to the field, avoiding assassins and trying to send his messages to the right people. They were a mix of science fiction, spy thriller and fantasy, full of wild stunts and last-minute escapes. Jupiter was always able to use his wits to get by when defeat seemed certain, and always in the end, there was some neat trick he could think of that would get him out of whatever the problem was. Jupiter was also kind of an overachiever, so that if terrorists had taken over a bank building, he was as likely to come in through a skylight as through any of the doors, even if the door would be safer. That's just the way these books worked.

Now I sit down, and I start writing out ideas. Starting with a threat.

A dream assassin?

Biological weapon?

A satellite is going to fall to earth and destroy one of the cities.

None of this is interesting to me. Maybe in the 80s they would be novel, but by now they have all been done to death. Not that that ever stopped anyone, but for an idea to hold the writer, he at least has to feel he has a fresh angle on the idea. Even though I know what I have decided to come here to do already, I am changing my mind about what it needs to be.

I haven't quite figured it out yet. I write down the words *Jupiter Blasts Off,* and already, I know that there will be irony in that title, that the book will not be what anybody is expecting. The first words of the book come to me then, right at the top of the outline. Maybe it's a line of dialogue. I don't know yet.

Our Jupiter is 50 years old.

My pen is poised on the next line. And then over the din of the space heater, I hear mooing—loud mooing, and a lot of it.

This is very strange because I don't remember seeing any cattle around when I parked. I think about it. There must've been some in the field beyond the yard, around the house. Then I hear what sounds like a voice.

I don't have any feeling of fear. I'm just confused because I'm supposed to be alone.

I turn off the space heater, plunging the room into quiet, and now I can hear a rumbling of engine and cattle lowing close by. I get up and I walk down the hallway, listening.

There is definitely a car outside.

Okay.

I realize now that I *am* a little bit afraid.

I walk to the window of the main upstairs bedroom and silently separate two of the strands of the blinds and look out and down. To my shock, below on the ground is a running pickup truck, lit up by its blazing headlamps bouncing off the exterior wall of the house.

Countless cows are gathered all around the pickup. I don't see any people, but the truck is running. How long have they been here, and I didn't hear anything? How long had they been here while I was wondering about what Jupiter's story should be? I continue to stare out the window until finally I decide to go down the stairs.

I walk slowly, even though of course there is nobody in the house, reach the bottom of the stairs and the kitchen, and turn right, walking through the living room until I reach the etched-glass front door. I opened the front door and then look through the storm door, but I don't see anything. I reach to my right and turn on a lamp, and it lights up the same front porch that I was just on about an hour ago. I don't hear the cattle anymore. I open the storm door and step out onto the porch. All is silent.

I go to the end of the front porch and look around to the side where just a few moments ago, there was a running pickup truck and a herd of cattle—and they are gone. My mouth is completely dry. I run my fingers through my hair. I cannot imagine how it is even possible that they could have gone so quickly or even who they were. Rationally, though, I'm already beginning to build a story that makes sense, because I know that my grandmother rents out the various pastures.

I gingerly step down the non-slimy west side of the steps and into the empty yard. I pull out my phone and find that I have two bars of signal and send my brother a text.

HEY SOMEONE WAS JUST HERE WITH A TRUCK AND CATTLE. BUT THEYRE GONE.

After a while, my brother texts back.

THAT IS PROBABLY THE NEIGHBORS JUST MOVING THE CATTLE.

Of course.

I feel ashamed of myself for being weirded out by this. As I go back up the steps I slip on the algae, falling for the first time.

Not a bad fall, but my knee smacks the wood and it hurts, and I whistle in anger more than agony. Walking it off, I get back up, reaching towards the door, then I look to my left at a utility shelf of random tools and other implements. I notice instantly that a number of things have been moved.

A grindstone that was on the third shelf is now on the second. This isn't some Sherlockian feat, I can just tell from the layout—for some reason, somebody has shifted the tools around.

I text my brother again.

SOME THINGS HAVE BEEN MOVED AROUND.

Dots, then:

SOMETIMES THEY LEAVE A CHECK.

Hm. I look at the grindstone and I tip it back, and underneath is a folded check.

Three hundred dollars, with a notation that says *grazing fees*, signed

Isabel Hardy.

I text my brother.

YEAH, IT'S A CHECK. THANKS!

With a little smiley face.

But I'm not feeling smiley face. I don't know why this whole episode has set me so ill at ease. It's not because I'm not familiar with farms or rentals or people moving cows.

No, I realize. What is setting me ill at ease is that somebody came up on the porch, moved items around, looked for something heavy enough to leave a check under, found it, moved it, and drove away. And by the time I realized they were here, they had already collected their cattle and gone.

This means several things.

One, I'm not as aware of my surroundings as I like to think I am.

Two, I am not nearly as well-attuned as my hero, Jupiter.

Then my heart skips a beat as I realize something else. I am thrilled to be having this harmless adventure, to have a moment of scintillating gooseflesh: *who was here and how are they gone so fast.* But also: this check is from Isabel Hardy.

That is thrilling itself because suddenly I remember her.

Chapter 10

Isabel Hardy is a name that I have not thought of in many years. In fact, I have barely thought of it since I met her in the summer of 1987.

That summer, I was fifteen years old and had come to spend my usual allotment of months on the farm, doing work for my grandparents and just hanging out in the country. At that point, the ranch house that I'm staying in now to write my book was still fairly new. My grandfather was retired from the Air Force and was busy farming, growing spinach, alfalfa, and soybeans. Soybeans were very big in the 80s. This was before the grand consolidation of farms that has eliminated most of the working family farms in Oklahoma.

My great-grandmother lived in the farmhouse and still made her own cobbler from the blackberries I would gather in a bucket that I keep to this day. She made most things from scratch- although she did not make her own bread, because she was plenty impressed with the sliced bread that you could get in town. We would take her to town every two weeks, climbing into an enormous Ford Galaxy and riding the eighteen miles, past the old WPA dam and back into the town- where I first met Isabel.

Isabel Hardy.

Isabel Hardy was the teenage daughter of one of the farmers in Nuyaka, which is the name of the farming community at the edge of which my grandparents' farm sits. The Hardy farm sat on the main road that heads for Hollow Hill.

I met Isabel because she had taken a job as a checkout girl at the supermarket in town. When I met her, she was a pretty girl with freckles, very slim, with curly brown hair that was pulled back in a ponytail. And she wore a green apron, the uniform of the grocery store.

I was more talkative back then, and Isabel was an easy person to strike up a conversation with (especially for a pretty girl). And so we started talking while I bagged the groceries she rang through.

"Texas, really?" I remember her asking. She crinkles her nose like the idea is distasteful as she hands me a can of collard greens.

"People do live in Texas."

"Is it like *Dallas?"*

I hear the italics in the name. *Dallas* is a soap opera about Texans. "You watch that show?"

She laughs. "Why do you ask it that way?"

I whip another sack into form and start lining it with cans. The woman checking out, in a green wool coat that dates back to the sixties, is staring at us impatiently. I smile. "I just—I never met a high school student who watched *Dallas* before. You watch *Dynasty,* too?"

She nods sagely. "*You* didn't answer my question."

"Okay," I say. "Dallas the city is… I guess… at least like the opening credits of *Dallas* the show." I hand the lady her groceries as Isabel counts out her change.

I could earn a tip if I took the lady's bags to her car but I don't want to leave the rhythm of conversation with this girl.

Looking back, I am impressed that Isabel took a job in town. It took a lot of commitment because the long drive was a significant burden. You would not only have to get your parents to be willing to put up with you taking the car for that amount of time, but you would have to actually do it, which meant a half hour commute either way, which is a big deal for a job that probably paid three dollars an hour in the 1980s.

As I recall, we only went out on two dates. My grandparents thought it was mildly amusing that it would be going out with somebody, but it was all fairly innocent.

We went to the movie house in town and sat in the balcony.

And I told her about a lot of things she had no interest in, like comic books I was collecting and whether or not the next *Star Trek* movie was going to be worth seeing. I made a point to brag about wrestling because I was on the wrestling team, although I was never the star.

The movie talk intrigued her because she was very interested in marketing and was already studying how movies were marketed. And I had never thought about it. So when I had the sense to let her start talking about herself, she would expound on all the different ways that movies are sold, how a message was sculpted to fit the audience it came into contact with.

Our second date was to the Fourth of July fireworks celebration in Hollow Hill. She actually went with her family, and I went by myself because my grandparents weren't really into that, preferring to have the family gather at the farm and shoot off fireworks on our own.

Isabel's folks had a blanket spread out next to the football stadium. Families from farms all over were eating hotdogs and coleslaw. The sun went down next to the bleachers, casting in amber a whole town chatting, the men in their khakis and white shirt sleeves, usually folded to their elbows, and cowboy hats. The fireworks were grand.

Although I had my own car, Isabel followed me to the WPA dam, which sits exactly nine miles from the gate into our farm and nine miles from town. There is a turn off at the dam, which is about sixty feet high and made up of enormous limestone blocks, damming a river to form Lake Hollow Hill. You park in the circular driveway, and then you can get out and if it's dry enough, you can climb the dam. That climb is not easy at all, because the blocks are three or four feet high.

I had climbed them several times with my brother. Although this day, I just got out and went to her car and helped her out of hers. Standing by her car, I took her hand and we kissed for a very long time.

I think of this and my entire body shivers. It is easy to forget, unless you close your eyes and will yourself to remember, that there was a time when you could kiss for hours.

But then I had to go back to Texas and that was the last time I ever saw Isabel Hardy.

I look at that name. I doubt it could possibly be the same person.

I look at the address on the check. 10485 Meansville Road. That sounds about right. Although I never actually went to Isabel's farm.

I shake my head, and then I go upstairs to complete my outlining, thinking about the strangeness.

The little desk with its low ceiling in the attic reminds me of a garret, and I am a character in a Lovecraft story, except that instead of summoning demons, I am going to summon bullet points.

I stretch, cracking my knuckles like Bugs Bunny getting ready to conduct an orchestra.

Our Jupiter is 50 years old.

Our Jupiter still knows how to talk to people in dreams, but he doesn't do it much anymore.

Our Jupiter hides how much he is afraid.

I am floating at the horizon, looking for an image, and into my mind floats a song by the Cure, the quintessential 80s band. I decide right then and there—without writing it down—that I am going to ignore that Jupiter was supposed to be a teen in the 90s. I decide without really saying to myself that it doesn't matter now.

In my brain, the song *Close to Me* starts playing, and I see it playing from the speakers of a family sedan.

The legal pad still says:

I

II

III

And now the music is dragging me towards the event horizon and I write OPEN—Jupiter drops off a check for daughter's tuition and they fight, interrupted by ROCKET ATTACK ON DORMITORY!!!

And I write, and write, for hours. There is finally a moment when I wake, and I have my outline.

This is success. Genuine success.

I tap the yellow pad with my pen and then walk down the stairs and out to the front porch, which is freezing, so I pull some boots over my bare feet and light a cigarette.

I have completed my first outline in at least fifteen years. I exhale smoke. I have not been happier in decades.

I smoke half the cigarette and crush it out, and go to bed.

Next morning I wake up at nine, and before I get to work, I want to check on something.

I am going to check on Isabel.

There is no phone in the house—no working phone—and I decide that I will do it in person.

Before I have time to talk myself out of it, I'm scraping a thin layer of ice off my windshield and driving over the ridge and doing the elaborate dance of gates until I am moving down the road.

Meansville Road is not far away. I drive for about 10 minutes until I finally turn onto a road and shortly come to a farmhouse at the address that I read earlier.

The entrance to this farm does not have a gate, since the people living in this house are here all the time. The many gates and locks on our farm are there because my grandmother has discovered that it is important to make it slightly difficult to get to the house. When everyone is gone, people will break in and steal things. This farmhouse is a two story structure very similar to the ranch house that I'm staying in. It is much better kept, with lime green painted trim and shutters, red brick, and a gravel driveway, with a new two-ton pickup truck in front – the very truck I saw last night. There is a large, white-painted porch, and lights blazing inside.

As I approach the front porch, I think that it would be proper to take off my hat. A gesture that I've seen my grandfather do many times. But of course, I don't wear a hat. I knock on the door. After a moment I see a shadow through the glass of the door, and then behind the storm door as the main door opens. I see Isabel Hardy and gasp.

"Yes?" The woman standing in front of me looks almost fifty years old. Her hair is curly and gray brown and pulled back in a ponytail.

She has a pair of horn-rimmed glasses that are on glasses-holders held over her shoulders and laying on her chest. She has almost no freckles. And at first, I can't really see her eyes, because she is looking down wearily, as though she were already tired of talking to whoever is going to be coming to her door at nine-fifteen in the morning. But as she looks up, still with no sense of recognition, I see crinkles of mirth around them. And I'm reminded of the 15-year-old girl that she once was.

I realize now that I've been moving almost entirely on instinct, and I'm not sure what to do next. But I do know, because I am the grandson of my grandfather and the son of my father, that above all else, you can be polite.

"Yes, ma'am," I say, as though someone has asked me a question. "I just wanted to drop by, because I got your check, and I wanted to let you know that I'm going to be staying at the farm for week or so—at Mrs. Dotson's farm."

She is nodding, in the way that one does when they're listening to what you're saying and waiting for you to get to some kind of point. And I think I've been pretty successful at giving her a point which is *I'm just letting you know that I am going to be staying there. So you will not be alarmed that someone is there.* Although this is a thin veneer of a point, because of course people stay there all the time. And now that she has dropped off a check, it is unlikely that I will see her again. Regardless, she is nodding as politely as I am talking politely. And then I hold out my hand, although there is a closed storm door between us.

"My name is Mike Dotson; I just wanted to say hi."

"Are you *Mike?*" This is the first time I've heard her voice, and it is lovely and husky and full of a strange sort of trepidation. She opens the storm door and steps out onto the porch. She seems to forget that I have offered my hand, and instead puts both of her hands up to her mouth and says, "Oh my gawd."

I go with this and say, "Do you happen to remember we met?" And she practically squeals and throws her arms around my neck.

"Why don't you come in?" she asks. Then she waves her hand. "Oh, well, actually it's a mess."

She holds up a finger and disappears inside, and appears with a couple of large metal bowls, carrying them with her out to the porch. "Boy, it's cold," she says, and she flips on a pair of tall metal heat lamps of the kind I keep in Colorado, right over either end of a porch swing. She sits with the bowls and gestures with her head for me to come with her.

Which I do. Under the heat lamps, it's actually quite nice.

"I like it this way, because I can almost pretend it's not winter," she says with a slight drawl. She keeps one of the bowls in her lap and puts the other two down on the porch. "Here, take some of these while we visit."

The bowl in Isabel's lap is full of raw string beans, and as though I do this on the regular, I follow her lead and take a handful of them. Without being prompted further, I begin snapping them.

Snapping beans is something that anybody who has ever lived on a farm knows you have to do. You snap them in half. You toss the ends away—here, neatly into one bowl—and you toss the part that people will typically recognize as green beans into the other bowl.

"So," she says, snapping a bean briskly. "What are you *doing* here?"

"Well, my grandma has loaned me the farm for a bit," I explain. "I'm working on a project."

"What kind of project?"

And I tell her that I am working on a book. And I am sheepish about it. Because this is of course the most obnoxious and silliest thing that any grownup could say. Her nod is sympathetic.

"Everybody wants to write a book sometimes," she says, and I do not bother to explain that I have written books before, but not in the last couple of decades, and now with my wife dead, I want to write more of them. Because honestly at this point, I can't imagine for all the world that she would be interested in that. And obviously, I have not had a great deal of success, because she doesn't know it already herself.

"So does that catch you up?" I ask after telling her that I have two grown children. I do not wear a wedding ring. And she does not ask me. I know exactly what she must be thinking, which is that I'm probably not married because I also have no tan line on my ring. So I must certainly be divorced, with the two grown kids. Law of averages.

"Let's see." She bites her nail in the most charming way possible. "Let me catch you up." She tells me that her parents are dead. She was married to Lyndon Merrinack, who is a police officer in Tulsa now. She doesn't mention kids.

We snap beans for a moment, and though I am not sure at all why I'm here, I am so glad that I have come. As we reach the end of the clump of beans that we are going through, she picks up the bowl and says, "So. You want to go to the dam?"

We ride out to the dam in my Matrix, both aware that this is a very strange moment, a very odd sudden date for two people of a certain age who had no idea two hours ago that we were going to be spending time together. And I'm also aware that I'm supposed to be writing a book. But right now, I'm driving out to a dam with a pretty girl and that feels almost as important.

It is seven miles until we reach the turn-off for the WPA dam of Lake Hollow Hill. We get out, tugging our jackets closed and walking near to one another.

The dam, which has at its front a pool that sometimes fills with water, is of course empty in winter, with no water flowing over it. The rocks are slick. But nevertheless, we silently decide to walk along the gravelly path next to the great stones, climbing up.

"I'd like to see what the lake looks like this time of year," I say.

As we climb up the path, we reach a point where we are blocked by shrubs and are obliged to step on to the great rocks of the dam itself. I climb carefully up one of them and then turn around and give Isabel my hand, and we climb up to the next one. We do this several times until we reach the top. There, we look out at the lake, which is gray and cold. And unprotected by the dam, up here the wind smites us fiercely.

Isabel runs her hand up and down my arm. "This hasn't changed at all."

"Nope."

I turn around and slip. And although Isabel grabs my elbow, she's not able to stop me. I fall, banging my knee on the dirt next to one of the stones. I curse, and then try to laugh, standing up awkwardly.

Now we have to walk down very gingerly, and I'm reminded that although I can still run—that photo in the Denver *Post* proves it—I'm not nearly as athletic as I once was. I stop for a moment to prod at my knee, and as I stand up again, I glance back down to the turn-off where we have parked.

Two or three men in a pickup truck have stopped to throw a bag into the garbage bin next to my car. It's another two-ton, with running lights on top. The men are wearing blue jeans and hunting vests. As soon as they have thrown their garbage into bin, they get back in and drive away.

Isabel and I climb together down and back to my little Matrix. I'm embarrassed for falling, though I can't really explain why, because of course anyone could slip. And we have gingerly climbed down the stones without incident.

But mainly I am embarrassed because I realize now that what I've been doing is meaningless. The time has gone by, and my body is old. And that there is no point in pretending that I can start over. By extension, I'm wondering is if it's even worth attempting to write or publish a book again. Because there is no point in pretending that I have my life ahead of me. The fact is, I have my life mostly behind me.

I give her a ride back to her house. And she asks me if I would like to come inside. As I walk her up to the door, I say "No, I have some stuff to work on."

Because the addiction to writing books is still there. And even though I just had those dark thoughts about how it's not worth it, I'm still going to try.

And then like somebody a lifetime younger, she gives me a peck on the cheek and puts her hand on my jaw to clasp my head. Then kisses me again. And I drive back to the house.

By the time I reach the gate, I am raring to work on the book.

Chapter 11

I NEED TO GET BACK to my plan.

It is now Sunday morning, and it is time to start writing the book. Trying to get yourself to start writing is usually for me a series of attempts to trick yourself into getting writing done. Last night, I did my outline. So I have it in front of me on my yellow pad, but the question of how to start an actual first chapter is never easy. One of the big reasons is that I am afraid that I will make a mistake, afraid to write something bad. But Aaron Sorkin is well quoted—I know this because I listened to a lecture of his on the way down—when he says that one of the ways to do it is to give yourself permission to write it wrongly. To say, "let's have a better version of this," and just write the bad version. There are a lot of words for that—some call it *dummy dialogue,* for instance, but you can just as well think of it as the rough draft.

The other thing, and I have read this advice and I've given this advice many times, is that I find it very important not to stop and fix what you're doing. If you start your story and your character is a white Irish cop, and then halfway through you decide that that character should actually be a black private detective, and not working for the cops at all, the best thing to do is make a note in the screen, or even on a yellow sticky note that says *go back and fix everything to make him a black detective.* And then you just keep going as though everything you've written so far already said that. Because the important thing is getting to the end. I say all of this, and yet I have not finished a book in twenty-five years. I am able to remember all of this advice, and I have utterly wasted years not following it.

Here's what I know about the day before me as I've planned it. Whenever I'm going to start, the day is going to be eleven hours long. It is now about noon, because I've already spent the morning with a woman that I haven't seen since I was a teenager. And so I'm committing to be writing until eleven o'clock tonight. At which point I will go to bed.

The way to get an incredible amount of work done is to divide it up. If this book is to be eighty thousand words, then over the course of five days, I need to create sixteen thousand words a day, just for the rough draft.

Assuming I want to sleep, I know that I can write fifteen hundred words an hour, so I should be able to do sixteen thousand words in eleven hours. The trick will be pretending that it's a new day after each chunk. The reason is that, after you write a thousand, fifteen hundred or two thousand words, or whatever your goal is, you will feel as though your brain has been spent. For that day, you've reached your vertical limit, and all writers have that limit—or at least think they do.

But what I've found was that you can always do another day's work—if you can just fool yourself into thinking that you've moved into another day.

And so now what I'm planning to do is: every hour I will write, and then I will get up and I will do something that divides the time, whether it will be a walk around the house or cooking something or making more coffee or even going out. Or even rewarding myself with one of the cigarettes that I bought. And then mentally, I will pretend that I have begun another day, and I will go back and start again.

To be clear, this is not something you could do for a sustained amount of time. It is the juice cleanse of novel writing.

And all along, the amazing thing is that with all that, I could still just fail to do it. I could still just not open up a new document, not type the first word. I could go out onto the front porch, and I could watch the freezing rain and fail to start again. I could try to see what will come in on the television near the couch. I could get on some boots and I could walk through the soggy fields across the hundred-sixty acres of the farm, out to the creek that runs along the western side of the farm. I could do any of these things as valuable hours slip by. I could miss the day entirely. That's the amazing thing about a creative endeavor: if you do it, you create something, but you could just as easily turn over and fall asleep.

And the only reason I am not turning over and going to sleep is that, somehow, I have forced myself to come all the way out here, and to recognize that I have more mornings behind me than I do ahead of me. I have allowed my time hunting down a girl that I barely knew to take up the morning. But if I start now, everything will have worked out perfectly. And I will be able to look at that decision and contextualize it and be proud of it.

What I need to do right now is to write the words to start the first chapter. I look at my outline, but the first words, what will they be? I once told somebody when I was working on the second of the three books I wrote when I was in my twenties, I said, *just throw a dart.* And what I meant was, start where you start, write the bad version, get it down.

Under CHAPTER ONE, my fingers hover over the keyboard. Then I remember I already have the first words.

Our Jupiter is fifty years old.

And I keep going.

The next eleven hours go exactly as planned. I write and then stop, and write and stop, as though eleven days instead of eleven hours have passed. Like clockwork, at 11:30, I stop, and go to bed in triumph.

Chapter 12

MY EYES SHOOT OPEN AND for a moment I forget where I am.

I can see a fuzzy red glare of a digital clock on the other side of the room. I know that it sits on a battered antique vanity. I find my glasses and look through the dark, it says 3:18.

Soft moonlight comes in through drawn shades, and the only thing I can hear is the grumbling of the space heater in the master bedroom.

I feel hot. It might be freezing outside, but with the bedroom closed up, the space heater turns the bedroom into a hot box. When I went to bed, it was so cold that I didn't know if I could get to sleep. I remember putting socks on my feet. And in fact, now that I feel my feet, I remember that I've put two pairs of socks on and several blankets.

Now, I reach down and peel off the socks, balling them in the dark and letting them fall to the floor.

Why did I wake up?

I feel cooler air against my feet and turn over, thinking with satisfaction about how in the morning, I'm going to start typing again.

As I close my eyes, I hear a distinct sound, recognizable anywhere, even over the loud hum of a space heater. I hear a car door close. Maybe a truck door.

That's not good at all.

Just last evening, I was shocked that a pickup was able to come all the way to the house without me knowing it. Now once again I hear a vehicle nearby. I'm supposed to be completely isolated, but instead, I am receiving visitors when I least expect them.

The only vehicle anywhere nearby should be my own Matrix parked in front. It's also possible that I haven't locked it. I don't think that Isabel would have come back at three o'clock in the morning. I suppose, for a sexually exciting moment, that it's possible. But no, that's not what people my age do.

I realize with annoyance and a little dread that it's possible somebody has walked up from the road to break into my car and take whatever's inside. I sit up, listening in the dark.

Walked up from the road is harder than it sounds. This house is hidden in a small copse of trees, barely visible from the road. And to get to the house, a person on foot would have to park by the road and climb a barbed wire fence, and then another, progressing slowly in the dark.

Still. It wouldn't be the first time in my life that I've woken up in my life to find someone breaking into my car. It has happened to me twice, in fact. So even though the car is difficult to get to, it is distinctly possible that somebody has found their way to it, just to steal whatever I have in it.

Or to break into the house, I think distantly.

I listen, sweat beading on my neck. I still can't hear over the space heater. So I stand up, crossing the room to find the switch on the front of the unit. The sound of the heating fan immediately cuts out.

It would take some real damn bravery to travel off the farm road towards a strange house with a car parked in front of it. With the nearest police station eighteen miles away, people take gun ownership here as a matter of course. So traveling off the road to a strange farm towards a house would require someone with the guts to face getting shot. *Someone desperate,* I think. Which does not make me feel better.

Briefly it makes me think about Glenn, and about my own cowardice, and I put that all away.

They'd be disappointed, too. The Matrix doesn't really have anything worth stealing in it. In my mind, I see the layout of the floorboards: a battered gray thermal lunch bag that I've been using for twenty years, a few protein bars, a Target bag full of trash, maybe a couple of old and probably nonfunctioning phone chargers, an ice scraper—which I'll need if I decide to go into town again. All told not a great loss if I have to lose whatever is in there.

But still, I'm in the middle of the country. And somebody just slammed a vehicle door, either theirs or mine.

There's no light coming under the door from the living room. I thought that I'd left the light on for all those great reasons, but I guess I forgot. I finished my day of writing, eleven days crammed into a grueling one, and pretty much fell into bed. So the house is dark, which would explain why the smash-and-grab guys would feel safer approaching. *I* wouldn't feel safer. No way. But *somebody* might. I keep listening.

I wonder if maybe I imagined the sound of the door after all. Half terrified that at any moment, I'm going to hear a window breaking, or the front storm door, which maybe I locked or maybe I didn't, or the front door itself, which is a Home Depot special with an enormous oval window of frosted glass.

I probably locked the door. Probably.

I pad over to the door in my sweatpants and bare feet, to listen at the bedroom door. Then I turn the knob and slowly pull the door open.

I investigate the living room. In the dim light, I can see the recliner, where I was just sitting a few hours ago. As I move slowly into the room, I can see left to the dining area near the kitchen where my laptop is. The computer screen on the dining table is glowing in the dark.

The whole front of the house is heavily windowed, although all the shades are drawn. I stand still, looking across the living room, able to see out the glass front door.

I still don't know if I imagined the sound.

I can see the shimmer of the Matrix reflecting in the porch light. I want to look through the front door, to get right up to it. The sweeps in the frosted glass design leave various streaks and loops plain with no frosting, clear enough to look through.

I haven't heard a sound since the sound of the car door closing, which I now realize I must have dreamed. I step towards the front door, reaching out my hand.

A shadow crosses the door, moving left to right as it travels along the front porch.

It is the shadow of a man. I gasp and then cover my mouth. In my mind, I see posters from 1950s Film Noir, always cowering women, often with covers pulled up over their breasts, one hand covering their mouth. That is what I am right now. A shrinking victim in a film noir, covering my own mouth after a gasp.

Adrenalin shoots through my chest and legs. *Oh my god. There's someone on the porch now.*

There's something else outside in the grass, a little way back from where my Matrix is parked. I see lights come on briefly and then go out, as I hear another vehicle door shut. And one more time. Someone—no, *two* someones—have just gotten out of a vehicle, just as the first guy had a moment before. Now finally I can make out a shadow of a larger vehicle behind my Matrix. And the moving shadows of men.

That one's on the porch now, and just crossed in front of the glass door. Do they even know anyone is here? I shrink back beside the closet that's really an underside of the stairs up to the attic rooms. I keep half of my body in the closet, nestled against old work shirts worn by my grandfather and never, ever moved. And I peer out.

I hear a few mumbled words, but I can't catch any of them. But now I see the first shape step back into view. Standing at the top of the porch steps is a man in blue jeans and a blue work shirt. He wears a baseball cap. He is pointing with his left arm, indicating the front steps.

I get it now: the man is telling the guys who just got out of the vehicle that the front steps are slippery. *That's the only kind we have around here,* I think, slippery front steps and slippery back steps that make the front steps look OSHA-inspection ready. I don't know if he has been here before to check out these steps, or if he has only now done his reconnaissance and worked out the problem, that the east end of the front steps are covered in algae, while the left end of the front steps are dry, except for the rain and ice, though they are a little rotten. The steps are an all-over nightmare, but if I had to choose, I would go down the west side, because that algae is going to get you every time.

Someone else comes into view and puts a booted foot on the lower step. The first man hisses a few scolding words, and then at his behest, this second guy slowly crosses the steps to walk up the west side of the porch. He's skinny, wearing rotten blue jeans and a T shirt of indeterminate color. I can see greasy hair and a goatee. He has work boots on, and he steps carefully, but he says something that I don't quite catch, but that the emotion of it is *you think you know everything.*

Now a third man comes up from whatever vehicle is behind the Matrix. This third guy is heavier, wearing dark blue jeans and boots, and an open collared golf shirt. He is heavyset, with a goatee and a baseball cap and a light jacket. He looks like a project manager on his break, like someone I would run into at Costco on the weekend. The first man repeats the gruff warning. And this new guy, who I think of as Costco, nods and steps across the steps to go up the dry side. His whole body is slightly bowed in deferment to the authority of the man in the blue work shirt. His shoulders are rolled forward, and I think idly that they're very much the way that my shoulders roll forward. Just as those poor souls in my family who worked in coal mines had the lungs of people who worked forever with coal, I will have the rolled-forward rolled shoulders of somebody who works on a computer. And so does he.

Now they're on the porch. Right on the other side of the door. I'm far back in the darkness of the living room, nearly in the bedroom. *Can they see me? If they looked?* I realize my mouth has gone completely dry and I try to swallow. My whole body is shaking.

Jesus Christ, Jesus Christ. What the hell am I supposed to do? Do I turn on light and make lots of noise? Like what, they're bears and would be scared away by noise? But maybe they *are* like bears, or some other wild animal. If you make a noise, maybe you're too much trouble and they go away.

I've heard on true crime shows, and definitely in commercials from people who sell alarm systems, that people who commit burglaries are looking for an easy score. And as they move down the street, if they see somebody has an alarm, or even a sign that just *says* they have an alarm, they skip that one and go to one that doesn't. Meaning that I and all of the neighbors of are engaged in a strange sort of weapons race, where each of us is trying to create a house that will cause the burglars, who we presume to be wandering up and down the street like Girl Scouts, are going to look at our house and decide that it is not as *attractive* as the next house. We are offering up our neighbors for murder and mayhem.

I can yell that I have a gun. I actually don't have a problem with guns per se—I have moved in my life after all from Texas to Colorado, from one gun-friendly expanse to another. But I didn't bring one. I *almost* brought my shotgun. You would think that having lived through a workplace shooting would make me reticent about any weapons, but the truth is I simply forgot it. In the end, I simply drove away from home and forgot to put it in the trunk. When I think of the gun, I think about a time a number of years ago when I was carrying a shotgun, and I went down those steps, and they were as algae-slick then as they are now. I was in a hurry.

And every time I went and put something in the car, while my grandparents yelled at me to do this or that, I carefully went to the west side of the steps down and then up for the next load, over and over again. But on the last trip, when I grabbed the shotgun to put it in the trunk of my grandparents Lincoln, somehow, I forgot. I quickly went down the east side. And I remember my feet flew out from under me. The shotgun was still in my hand, my back colliding with the wooden steps. I wasn't really very hurt, because I was young and pretty supple. And because I'm not the kind of person who would be stupid enough to carry a shotgun with my finger on the trigger.

But it's funny that I have not thought about that, since it happened some time around when I met Isabel.

But no, tonight I don't have a gun. What I should do is make a call, I should call the police. They're eighteen miles away in Hollow Hill. My mind shoots through the house and I remember that I left my phone sitting on the washer in the laundry room. To get there I'd have to walk through the living room, and there's a good chance they might see me cross, even though it's dark. A *very* good chance, especially if they press their faces to the door.

These men that I don't know, who have come to this place in the middle of the night, if they press the flesh of their faces up to the glass of the front door, would see a middle-aged man in a T shirt and warm up pants, slowly crossing in the darkness towards the kitchen.

But it's still the best bet. I have to get to my phone. Next to my head, an ancient rotary phone, still attached to the wall as a permanent ornament, mocks me. It has notes on it. There's something that says *Ruby called 10/11/76*. It is astonishing to me that in all this time, my brother and grandmother have not bothered to pull down a sheet of paper that says that somebody named Ruby called on the first day of October in 1976. *Why is this phone still here? Why is the TV Guide still here?* Right now I'm thinking, *why am I still here?*

A shape fills the door as the first man leans on the screen, elbows splayed out, to press his face against it. The man is looking through the mesh and through the glass of the door, right in my direction. I freeze. Am I visible? I have no idea. The shadowed face turns left and right, scanning the room, possibly seeing nothing at all. Only vague shapes of tables and a recliner. The man pulls on the storm door and it makes a thudding sound. So I did lock it.

But of course it won't hold. Of *course* not. Already, I can picture it in my mind. To get that storm door open, the most you would need is a screwdriver. Just stick it into the seam and *pop* and it would open.

The man says something out loud, not loud enough for me to hear, but at a conversational tone. His nonchalance makes me all the more panicked. *Shit, shit, shit.* My heart pounds. I need the phone.

Fuck it. I'm going to run to the back, to the laundry room, and get the phone. He pulls on the storm door again. I step into the living room. I am more terrified now than when my best friend was killing people in my own office building. Because this is different.

I'm moving. If the man sees me, or if the other two are looking through the cracks in the windows and see me, I can't do a thing about it now. I don't run, though. I walk slowly past the recliner, past the door with the man tugging on the storm door, left to the dining area and into the kitchen.

I pass the kitchen table in darkness and smack my bare toe and my knee on a wooden chair, very hard. Pain shoots through my foot, and I yelp as the chair clatters into the table, setting it rattling on its legs. A ceramic rooster falls over loudly, clacking against a saucer. I keep walking, wincing with pain. *Shit. They can hear me they can hear me they can hear me.*

I reach the stove at the entrance to the laundry room at the end of the kitchen. On the other side of the laundry room is the back door, and I freeze.

I can see through the glass of the back door into the night. This door doesn't have an entire glass oval like the front, just a smaller square window at about head height. The moonlight and the yard are just a sliver—over the shoulder of a man who is standing and looking through the back-door window.

One of them, while I was concerned about the front, has come around to the back. There is no time to move as the glass window shatters, the feeble wooden stocks of the window punching in as a brick punches through it. The brick falls to the floor in the laundry room, bouncing in the darkness and landing next to the oven at the entrance to the kitchen. The man who has used the brick reaches through the window, feeling for the lock. His bare hand, at the end of a long, bare, scrawny arm, moves, sliding across the slickness of the door.

Somewhere in my mind I know this stranger is *very* vulnerable right now. I could hurt him many ways—if I could even think to do it. I could pick up the brick and smash his fingers. But I am frozen. He finds the lock instantly, because he has done this many more times than I have done what I am doing, which is *nothing* as I watch somebody break into the house. He twists the lock. I begin to fall backwards and then lurch forward, my mind bringing back to some kind of consciousness, scrambling for the brick. I find it and pick it up, feeling little bits of glass on its pocked clay surface.

The door slams open, and the man comes into the laundry room. For a moment, I see the blue light of my cell phone blinking on the white skin of the washer. I manage to form words as I back up with a brick. "Get out. I have a gun."

I know this sounds crazy and silly, because what I'm holding is a brick, and I'm not even holding it like a gun. We live in a country where men who are holding objects in their hand get shot all the time. And the cops say *I thought he was holding a gun,* but I can guarantee you that nobody would observe the way that I'm holding this this brick and would think that I'm holding a gun.

In the darkness, I can see the scrawny guy, the one with the T shirt and the work boots, and he shouts at me: "Bullshit!"

And at that moment, I do everything that a middle-aged, midlist novelist has been trained to do. I turn and I run.

I scramble back past the refrigerator, and I have a decision to make, my brain stumbling over itself. *I can't die. I have a book to finish, and it really just needs one major draft.*

I can't run to the front door. I see the shape of the first man outside the door's glass.

I turn instead and run up the stairs, up to the attic where I was writing my outline the night before last.

I get up to the door at the top, rip open the attic door and I slam it behind me. There's no lock, but it's a solid old door.

Before me is one of the beds where family members sleep when we have Thanksgiving out here. I press my back against the door, staring at the queen bed and scanning for anything that I can reach. I see an old radio, blankets, a random wooden chair. All I really have is the brick.

The man hasn't followed. I can hear voices in the living room below. And then there's a sudden noise that I have only heard on a stage.

The thought instantly comes to mind, although I am not worthy of the thought. There's a moment in the play *The Diary of Anne Frank.* The family who we've been following throughout the play, have been living in the same attic for years. And now at a moment of tension, we can hear people below. And then all of a sudden, the jig is up, and there is *running on the stairs.* I have never heard anything more terrifying than hiding and hearing people running upstairs.

That is what I hear now. I press my back against the door and close my eyes. A heavy weight smashes into the door and throws me forward several inches. I try to push back against it. *Please* I think, because now I am a coward. I hear steps on the stairs again, as if the guy is going back down a few steps, and then I hear wood creek.

Then he is coming again, running faster, and he's going to hit the door hard.

I fall out of the way and I let the man come. The intruder slams into the wooden door and flies through instantly, sprawling his legs, trying to compensate as he careens toward the queen bed. I leap after him with the brick raised, bring it down, but my fist brings the brick down on the bed, smashing my own knuckles and missing the guy by a mile.

And then I feel fingers on my shoulders. Someone else grabbing me from behind.

And I might be screaming but I have no idea. I can no longer think clearly. I see a swirl of dark visions. I fight like a lunatic, and the man behind me yanks me back and throws me and I am falling, fingers slapping against the side of the stairs. My head hits one of the risers on the way down, and all goes dark.

Chapter 13

WHEN I WAKE UP IT'S bad.

I've written a lot of bad scenarios. When I was writing, before I stopped, I used to receive letters from readers around the country who told me they were on the edge of their seats, whether it was in the *Dream Tasker* or the *Fearless* books. For instance, when I had my hero Jupiter Chris escape from a bridge under which he had been hung by his wrists, Jupiter flipped up and untied himself, holding on to the ropes with his ankles.

I heard that they loved the one where Jupiter got thrown out of an airplane in a straitjacket. At that time, my walls were lined with books about how to affect daring escapes, how to make an oxygen tank out of your shirt, how to survive a plane crash, how to fall from a building. I absorbed and used those lessons dutifully, was a known prince of getting out of bad situations. In fiction I haven't touched for twenty years, in bullshit on paper.

But I'm not Jupiter Chris, *Dream Tasker*. I'm a barefoot middle-aged man in terrible shape. And when I wake up, I'm tied to a chair. I'm blind. Blind because, I realize the instant that I open my eyes, I've lost my glasses on the stairs. I feel a rush of panic as I look left and right. I beg for my vision to come into focus.

Without my glasses, I know everybody by their shapes. But if I take a book in my hands, I have to hold it until is about an inch or an inch-and-a-half away from my eyes before the words come into focus. My world is an impressionist painting of moving shapes. I don't even have the clarity of an actual blind person accustomed to using my ears and hands alone.

That was why my mother filled my world with ways of seeing the invisible—the flower decals on the glass, brightly-lit cups, as my vision worsened to the terrible—and not terribly uncommon—awful near-sightedness that it is now.

What I see before me is a room lit by a chandelier that appears as a series of fuzzy orbs near the ceiling. There are three shapes in the room, none of them clear, they're just swipes of color. I know that they are the shapes that chased me upstairs.

My wrists ache. I look down to my sides to see my arms as nothing but a swatches of flesh color next to my body, vaguely darker at the wrist. But I can feel that my hands have been tied to the wooden chair I'm sitting in. The darker patches are straps. Maybe shoestrings.

Oh my god, oh my god, this is how I'm going to die. I think again about being up on the dam, and how I slipped. And what I must have looked like in front of Isabel. What an idiot to come all this way, and nearly kill myself. And now, what an idiot in general.

My kids are going to have to fly my body back if they ever find it. How stupid I would feel—and that's impossible to make sense of: *how stupid to be dead.* Worse, how stupid to be injured, injured badly, in a coma, lingering for years or puttering around the house with a damaged brain and looking at my old books and saying, *somehow, I wrote those.*

The shapes, barely visible in my vision, move about, making the carpet creak against the pier-and-beam foundation. I move my wrists, trying to alleviate the sting of the bindings. They're going to kill me, probably take whatever they can find, which won't be much: my laptop and iPad, the keys to a beat-up old Matrix, and they'll shoot me in the head, or they'll cut my throat.

Cut my throat. How many times have I written that phrase or described it from other books or terrible videos on YouTube? And now that's going to happen to me. I don't want to be cut. I read once that in the movies when somebody gets stabbed, they barely make a noise. They fall over, and then Hercule Poirot comes out, and he starts investigating. But in real life when a person gets stabbed, it hurts, and they're still alive. They beg not to be stabbed again.

"So here we are." The sharp voice cuts off my reverie. I look forward as one of the shapes, the man who is neither scrawny nor fat, the one in the blue work shirt, comes to stand in front of me. He is a fuzzy swatch of blue floating in my vision, blue with a blurred, pale face and a baseball cap.

"Here… here we are," I repeat. What am I supposed to say? I can see the man's hands and they don't seem to be holding anything, but *I'm going to die I'm going to die I'm going to die.*

What do they always ask in the movies? What do… "What do you want?" I ask. "Why are you doing this?"

"It's cold outside." The man who I'm now thinking of as Blue says. Blue turns and looks at the others, as though he's making conversation with them and not with me at all. "You got it cold in *here* too, does it warm up?"

I try to process this question, but my brain is swimming too fast. "Does it… oh! There are space heaters, but no it's, it's cold, it stays cold." I am off to a great start.

"You don't live here."

"What do you mean?" I respond. My voice is whining, and I hate it. I'm not a man at all. I'm a shadow of a man, a child in a giant, fat body. Just listen to yourself, you blind, fat, worthless, *midlist author.*

Blue sits at the edge of the recliner to my left, and he comes a little bit sharper into view. "I mean… this ain't your house, right? You don't live here."

"I'm…" What is the meaning of this question? Why would they want to know if I live here? I finally decide to answer with what I'm doing. "I'm getting some work done." That sounds like I'm getting plastic surgery, I realize madly.

"Well, whose house is this?" Blue asks. Like he's a little amused and a little pissed off.

"Can I have my glasses?" I ask, and I instantly regret it, because now they will know I am blind. But my words and me are not working together today, they are like a mine train rolling away too fast. "I need my glasses."

Blue pats the air, as if calming down a child. "We'll get your glasses. Now answer my question. Whose house is this?"

"This is my grandma's house," I say, and I wince at the childish wording. "My… my grandmother's house."

The man nods. I can't make out any movement in his eyes. They're just a pale dark blur in his face. "Your grandma alive?"

I hesitate a second and then I say, "What? No." It is my first lie to these men, and it makes me feel good. It gives me a tiny amount of strength, and the strength surges through my body. "She's dead. We just—no one uses the house." Now I'm gaining confidence. "You can take anything you want." I add this last bit as though I can bargain, as if they don't already plan to take whatever they want. As though there would be any reason to tie me up the way they have if their plan were to steal an iPad. The strings cutting into my hands remind me that bargaining is for shit right now.

"Not much to take!" Blue laughs. Like we're all friends here. "I see the iPad over there, and I guess that computer. But that ain't much."

"What do you want?"

"That's a good question." Blue takes off his cap, and there's a flurry of movement as he runs his fingers through blurry, medium-length brown hair. "Let me ask you something. Mr…"

"Dotson," I say. "Mike Dotson." Why I tell the truth here I have no idea. My imagination is failing me. I could have said "Max Ortega."

"Okay, Mike?" Blue leans forward. "What do you do out here? What are you working on?"

All at once and unbidden I start to shake again. I have never felt this before. I cannot get my mouth to work. I cannot get my shoulders to stop shaking. I feel as though I've been plunged into a frozen lake.

"Calm down," he says. "What are you working on?"

I try to get a hold of myself. I look for words. I try to find strength in words. Finally I get my mouth to work. "It's just a project," I say, "it's just some writing."

"Some *writing*," he repeats. Blue sighs. "Well, okay. So, you do this writing for people or…"

"For other people, when they pay me," I say, which is as close to a joke as I can get. And I'm terrified for a second that Blue will hit me, that I'll flip onto the floor. I cringe and see all of that happen, but it doesn't happen.

Blue just nods. "Okay, I get that. You're a consultant. See—that's what I am. I'm a consultant."

This strange, modern word, *consultant,* calms me a little. "Okay," I say. What am I supposed to say to this? Well, what would I usually say? "What kind of consulting do you do?"

It's something you'd hear at a cocktail party. The sheer normality of it, though, gives me a strange, warm feeling, a few degrees of safety.

"Well, now that's a *funny* question," Blue says. "See, I don't know how well you know this area…?" He pauses as if waiting for me to fill in something, but I'm straining so hard to follow what he's saying that I can't find the right response.

I want to, though. *The area of Oklahoma? This area where I'm eighteen miles from the nearest police station. I know it okay; I've been coming to this farm since I was a little kid, my grandparents owned it since the 40s, before that they owned another farm. I've even driven a tractor on this farm, nothing serious, you understand.*

"I know it okay," I say.

"All right, then," Blue says. "So maybe you know and maybe you *don't,* mister, what you say your name was?"

"Mike Dotson."

"Maybe you don't know, Mr. Dotson, but this part of the country has been hit pretty hard, recessions and all. So, a guy comes from around here, he's got to be a kind of a creative guy, an *entrepreneur.*"

I am utterly terrified by his use of the word *creative.* It's a word that has been used to describe me many, many times. But I do not like a man describing himself as creative while I am tied to a chair. I try to see through the blazing red in my mind.

"I understand. Recessions," I say. "I can give you money. Is that it? I don't—I don't have much, but I can. I don't have much *on* me, I never *do* nowadays but I can go to the bank, and I can pull out cash. I'm not rich, but I can do that."

In my mind, I think: *Kansas.*

There's a story I heard a few years ago, probably something that I saw on a true crime television show. There was a family held in a basement. And at some point, the robbers let the mom go to the bank to get the bad guys thousands of dollars. And when she got to the bank, she even passed a note to the teller that said *My family is being held hostage in our basement. Send help.* But the teller hadn't noticed it. And after she brought the money back, everybody died. The end.

"You see this fellow over here?" Blue gestures with his head towards the larger guy behind them, the one in the golf shirt and the baseball cap. The one I thought of earlier as Costco. "He's my client—you can call him Ryan."

"O… okay."

The blur that is Ryan is standing awkwardly, and now sort of waves. It is amazing how little strength is in his wave. It's sheepish, as though he is at a mixer that he doesn't want to be at.

Blue leans forward, close enough that his face comes into focus. "I don't need your money. I got *his* money."

I swallow painfully. I try to think of anything to ground me. I try to feel the cold in the room, but I don't feel cold. I feel hot. And I feel scared.

Blue goes on, nodding, a look of solemnity in his tan, lean face. "So, what sort of consulting do I do? I help people like Ryan get their balls back." He laughs, and he slaps my knee. Now apparently really getting into it, Blue straightens back up, spreading his arms. "You ever hear of a cattle drive, Mike?"

A cattle drive? Despite my years on the farm, my first thought is of a movie. "Like in *City Slickers.*"

"Yeah!" Blue points. "Yes, indeed. Well, this is a little like that. Someone don't do much work with their hands, you know, they *lose* a little something. So what *I* do is I lead someone like that out *here*, like *City Slickers.* Like on a cattle drive. But it doesn't take three weeks! No, no. It just takes one night. And we don't drive cattle, Mike. We kill someone."

I start to scream like an idiot or a child. I yank against the chair. I rub my hands raw as Blue sits on the edge of the recliner, coming close enough that I can see his smile, until he leans back and away.

Costco, or Ryan as he's known now, doesn't seem to know what to do with his hands while I am flipping out, and he folds his arms in front of him.

"Hey!" Blue says, snapping his fingers at me. "Hey! Cut that shit out."

And I stop screaming. At least I think I do. I am moving in and out of my body now, as though I heard myself screaming and now, I don't hear it anymore.

Out of nowhere there is a blur and I feel a sharp blow across my face. *Whack.*

I breathe hard, and my cheeks burn. And I taste blood where I bit the inside of my lip. This is how much of a coddled life I lead. I have not been struck since I was in the fifth grade. I have gone my entire life with anybody striking me, except for a bully, when I was very small. I look down at my arms tied next to my legs, my brain only half working. I'm not getting out of this. Mr. Blue is a consultant, and he consults in killing.

"But why…" I whine. "How do you even know me?"

"Well," Blue says, "you fit a profile. We saw you wandering around the old dam, like a tourist, which there ain't none around here, and you clearly have this out-of-state car. So, here you were. It was lucky, too, because it's a risk, it's risky driving up to a farmhouse at night."

"Yes," I agree, as though he's asking for my approval.

"And there was a woman with you? Is she here?"

This question seems to come out of nowhere. And for a moment I can't even remember what he's talking about and then I say, "No… no one's here."

"Okay," he says. "That does seem to be the case. I was pretty sure that you wouldn't give us much trouble." He slaps my knee, like this is obvious.

"You're *talking* too much," the scrawny shape behind him hisses. "Ryan here says let's go, he wants to get *goin'!* Don't you, Ryan?"

Ryan mumbles something.

"What's that?" Blue turns around and moves a little more out of focus.

Ryan is looking down, whispering, but I can hear him. "I said, could you stop saying my *name?"*

Blue laughs. "It don't matter, Ryan, because you're gonna kill him. See, so then it don't matter that he heard your name."

"But you're *talking* too much," the scrawny one says, "We gotta move it. I want to get back to town, I got that thing."

"No," Blue says. "We promised Ryan an experience, and it's not going to go like that. We can make this an experience." They confer for a moment with close heads. This blurry consultation completed, Blue turns back and looks at me. "You know, Mike, he's right. Boy, is he right. We *shouldn't* waste time, my boy here wants to catch Trivia Night at the casino on 75. Ain't that something?"

I can make no sense of this. My death is being negotiated around whether Scrawny can correctly state how many seasons there were of *Mama's Family.*

Blue turns back towards his client. "Hey, Ryan. After this, are you going to join us for trivia?"

"Let me go!" I scream, "Please. This is crazy. I have, I have a family. I have two kids."

Blue is standing still, again conferring with the other two, and he turns back and says, "That does sound sad, Mike. Yes, it does. But you know, people have sad tales *all* the time. I'll bet you drove past a whole heap of them as you came through that rat's nest of an old downtown on your way out here. *Sad, sad,* but you know the magic of someone's sad tale, Mike?

I stare. "I… I have…"

"The magic is that if you just drive on, it's like it *don't even exist."* I stare and Blue nods, as if he has profoundly impressed himself with this bit of wisdom. And I have to admit, there is some truth to it.

He puts his hands in his pockets with a dramatic sigh. Then he withdraws one hand and turns to Ryan with something that glints at the end of the blur of his arm. I have no idea what kind of knife it is. But I begin to grunt and fight, trying to yank my hands free. "Go ahead, Ryan."

Blue hands the knife to Ryan, or tries to, but Ryan just sort of lurches back, his arms folded as he stares at the blade. All of this is barely clear, a pantomime of smeared color. Blue reaches out and puts his hand on Ryan's neck, massaging it. "Come on." Ryan takes the offered knife and just stares at it as Blue points. "Now you're gonna go over there and you're going to cut this guy's throat. Grab them by the hair. That makes it easier."

Chapter 14

RYAN HAS BEGUN TO WALK slowly towards me.

"Hang on a minute," Blue says. Ryan stops. "You know, it's occurring to me. Maybe we're going about this all wrong. In fact, suddenly my abilities as a consultant are being severely called into question, 'cause after all, you can't get your balls back just with one sudden shot." He looks toward me as though I will surely agree.

"I have to give a man a certain *service*, Mike. Ryan here isn't in much of a hurry. And I think that's because he is owed a certain product for his money." He comes back towards me, crouching. "I think that we need to make a night of this."

I am utterly terrified by what Blue is saying. And yet at the same time, I feel a sense of extreme relief. Because for a moment, I believed that it was all over. And now I am still alive.

I'm living a life where every moment now is a gift. And I am so capable of fooling myself that now that Blue is talking again, I want to believe that somehow this is good for me. That maybe it will enable me to get out— because although I am afraid that I am going to die, I don't really believe it. I think no one does. I think there is something in us that insists, up until the last possible moment, that we are not.

"What are you talking about?" I ask.

Blue takes the knife back from Ryan and returns to crouch in front of me. I hear the wooden chair that I am on creak as I bodily shrink away from him, and I realize once again that I'm trembling. He taps the point of the knife on my knee, *tap tap*. As though he were thinking, thinking with a knife.

"I think it would do a lot of good," he muses, "for Ryan to hear you *scream*. But what exactly are we going to do?" He brings the knife up towards my face, and I shrink away, gasping. There is nothing I am going to say now that is going to have any dignity. And in fact, whatever I am saying is beyond my own consciousness.

"Please," I hear myself say, "please don't," as I feel the steel of the knife against my cheek. He scrapes the blade very lightly. Not even cutting.

"Look at how he shrinks away," Blue says. He is narrating to Ryan as though I am a bug or a cadaver in a medical school. I am a creature in a film clip that a critic is showing to his class. "Look at the way he reacts to the steel. And I ain't even cut him yet."

No, not a bug, I think wildly. I'm an animal being captured and tagged on Mutual of Omaha's *Wild Kingdom*, where someone would jump out of a helicopter and wrestle down and tie up unsuspecting wildlife. I'm a loose deer, bug-eyed and terrified.

Then suddenly Blue takes the knife, and he swipes the air with it. I don't even see the movement, just a flash of metal and then suddenly I feel a screeching, slicing pain in my ear.

I breathe and scream, *"Stop, stop, stop, stop, stop."* And I feel blood trickling down my head. My brain is like a computer on a spaceship in a movie, calling out damage reports. My senses are telling me that he has cut through a piece of the cartilage of my ear.

Tears come to my eyes.

"What do you want to do?" Blue says. "Do you want to maybe cut off an ear, or maybe an eyelid? He reaches out and I can see his fingers suddenly come into close focus. I move my head back and forth but grabs the top of my head and with his other hand, he reaches and grabs my upper eyelid. I can feel his fingers against my eye, and I am screaming.

As he pulls my eyelid, he says, "I could just slice it right off. You want to see that, Ryan? Would you like to do it? I could hold it, like this. It might be some work, but you'd be able to get the blade in there."

I am babbling incoherently. I am in another world.

Blue lets go of my eyelid and strikes me hard across the face.

I fall sideways, out of balance as the chair wobbles. I don't have power over my own weight and crash sideways to the floor, my head pointing towards the door. My arm is being crushed by my own body and the chair. Everything hurts.

"I think what we should do is start with some meat," Blue says. "He's a heavy dude. We could cut off some flesh."

"I can give you anything you want," I cry from the floor. "Anything you like."

"I've always wanted to cut off somebody's nipple," Blue says. "I have this idea that you could cut it off, and then you could *dry* it. And then… if you had a bunch of them, you could lay out a collection, like on the dashboard of your car. Or maybe it could be just a souvenir." He snaps his fingers. "For *you*, Ryan, it could be what you take home. Maybe we could poke a hole through it, and you can make a necklace of it. And you can take it out at night and wear it."

Distantly, *take it out at night and wear it* lights up something in my mind. It is probably not going to resonate with Ryan. I don't know much about this Costco warrior, and I don't know what would have compelled him to decide that he wants to hire a consultant to take him out into the countryside and kill somebody, but it's a very particular kind of person who wants take a piece of flesh and *wear it at night.* And that kind of person is Blue.

I can feel the blood streaming, gathering in the folds of my ear. As I lay on the floor, Blue gets down next to the chair and almost nonchalantly slashes the knife across my ankle, through thin skin on bone. I feel the blade scrape and scream in agony. I am sobbing.

Blue says, "Let's get him up and get started on this right. Ryan, I expect you to start holding this knife. Maybe the first thing we should do… now that I'm looking at that ankle," he says, "maybe we should work on his feet some more. That seems like a good place to start."

I'm babbling again as they lift me back up. Ryan is holding the knife and I see him physically shaking his head and I'm filled with such loathing for him. Even more than Blue. Because Blue is an animal. But Ryan feels like… like family.

I start directing my babbling towards him. "Ryan, please, you've got to—you've got to stop this. You've got to go away. Maybe they'll listen to you."

I'm talking to him as though I am one of his kind, in a way that I am not one of Blue's kind. Blue seems to get frustrated, now. He huffs and I see his blurry arm and his hand grabbing Ryan's hand. He drags Ryan forward.

Blue pulls Ryan down to crouch with the knife just an inch or so from my bare feet. And Blue says, "You just push it in. Like it's a ham."

Ryan is shaking and his voice quivers. "I dunno, man, I dunno."

"Ryan," Blue says firmly. "We're gonna do this, or you're gonna regret it and not in all the ways you're expecting. Come on now. Now try the toe. Like a little carrot."

Ryan bends forward and he puts the knife against my little toe.

"Just slide it in right between the toes at an angle. It'll snip right off."

As I feel the steel against my toe, there is a knock at the door.

Chapter 15

I HAVE ONLY BEEN STRUCK on two occasions before.

In the fifth grade, the thing I like best is to be outside.

It's a Saturday in a hot September. Killeen, Texas, a community just off of Fort Hood, the largest base in what we then call the free world. My father is in the Army and the neighborhood is heavily made up of Army kids. I am overweight and twelve years old, with unkempt blond hair and glasses.

On Saturdays, I like to ride my bike through the streets of the neighborhood and on some of the dirt trails between the houses and the more developed parts of town.

My meandering route is something out of a Ray Bradbury story. I ride to the edge of the neighborhood, then through the parking lot of an apartment complex, and then into a park, through the park and then through a graveyard, and then into a larger park. The big park is always alive. At Long Branch Park, you can find a veritable parade of muscle cars and ragtops, all lined up along the curb and baking in the sun. Soldiers bring their cars there and wash them from buckets, the chrome and paint glistening, the whole place awash in foamy water and boomboxes playing rock and roll.

From Long Branch I would ride to a railroad track and follow it until I would reach the shopping center where there was an arcade, a hot dog place, a used bookstore, and a grocery store. It is a perfect circuit.

This particular Saturday, I'm not riding my bike, but walking along the sidewalk at the edge of a dirt bike track. Basically just a big undeveloped lot.

I realize at some point that there are four boys, all slightly older, eighth and ninth graders who have appeared ahead of me. They are walking, one of them rolling a dirt bike along. I don't know how they just suddenly came into view. Maybe they came from Long Branch park nearby. But all of a sudden, they're walking towards me. I am completely exposed on the sidewalk walking along the dirt path.

The boys walking towards me on the sidewalk are intimidating and they stare at me. And then as I reach them, I begin to walk past them, moving off the sidewalk.

"Hey, hold up," one of them says. Like me, he has sandy hair, and he is tall and lanky. The other boys are nondescript to me.

"Huh?"

The leader says something that I don't understand at all. "We think you did something to one of our bikes," he says.

I just want to be away from these guys. Because every moment that I'm near them, I sense that I'm going to get hurt. And I am absolutely incapable of protecting myself. I am round and soft and slow. This is the biggest problem above all else: physically, I am extremely slow.

"Bobby here says you did something to his bike," Sandy says. "He says you were throwing dirt clods at his bike."

I am not able to follow this absurd story at all. But I'm living in a world, in a time of my own life, when I still firmly believe that reason will get you everywhere. So I try some of that. I say, "I don't know... I don't understand."

And the guy says, "Are you stupid?" And I say no. He says, "Are you retarded or something? I just said Bobby here says that you threw dirt clods at his bike."

I stare, trying to think of words. But none of them are coming because this whole conversation is completely bizarre. I have too many questions. Why would these guys think that I threw—and the very word makes me roll my eyes— "dirt clods," which are basically big hunks of dried mud, at this guy's bike. And why, if I did, would that have even hurt the bike? Under what circumstances would throwing dirt clods at a bike hurt it? And more, why would they confuse a guy who *did* throw the dirt clods with me? Because I'm just walking down the street?

"I didn't!" I insist. Sandy turns to the guy that I assume to be Bobby, who has jet black hair and a Members Only jacket and a pudgy face.

Bobby says, "Yeah, I think so."

"What do you think about that?" Sandy says to me.

I stammer, "I don't know... I have I have no idea."

"What is he supposed to do?" Sandy responds, "If his bike doesn't work?" He points at the Bobby's bike, which looks pretty normal to me. It's a dirt bike with a big vinyl seat just like any other dirt bike. It is exactly the same bike that everybody rides. Although I am not riding a bike today, and with every second I am regretting that more.

I look at the bike and say, "I guess I don't know... but if his bike is in need of repair, then..."

"*In need of repair?*" Sandy shouts, and he gets close to me. "What the fuck kind of thing is *in need of repair?* Why do you *talk* that way? What the fuck is the matter with you?"

And then he whacks me on the side of the head. My glasses fly off and fall down, and I reach down and to pick them up. Bobby says, "We're going to be watching you. We don't trust you."

I say, "Okay."

He tilts his head. "Where are you walking?"

"That way." And I point towards the park, because through the park is the graveyard and then the railroad track and then another park and then the shopping center.

Sandy says, "You walk that way then. And don't look back. If you look back at us, we'll see you."

"I don't understand what..."

And then Sandy makes as if he's going to hit me and I flinch. "Don't look back." He gestures and the other boys begin to follow him, and they walk away. Now they are behind me and I start to walk.

I walk a hundred yards, and then two hundred yards, nearing a cross street. On the other side of the cross street is the park.

This next thing I do still amazes me, not because it is brave, but because of how passive and stupid I could be. They had given me simple instructions.

I reach the corner and I look back.

The five guys are about fifty yards away. I flinch as they break into a run. Almost at once they surround me again. I so want to be done with this.

"What did I say?" Sandy says.

"I don't know."

"The fuck, are you stupid? Is that what's wrong with you? You talk funny for someone so stupid." And he smacks me in the head again. My glasses fly off again, and I picked them up, starting to cry. "We *told* you not to follow us."

When I stand up, I'm holding my glasses against my stomach because I haven't even put them on yet. Then he hits me so hard that my vision goes red and I'm lying on the ground.

I don't even hear them run away.

I'm tied to a chair and someone is about to cut off my pinky toe, and for a moment I don't hear my captors at all. But they are not gone, because nobody has gone. This is the reality that I have become aware of.

I have managed to grow up and I've learned almost nothing from my time as a child. I was vulnerable as a kid to random young men who could follow me and terrorize me and hit me and make me fall down. And I'm still just as vulnerable. Nothing has changed.

Those of us who were sheep in school fool ourselves into thinking that as we go through our lives, the balance of power will change. That because of our money, or because we have a good job, or have plenty of friends, or because we have a wife, that we're more valuable now than we were then. That we are able to exert power over those who once exerted power over us. But the reality is that all of those vestments are impermanent. They're like jackets that we've put on, like paper on the wall. They do not make us able to hit back when somebody hits us. They do not prepare us for the bullies that are actually still around everywhere.

We are still sheep. We just managed to build lives where we rarely are reminded of it.

The only reason they have not cut me again is that *there is someone at the door.*

Chapter 16

THE WORLD HAS SUDDENLY SNAPPED into a strange kind of focus, because all three of us, Blue, Scrawny, Ryan, and me, have turned our attention towards the door, because there distinctly has been a knock on the frame.

I see a shadow outside. The guys have pulled a thin curtain, usually bunched up, across the door, so it's not clear who the person is.

It is possible, although it strikes me as not likely, that the person cannot tell anything strange is going on. Only that the lights are on. I have no idea if whoever is out there has heard anything. Moreover, it is around 3:45 in the morning.

Blue puts the knife back against my throat. Whispers. "Who's that?"

"I have no idea," I say, a little loud. He repeats it and I say the same thing again.

Now Blue unties my hands. The loosening of the bindings and the sudden free flow of blood actually makes my wrists hurt more. "Go look," he tells me.

I get up unsteadily, adrenaline making my body shake. My fingertips feel cold and my shoulders tight. I roll them. Even walking feels awkward. It reminds me of being an actor on stage. Because I know that everybody is watching me walk, and I walk like someone who's forgotten what walking is supposed to look like. Do I walk on my heels? On the balls of my feet, like I'm sneaking? I step across the carpet towards the curtain that hangs across the Home Depot door with its large etched-glass window. I peer out around the edge of the curtain.

Standing under the bright light, blurred but recognizable, is Isabel Hardy.

She is shifting from foot to foot, wearing blue jeans and a work shirt. She appears not to have seen me looking through the curtain. I cannot for all the world imagine what she is doing here. Instantly, I think of all the different things that I could do now. I could begin screaming. I could turn and run for the back door. I could open the door and invite her in.

The first one undoubtedly would result in my sudden death. The second one would probably result in her eventual death. And the third would be both of us to my captors. And because I'm still alive, I'm still full of hope that I'm going to stay that way. Every interview I've ever read with a serial killer tells me that this is how people always behave. They make choices based on a hope that they will stay alive.

I turn around and look at Blue. "I need my glasses."

He makes a harrumphing sound, but I win this one. I see the shadow of his hand pass them across and I take them from him. I put them on my face, and the magic of vision suddenly fills my world like glorious, sweet water.

I turn around and look out the curtain again. I didn't need my glasses to know it's her, but I'm bursting with joy to have them anyway. And it is her.

I turn around and say, "I think it's my grandmother's tenant, tenant of the farm, they rent the pasture for the cattle." I say this remarkable sentence because suddenly it occurs to me that *my grandmother's tenant* makes it sound like my grandmother is alive. Which she is, but I earlier told them that she is dead. And I don't want to be caught in a lie, especially a stupid, unimportant one. But Blue doesn't seem interested in that.

He says, "Do you know her?"

And I say, "Not really." But I'm remembering that he saw her on the dam, and I'm not sure if he's going to be able to put that together, and I don't know if it will matter.

He says, "Get rid of her."

"What do you mean?"

"Just tell her to leave. You don't have to be nice about it. In fact, if you're *not* nice, maybe she'll go."

I nod.

Then he adds, with the coolness of a literary agent: "Mike. You try to run, you both die."

I turn around and unlock the door as the men move back out of sight. I open the door and poke my head out. "Isabel."

She stares at me as though confused, even though it is such a weird hour that *I'm* the one who should be confused. But then I realize what she is looking at.

I am completely awake, and all the lights are on, and I am sweating, and I just now remember that my ear is bleeding profusely.

She shakes her head, her eyes wide. "Are you *okay?*"

I reach for my ear. "Oh!" Like *this old thing?* "Sure, I just had a little… kitchen accident. What's up?"

"You should look at that!"

"I will."

"Let me come in and help you."

"Isabel…" I shake my head. "What's… up?"

She seems shocked that I have not accepted her invitation to herself, but she rolls with it. I see her maintain her dignity. "I'm sorry, I… I didn't mean to interrupt you. I was already up and working in the barn and I thought I'd drop off the lease, your grandma had some changes she wanted. I figured I'd leave it for you… I saw that all the lights were on. But honestly, I thought that you would be asleep. Is everything okay?"

For a flash of a moment I wonder if that's true, if honestly she thought I would be asleep, or if honestly, our hot date of snapping beans and falling down has bewitched her, and she's hoped to find me awake. But I move past this fantasy.

"Everything's fine." I'm thinking of Kansas. The mom had a chance. She handed over a note. What do I say? I reach for the first absurd thing that pops into mind. "I'll, um… I'll be by to pick up the motorcycle in the morning."

She blinks and bites her lip. Finally she says, "Okay." She turns around and walks away. She stops at the top of the steps and turns around to hand me an envelope. "Here's the lease renewal for your grandma." I say thanks, shut the door, and she is gone.

One thing I'm glad of is that I have kept her from being slaughtered.

Although I'm afraid that just like the woman in Kansas, I have not helped myself at all. I am hoping now that she will take my weird motorcycle reference and run to the police with it.

I turn around. "She's gone." Blue, Scrawny and Costco come out of the bedroom.

Blue looks at me. "What was it?"

"Tenant was dropping off a lease." I hold up the envelope. I put it in the pocket of my warmup pants.

"All right, you did good," he says. "Now, where were we?"

I take this opportunity to run. I am barefoot, but I'm not interested in staying here a moment longer. Now that Isabel is gone, I feel as though I don't have to be so careful. I run straight through the kitchen towards the laundry room. I make it all the way to the back door next to the washer and dryer and even tear the door open. I look out on the frozen rain falling on the back deck and the metal steps stairs where I spent an agonizing amount of time getting the water turned on properly. I get as far as the open door when their arms are on my shoulders again.

They are dragging me back, kicking and screaming. Once again forcing me into the chair. Blue puts the knife against my throat again and once more, I am docile. Blue says to Scrawny, "Get some more rope and tie him good."

Just then the front door shatters.

Chapter 17

ISABEL MOVES LIKE SOMETHING OUT of a dream. And other than the strangers who have made their way into the house tonight, I have never seen someone move the way that she does. I realize I'm drunk on adrenaline, but she seems more like something pulled from one of my books.

Even though I spent the previous morning with her, and we went on what I would have to count as one of the first dates I've been on in many years, she is still very much a stranger that I knew briefly as a teenager.

The bullet that she fires through the glass shocks everyone; even Blue cries out and twists away from the flying shards. She yanks open the still-unlocked door and runs straight in. The three men fall back in disarray. If they have guns, they have not drawn them yet.

Isabel has a pistol in one hand and grabs my wrist with the other, pulling me up with remarkable strength. It's a moment that I've seen a thousand times in movies, and that I've even written in books. And because the world is sexist, it usually goes the other way. The guy runs in, grabs the girl by the wrist and pulls her, as though she is unable to run on her own.

I am actually very close to being unable to run on my own.

We head out the front door. I have so many questions and there is not a moment to ask them. But as she is about to run down the front steps that she just walked up, I stopped her and say *over here*, moving her to the west side of the steps which are not covered in algae.

It is raining frozen pellets again.

The guys reach the door as we run for her pickup truck, the big one she brought earlier, and jump into it. She gets behind the wheel and I'm on the passenger side.

A shot rings out. I look and see Scrawny on the porch, moving with long gun that he must have had hidden.

And then the most glorious thing: looking very much like myself when I was teenager, he steps on the top step and his feet fly out from under him. Scrawny lands hard on the steps, the gun firing again, the bullet going wild.

Blue is standing on the porch with a pistol. The rain is bouncing off of the top of the truck in little glass pellets.

Isabel starts to drive and the moment she puts the pickup in gear she says, "What the heck is going on?"

"I don't know," I shout. "I don't know who they are."

She is backing up towards the open gate by the house and whips around to head through it. The gate lies on the ground and we drive over the barbed wire. "What do you mean you don't know who they are?"

I am looking back. Scrawny isn't on the porch anymore. "I mean, I was writing. And then I went to sleep. And then when I woke up, these three guys broke in." I can't believe it. I can't believe I'm alive.

"What? Who are they?" she asks again.

"I don't *know.*" I wring my hands. And then I do my best to explain, but it all sounds absurd. "There's three of them but I think two of them kill people for sport or something, and they charge the third guy money. I'm actually not really clear on it. But they were about to torture me."

"It looks like they did."

"Careful here, careful," I say, pointing to guide her up onto the ridge, because the ditch on either side is liable to get the truck stuck. All around are signs of a crazy winter, ice and a few patches of snow, slippery and cold.

We pass a pond on the left, and I remember when I was a kid one winter, when it was frozen solid, going out and laying in the middle of the pond. I got in trouble with my mother, because it is rare that such a pond would actually be frozen solid. Nevertheless, I felt pretty confident about it, because I had seen the horses walking out on the ice. And if a horse can walk on a pond, a twelve-year-old can.

We're driving on the ridge. I noticed a pair of headlights turn onto the ridge far behind us, and the pickup truck with its running lights is following.

"I don't know who's in it, but they're behind us."

Isabel drives about a quarter mile atop this ridge. Coming up ahead is the left turn to take the path out to the road. As a tenant with her own key, she knows this as well as, if not better than, me. Because while I know this farm mainly from my time visiting it as a child and a teenager, she comes here twice a month to leave a rent check. Nevertheless, we are driving fast. The wheels slip and slide atop the ridge.

Gnarled trees light up white. Unrecognizable farm equipment, plows of unknowable age, parked against barbed wire fences and gradually fused with trees. Up ahead where the turn is, there are several barns in a complex that makes up the working section of the farm—a series of barns, the old house which lies in ruins, a tractor barn, an old combine harvester, and more.

Isabel is wide-eyed, gunning it and looking in the rearview mirror. She's not an action star, I realize, she's a real person who's high on adrenaline now and driving too fast.

"They're gaining," she says.

"Look out," I cry, "This is your turn, turn *here.*"

She hits the turn too fast and the truck slides, the wheels coming off of the ridge. And for a moment, the bottom of the truck scrapes on the mud. We're about to get hung up. But she guns the truck and compensates, swinging the wheels around. But this causes the whole truck to whip down into the ditch. At once we lurch, my body flying against the dashboard.

Because we are stuck.

Chapter 18

"WE HAVE TO GET OUT," Isabel shouts.

The truck is sitting at an angle on the side of the ridge. I look back out the rear windshield of the pickup cab and see the other truck coming fast. It is possible that cannot see us. But they will be on us very soon, right above where we have run off. Isabel's truck is in the mud and at an angle in the ditch that, with the pursuers' running lights, will be impossible to miss.

I groan, my body pulsing with the impact against the dash. I scramble to find my glasses, which have flown to the front of the dashboard. Finding them, I open the passenger side door, and it slams against the mud. There is barely enough space to haul my flabby body through and out. My sweatpants get soaked as my knees land in the grass and sludge.

Inside the truck's cab, Isabel says *shit* as the lights come on, and in a moment, she switches them off.

To find my balance I have to put my hands into the mud, caking them and freezing my fingers in the frost. As I do, a visceral thrill races along my spine, because I know there are countless wayward bits of barbed wire and rock all over the farm, and if I slice my hands up now, we will not be able to stop and worry about the cut.

It is freezing cold, with pelting rain falling out around us. Isabel has gotten out the other side, and now she appears around the front of the truck. I get to my feet as she gestures, *come on.*

But then the truck that is pursuing us zooms past on the ridge and we crouch low. There is no way that they do not see our truck here, I *know* that they must see us, and I say this aloud.

The pale truck stops up ahead at the turn we were headed for and idles, its engine chugging. I don't know what they're planning. Maybe they're looking back, trying to see in the dark, to tell where we are.

"We can't stay here," I say. Our truck is the one thing that they can see.

Next to us at the edge of the ditch is a barbed-wire fence lined with trees. And I know that on the other side of it is a long, rectangular field. If we follow that field, eventually we will come back to one of the main roads that runs along the southern edge of the farm. I know all of this because I have walked it thousands of times. "This way," I say, and we run crouched up the side of the ditch, not looking back at the men in the truck. If they have gotten out to search for us, we have not heard it.

Under cover—we hope—of a clump of trees, we take turns going through the fence. Climbing over barbed wire fences is something that everybody who has been around a farm most of their lives knows like the back of their hand, because fences and gates are a constant part of your lives, like the need to breathe, or to replenish food and fuel. The way to go through a barbed wire fence is to put your foot on one of the lower wires and use your hand to pull up one of the upper ones, so that the person you're with can crawl through. And then you do it again for the other guy. A variation of this can be done if you're alone. If the fence is low enough or loose enough, you can just push the whole thing down and climb over it. Regardless, I have learned over my life to be careful; you need to climb over and make sure not to get the barbs of the wire caught in either your clothing or in your skin.

I have often thought about the fact that barbed wire was invented not for farms, but to terrorize and maim soldiers in war. Those World War One soldiers who were caught in barbed wire, or saw bodies bound up in it during that Great War, spent their entire lives traumatized by their existence. And yet it was repurposed as an important means of managing cattle and land, and for the demarcation of ownership in farms around America. It is one of the ugliest tools of the heritage of war, and it is a part of our everyday lives.

The wires of the fences on this farm are loose. I push down the top wire and Isabel stretches her long legs over it. And then I do the same, being careful because I am barefoot and wearing sweatpants.

We begin to run along the pasture, Isabel now following me. The ground is frozen and covered in rocks which are torturing my feet, and I am constantly in fear that I'm going to put a foot wrong and slice it open on something sharp. Instead, what I get is constant but unbleeding pain. As we run, I try to aim my feet at frozen and flattened hay, but there is no light to see. Isabel and I are dark silhouettes to one another.

As we move towards the south path, I hear the slamming of the pursuers' truck door. "Wait, stop," I say as we near a tree and crouch. The leafless, gnarled tree seems as good a place as any to take cover and look back toward the ditch. Looking back whence we came, we see a silhouette in the night shining a flashlight as he moves towards Isabel's truck. His torch beam bounces off the glass as he whips it around the cab and into Isabel's truck bed. He then shines the light towards the line of trees and fence we came through. But with the sleet and rain, the light does not penetrate enough into the field to come anywhere near us.

Isabel has her hands on the gnarled limbs of the tree, staring at the pursuer. "I don't understand this at all."

"Neither do I," I say. "Come on, let's head toward the old tractor barn." She follows me, although it is unlikely that she knows the nest of buildings on this farm well enough to tell one from the other.

We move away from the tree and steadily along the field towards the southern road of the farm. When we reach it, a car-wide dirt path running all the way west to the creek that is the boundary of the property, we turn left and head towards the black silhouettes of a large barn.

Before us is the enormous wreck of a combine harvester that has not moved in close to two decades. The combine is like a vast metal lobster, a giant tractor on steroids. Its wheels are the height of a man. There's a cockpit up top that you sit in, a wide rolling-pin kind of structure towards the front. This piece of equipment is the kind of thing that farm accident stories are made of, with countless little metal teeth for ripping up grain, and in the back a big hopper into which the grain can be poured.

The tires are not just flat but rotten, and the roots of nearby trees have crept through them. The combine, like other pieces of equipment on the farm, are becoming one with the land. As we reach it, we are once again close to the pursuers' truck.

We hear a shuffle on the path and suddenly Scrawny is coming towards us from a clump of trees.

"I see you!" he says. "You can't get away."

I'm not sure if he can see us at all or is guessing and working off sound. I cannot tell if he has his gun, but he does have a flashlight, which he whips towards us. Isabel and I duck behind the combine, gingerly crouching next to the long wire teeth of the rolling pin. We are silent as Scrawny moves along the side of the beast.

Earlier tonight, I was thrilled that I would be able to tell people I wrote a book and dealt with cold. I have completely overflowed my reservoir for adventure.

There is nowhere to go, because of an enormous blackberry bush beside the combine. All we could do is turn back, run for the field or the southern path, and in so doing, even in the dark, we would be exposed. I look at her and I can imagine what she must be thinking. How did she get into this? She came to drop off a lease and now she is running for her life, fleeing consulting psychopaths from Tulsa.

"Do you have your gun?" I ask.

"Shit," she whispers. "I lost it in the truck."

Finally Scrawny reaches the front of the combine, his flashlight sweeping the ground in front of him.

He is getting closer.

I have to do something. As soon as he rounds the front of the rolling pin, I gasp in fear and run out.

My intention is to leap and grab him around the waist, as though I am an eighteen-year-old right tackle on a football team, except even when I was eighteen, I did not play football.

And the idea of my making an actual leap of any athletic kind is preposterous. The *Post* showed me leaping in the air, but in fact I was leaping off a curb. What looked athletic was plain old gravity.

This is too. I fall forward. I hit the ground, but my shoulder does connect with his right shin and he topples sideways. He kicks me in the shoulder, and

I crawl over him, enraged. He is a skinny figure in the dark, in the mud and gravel, and I grab for his flashlight hand.

I grab his wrist and I yank on it, pulling him with my weight, whipping his body across mine towards the combine. Scrawny smacks his head and left shoulder hard against a cluster of iron pipes and equipment on the side of the combine. He yelps, and when he goes down, he whacks his head on the fender of one of the enormous tires.

He lies in the frozen mud. Isabel and I run for our lives.

There are several barns to choose from and I point towards one.

Having at the very least knocked out a man, I'm going to take Isabel to where I once hunted wood bees.

Chapter 19

MOVING INTO THE BIG BARN at night is a challenge, because there's wire and boards all over the floor and we're trying to move silently. We move past a feeding trough and the inoculation chute towards a door in the side of the barn.

The barn is enormous, black wood so old that in the daytime it appears to have become one with nature like the combine harvester and the Ford Ranger near the ranch house that are merging with the trees. We move out of the cold, pelting rain into the shelter of the barn. The clay ground is cold beneath my bare feet. But I can deal with the cold. All I really want right now is safety.

Isabel surveys the place. "I've been in this barn before," she says. "Your grandmother showed it to me when I came to rent the pasture.

I nod. "I used to spend a lot of time here." In my memories, my time in this particular barn is always one of sweltering heat. The air would be filled with wood bees, enormous fuzzy bees so large that they laze in the air and constantly struggle to keep themselves aloft. So slow that you can hit them with a two by four, which I would often do for sport, and which my grandfather encouraged because these bees drilled into the wood like termites.

Near where we are standing, lit by dim light, is a wide, shallow trough. We tilt our heads to the side, listening. But we don't hear anyone. Scrawny may be dead, but there is still Blue and Ryan.

"It's strange," I say quietly. "He didn't seem *that* injured when he hit his head." I put the thought aside. "We need to get your truck out," I say. "We can't go all the way back for my car."

"How long can we wait here?" Isabel agrees. "They'll come looking for their friend."

"Or… maybe they'll leave," I realize. "This isn't the way it's supposed to have gone for them, so maybe they'll cut their losses."

"If so, they'll need their truck."

I agree with that. And we have not heard their truck move. The whole farm has become quiet. Even though it is desperately uncomfortable to sit down on the cold trough in my wet sweatpants, I need to rest. So I sit and slide back, leaning my back on the wall. Feeling the prickliness of cold against my body.

"Hey, you were like a superhero back there," I say.

Isabel turns in the dark and runs her hand over her ponytail. "You were too. Running out of the truck like that. Bashing that guy against the combine. That was pretty great."

I chuckle a nod. This is not at all how I expected my evening to go. I am on a clock. My plan was to write Monday—today, I suppose—as much as I did the first day. A solid eight hours of sleep is necessary for that. This will be the second morning that Isabel Hardy will have disrupted my schedule. I feel the crinkle of the envelope in my pocket. "You really came just to drop off a lease?"

She scoffs quietly. "I don't know. I did come to drop it off. But I was just kind of wondering if you'd be awake."

"At 3:45 in the morning?"

"Well… you said in your author's note that you tend to write all night."

This makes my eyebrows raise, and I tilt my head.

She raises her hands in the dark, a mock surrender. "I know, I know."

"My author's note?"

"Yes."

I'm searching my mind, flipping through pages I wrote long ago. "The author's note in the first *Dream Tasker* book?"

"Ugh. Yes, so, yes, I knew that you were a writer." The way she says this, I know that she is rolling her eyes. Her silhouette moves against the blue outside, her voice mixing with the rattling of freezing rain. Every time we speak, bursts of steam fill the air. "I remembered you from when we went out. And when your grandma told my mom that you were writing books, I *did* get them. And I read *all* of them. I even read the *Fearless* books, the ones under the Ortega name. So yes, I remembered."

"Why did you act like you didn't know?"

"I don't know," she says, "I guess I just didn't want to seem like a stalker."

"By dropping off a rent check? I'm the stalker," I point out. "I came to *your* house."

"That's true. I guess I could have been a stalker if I wanted to."

I sigh. "I *did* use to stay up all night to write. But the truth is it gets harder as you get older. And I haven't written in a really long time. So I'm just going with an assumption that I need some sleep. I'm writing by day. Yesterday was a really good day."

We're both on alert, putting off going back out, waiting for noise, or a truck heading out to Dentonville Road.

On the wall I spot a pair of old sacks once used to carry fertilizer. I tear both of them down. The burlap sacks are rotten but thick. I shake them, feeling for snakes or anything else. Look in.

"What are you doing?"

"I'm making myself some shoes." I tear a strip off the top of each of the burlap sacks. I don't put a foot into each sack to wear it like a sock—I lay each sack down and put my bare foot into center, right on the feed label. Then I lift the sack around my foot and use the strips that I tore off the tops of the sacks to bind them. I admire my work, tilting my new, burlap moccasins left and right. They will definitely get soaked. But at least I won't be barefoot. It'll do for now. My feet instantly feel warmer and, in the darkness, I put my hands on my hips as though I'm a very accomplished person.

"So tell me what it was like," she says. "Like, how did you wind up doing the *Fearless* books?"

"You may know more than I do," I say, "if you've read the interviews that I did."

"Tell me," she says. She's closer now, taking my hand.

111

"Okay. Let's see. The *Fearless* books were the brainchild of Niles Peary, an executive who ran the movie studio that had created them. It was his idea that I would use a pseudonym."

"I seem to remember some fight. You and an editor?" Like she's narrating as she searches around her mind.

"Oh, god," I say. "Yeah. Not really an editor, an executive. I think I blabbed about that in an issue of *Publisher's Weekly.*" Though I never think about it, this fight is still very close to the surface in my mind. "So look, I'm in my mid-twenties. Any argument about my writing tended to make me very sensitive. Kind of a prima donna. And it's a tie-in series, it pays well—they did, back then—but you don't control everything the way you do if it's your own book. And so one of the arguments we got into, the one that made the magazines, was just… weird," I say.

"How weird can it get? You're writing about teenage spies."

"Yeah, well, it was this thing where Mr. Peary wanted the bad guy in one of the books to be named after—I think it was a girlfriend or an ex-girlfriend. And he *insisted*. And none of the lawyers were involved in this because this was a pet project of his."

I stop and think, because I want to make sure that I'm telling it right, even though it doesn't matter at all. "I don't remember if I agreed or not. But anyway we kept changing the name back and forth. I'd change it back to something generic, and he'd change it back if he could get involved at the next editing stage. I mean, I didn't want to be accused of making a bad guy out of this guy's ex-wife or whatever she was. And then, if you can believe it, before the book went to press, he changed it back *again*." I'm almost laughing now, and I remember to get quiet. But it's the first time I've felt like laughing in many hours.

She kisses me, and her body feels warm. She leans back against me and we look out through rotten boards at the darkness. "So is that what came out? You made a bad guy of the ex?"

"Ah," I say, my hands on her shoulders. "No, because I caught it at the last minute. And so I changed it back one last time. And so the version that came out," I say, tapping the air as though I'm tapping a desk in front of me, "is the one that *I* wanted."

"Well, that's what's important," she says, and I can hear her smile. She tilts to look back at me and kisses me again. "So do you remember what the name was?"

I sigh. "Oof. Who cares? I look out the window and get us both on our feet. "What?"

"I'm just thinking if their truck is still there… maybe we can use it."

"Don't you think they're watching it?"

I go forward in the barn and she follows me through a wide door into the next room, which has slats in the wall that look out towards the combine and the truck nearby. I can make out the glint of the pale metal on the ridge. "It's still just sitting there. Look, there was the scrawny guy. Assuming he chased us alone—and that's a good assumption, because no one else got out of the truck, and the other guy, the boss, would have if he'd come in the truck with him—then that means the other two are back at the house. And the truck is right there. We should try to go take it."

"They could be on foot anywhere between the house and here," she says. "Why don't we just wait for light and then we can see if we can move *my* truck."

"Your truck is stuck in the mud; I don't know in the morning we'll be able to move it."

"I *don't want to go out there,*" she hisses. "I'm not… I can't do that again."

Meaning: don't think of me as Linda Hamilton. I can only do so much.

"Sit down," she says. "There's got to be blanket or something in here. I don't *know*. Just… tell me more stories about fighting with studio execs."

But I'm not listening. "I know that we can get it." I am sneaking out the front of the barn and looking around, moving towards a fence. I look off to my left towards the combine harvester and an enormous pecan tree. I do not see anybody moving. I'm not going to go to the combine and see if Scrawny is still there next to it or if he is moved somewhere else. But I don't hear anybody around me.

I hear Isabel coming up behind me. She has decided to get back in the game, and it's important, because we can't just sit there.

We move towards the ridge. Finally we reach the light-colored pickup truck that Scrawny was driving.

"I don't know," it might not even open," she says. I put my hand on the handle and pull, and the truck opens up. I'm standing on the side of the ridge at an angle because the truck is wide enough that it takes almost the entire top. I have to climb up into the driver's seat. I look down at Isabel.

"Are there keys?" she asks. But there aren't. I curse. And worse, the lights have come on. *Shit.*

I reach for the dash, finding a button and turning the lights off. Jupiter, the hero of my books, never would have let it come on in the first place.

"They'll be here any minute… any second," she says. I know she's right.

Probably Scrawny, even if he has regrouped with Blue at the house, saw the lights of his cab turn on. For that matter, he could be right behind us. He could even be in the pickup bed or crouching behind the truck.

Where *is* he?

I know it's unlikely to find keys, but I reach into the glove box and open it up. What I expect to find at best would be a pair of keys, laying on a whole bunch of meaningless crap of exactly the kind that's in my own glove box: registrations and old light bills.

But the glove box is almost completely empty, so bare you can see rug lining. Empty except this: a long white card with perforation on the side.

I look at it and make out that it is a rental agreement with the customer name of Brian McMurtry.

Brian McMurtry? I wonder if that is the name of Scrawny, or the name of Blue.

I wonder, if I were Blue, would I rent the truck to take my client out on safari? But then I remember that he called himself a *consultant*. And it is very possible that he wants to put up the best front for his client. And so, if that means renting a nice truck to pick up his Ryan in Tulsa and drive them out into the middle of nowhere, then so be it. It is indeed a nice truck. But what I haven't found are keys, so we need a new plan.

Chapter 20

I LOOK TOWARDS THE RANCH house where the lights are still burning.

I don't want to go back into the barn that we just came out of. I left Scrawny too close to there. In my hand, I am idly swiping my thumb and forefinger across the piece of paper I took out of the empty glove compartment. I look towards the old farmhouse, the one that lies in ruins. I can't see it right now because it is still dark, though it must be about an hour to sunrise. And there are a number of trees and barns and several gates between us in the farmhouse. But I think it would be a good place to hide.

"Farmhouse," I say, tilting my head towards it. It is next to Dentonville Road, though hard to see from there. Part of me thinks if we can get to the farmhouse, we may as well run for the road, and—what? Walk the road for miles? Waiting for them to come and run us down?

An engine fires up in the distance. Something I haven't heard before—not tonight, anyway. From the direction of the ranch house comes a droning, high-pitched engine whine, and suddenly there is a shape moving away from the ranch house and out towards the ridge. It swiftly turns as it passes over the ranch house gate and swings in our direction with headlights blazing before it. It's a four-wheeler ATV, with rider.

"I don't understand," I say, "I don't remember there being another vehicle." But of course it's possible. When I awoke, I saw my three captors in the front with their pickup truck. They could very well have had another vehicle around the back of the house. Because what do I really know about them, or what they have in the darkness? They could have hidden this little ride behind the old pickup truck across the back yard, or even parked it just forty yards away from the house, far enough to be lost in the darkness.

"Come on," I say, as the four-wheeler closes the quarter mile between the ranch house gate and the pickup that we are standing next to.

Running and crouching, I lead Isabel through a tall open gate next to a large tractor barn.

This is the tractor barn where my grandfather fell in his mid-fifties and broke his leg, a painful break that would haunt him for the rest of his life. It is also here that I remember finding a stash of 45 RPM records and paperback books put for storage but never protected, ruined by the elements over the years.

We cross the yard by the tractor barn, and now we're into the oldest part of the farm that I know of. In the darkness I can see the old house, huge parts of its roof caved in. It is a single story farmhouse with a front porch and an enclosed back porch, a place that I spent many hours when I was a child. That was before the ranch house was built and this place was allowed to fall into complete ruin.

It is a mystery to me that it has not burnt down or been destroyed or plowed under by my brother or my grandmother. Instead, it just sits there.

We go to the main door, a glass storm door with a wood door behind it, with a large glass window. Both are locked. I don't want to try to break it right now, because we may need this door's protection. Instead, we hurry around the back of the house to find one of the bedroom windows. I don't hear the four-wheeler close by now, which means they must have stopped by Scrawny's pickup truck. It may well be Scrawny on the four-wheeler, but it may be Blue. It is unnerving to me that we have not seen Scrawny since I bashed his head against the combine harvester, and I have no idea if he is still laying there or if he has gone back to the ranch house to regroup and then come back again. I definitely do not fear that the rider of the four-wheeler is Ryan, because I have a good sense that Ryan is as in over his head as much as I am.

We find one of the bedroom windows fairly low to the ground. It is large, so that it could be opened up in the summer to let air in. The paint on the wood lats of the wall are so peeled that the curlicues of old paint look like infinite rows of snarling teeth.

I put my hand on the windowsill and try to push it up, but it's jammed. "See if you can help me with this," I say, and Isabel and I put our fingers on the windowsill and try to push it. After a moment it becomes clear that the window itself is going to give way before the frame does, and we have no choice but to break it.

In the movies, and in books that I myself have written, what usually would happen is the main character would bash the window with his elbow. But my elbow is bare because I'm wearing a T shirt. Rather than peel off the muddy shirt and wrap it around my elbow, I simply look around and find a large sandstone rock. Gripping it, I shield my eyes and slam it the rock against one of the windowpanes. We break the glass and then push the wooden frame of the window through. The wood is so old and rotten that it breaks less than it bends and crumbles.

We climb into the bedroom. It never ceases to amaze me what this abandoned place looks like. Isabel breathes unhappily as she looks around in the extremely dim light. There is still art on the walls. There is still furniture in the room. There are still beds for guests here. This entire house was closed up when my great grandmother moved into a nursing home, and no one has dared touch it. So the elements are molding and crumbling it.

"We need to find a place to hide," Isabel offers. No sooner do I step forward into the bedroom than the floorboards collapse under my feet. My foot falls several inches, jamming against the crumpling boards, and I fall backward, landing on my ass. I scramble as my jagged burlap shoes catch in rotten wood and nails. I am lucky that I do not lacerate my feet. I tell Isabel to stay back.

She sticks to the wall. Luckily, there is only about half a foot below the floorboards. But the floors are completely rotten, so we will need to carefully move along the walls and hope for the best if we hope to move through the house. Maybe this won't be the right place to hide after all.

Isabel gasps, and as I look down, I feel a strange, fluid motion against my hands. And then I see a swarm of small black snakes, squirming over my fingers. Instinctively I shriek and yank back my hand, little snakes flying into the air. *Oh my god. Oh my god.*

"It's okay!" she whispers. "It's okay, they're rat snakes. They're harmless." But I am already scrambling up as a deep, basic revulsion makes me shake.

I pull free and join Isabel at the wall, and both start creeping towards the center of the farmhouse, the den. I am shaking, and Isabel touches my shoulder.

"Let's hide," she says. I can see her struggling to stay on top of emotions that are bucking within her. We are struggling not to drown in panic as we try to stay alive. "Let's, let's calm down and get our heads around us and figure out the next move."

We enter the den. This small room, which is next to the windows that look out onto the front porch and then out to the trees lining Dentonville Road, is a room that I spent many years in. It is the room where I saw the *Star Wars Holiday Special* in 1978, when there was no ranch house. This is where the family would gather at the farm.

There is still a very large couch against the windows and an easy chair against the corner. Both of them are collapsed and rotting. Testing each step as though we are walking on ice, as though we are walking on a frozen pond, I lead Isabel across the living room. And then finally I slide down the wall. Sitting next to the couch. If someone were to look through the front windows, we may well look like muddy lumps of clothes.

Isabel slides down next to me. I reach into my right pocket and pull out the piece of paper. "McMurtry."

"What is *that?*" she has not seen the paper before.

"This was in the glove box of that truck. It says McMurtry—I think Blue is Brian McMurtry. I don't know. It just seems so funny that he would rent a truck. I guess it makes sense though." She doesn't have any response to this.

She breathes, nodding to herself. "As soon as the sun is up, we'll be able to see what's going on with my truck and we'll be able to get out of here."

"If we can get to it," I say. "I'm tired." I'm looking around in the dim darkness. There's so much dust in the air that my nose is closed up and I sound like Rudolf, the Red-Nosed Reindeer.

"You're right, it's good to rest."

I think about the guys back at my grandmother's ranch house. "I'm gonna lose my computer," I say. "And I got all that work done yesterday." I can't believe that I'm thinking about the loss of a day's worth of writing when I could lose my life, and when my adult children could lose their father. But it's true. The loss of the writing is forefront in my mind.

She pulls her feet under her legs. "It was going that good?"

She leans her head on my shoulder. Across from us is a crocheted doily on the arm of a collapsed armchair. I remember it and I'm shocked it hasn't moved. But then maybe my grandmother has her own logic, her own mystic reasons for closing up this place and letting it turn, slowly but surely, to dust.

"It was," I say. "It was one of the best writing days of my life."

She sits very quietly. "You bring back the old bad guy?"

"Who?"

"Oh, the one with the name you can't remember," she says.

"This isn't a *Fearless* book. No, I left all that stuff in the past. Everybody's going to be surprised about this book."

After a while she says, "Was that fight why you never published another book?"

I don't have an answer for that because I have thought about it a lot.

"All about a stupid character name," she sighs.

"Yeah," I grumble. "What was it. Ally, Alice, Alexis…something."

She is still, listening to me try to capture trivia, her hand on my chest.

I freeze as the four-wheeler roars, arriving at the front of the house. We've both gone rigid, but I have to look.

Slowly, I poke my head up next to the couch to peer through the front window.

I see a shadow in the front yard next to an enormous line of fir trees that create a natural barrier between the yard and the road. Then the shadow steps up on the porch, just yards away from me. Unlike the floor inside this dilapidated wreck, the front porch is made of cement. It is surrounded by wooden columns with a wooden roof.

The man on the front porch is tall and bald. And even in the light, I can see that he has a complicated and ornate tattoo on his neck. Therefore, this man who I will call Tattoo is not one of the people who held me at the house. This is deeply disturbing.

"I've never seen this guy before."

One thing is clear: he is carrying a gun which he holds down in front of him. He moves by the front window, peering in, but he does not see us crouched directly below him.

He steps back to the entrance of the porch, back down the steps, and around to the side of the porch, where he is looking through a window next to the well.

This well is not what people think of when they think of a well in the country. It's just a ten-inch-wide iron pipe that sticks up out of the ground. By the time I was a child, it was not used for water anymore. And what *I* usually used it for was throwing fireworks into it. I would throw firecrackers in and hear them drop far down until they burst with a ringing and hollow explosion. Or I would take a bottle rocket, light it, drop it in the well, and the rocket would fall. And then sometime before the rocket reached the water far below, it would ignite and fly back up out, rifling through the pipe and then soaring into the air, barely missing the overhang of the roof as it passed.

My great-grandmother and grandparents never knew that I did all that and probably would have been furious, even though the well was never going to be used again.

The man with the gun comes back to the porch, moving fast and grabbing the porch door handle. It too is locked. But it will cause no problem for him. We need to move. The first thing to do around anyone with a gun is to get the hell away. This is true in workplace shootings, and it is true in school shootings. And it is true right now, sometime in the wee hours of the morning in Oklahoma.

The problem is if we move right now, there's a very good chance that he will see us. We have no choice, though. We can't crawl across the living room towards the back. But we can crawl along the couch into one of the other bedrooms. I point towards the door into my great-grandfather's old bedroom, with its window right over the well.

Isabel nods and starts to crawl towards the bedroom. I crawl behind her, and just as we do, we hear the porch storm door wrenching open. Then there is pounding on the door. He slams against it and the door flies off his hinges. As we move into the bedroom, Tattoo is coming for us.

Chapter 21

HE MOVES IN VERY FAST, this Tattoo, this stranger who I've never seen before. After just a few hours, I have come to think of Blue and Scrawny and even Ryan the middle-manager type as old friends. Tattoo tears through the front door like a bull. It doesn't surprise me in the least, because the wooden door is very light and never reinforced because there is no way that you would want to steal anything from this house. He bashes the door down like sheet rock.

By now, the slightest glow of morning light is beginning to come in from the window in my great-grandfather's bedroom. I am terrified, once again hiding. I think for a moment about getting into the back bathroom into the bathtub. But I do not think for an instant that he would stop before tearing through—or even shooting through—a shower curtain. Instead, while the door is coming off its hinges and making noise, while the floorboards are crunching treacherously beneath his boots, so that he is practically wading in the rotten floor, we find a vanity with a wide mirror and move it. As we crouch behind this polished old vanity, pushing it three feet from the wall, it is shocking to me that no one has removed it from this house. Another thing I will have to ask my grandmother about someday.

What is it that caused her to lock the door in this house and let it fall apart this way? I think I know it is not a betrayal, or a slap in the face to her own parents. I think it is a profound respect, it is the speech of grief itself. In her decision to lock the door and watch the house fall, she is saying that in the blink of a cosmic eye, all will be reclaimed. The fact that it is taking fifty years for the house to fall apart is nothing. For someone who loves God as my grandmother does, it is meaningless. There was a song she used to play for us, *Ain't a gonna need this house no longer.* And so, and so.

We crouch behind the vanity as Tattoo comes into the room. He walks slowly now, carefully sweeping his feet as the floorboards crack. I cannot see him, but I hear him. He walks right past us and into the back bathroom. If it were brighter, and he looked towards us, he would see us crouching behind the vanity, especially given how far it has been pushed from the wall.

I hear him moving around in the back bathroom, behind us. He pulls back the shower curtain, which rattles until the curtain rod collapses, clattering in the porcelain tub. There is a back window above the shower. Although I do not see it, I know that he is looking at it to see if anybody crawled out. But of course we have not. There is certainly no way that I personally would be able to climb up and out a narrow bathroom window.

He comes back out and he stops for just a moment beside the vanity. He turns towards us. We are enveloped in shadow, and he is right in front of us. And I have no idea if he sees us. We are frozen.

Isabel's knees are against my ribs as we crouch. I'm hoping that the angle of the vanity makes it look as though somebody started to move it, and then abandoned the task long ago. He is staring right at us and then he moves on. I hear him move back into the living room and then into the little bedroom, the one where we came in through the window. I hear him stop his feet, kicking plaster. No doubt he is looking at the busted window right now. He turns around and walks back into the living room. He has now explored almost the entire house except for the kitchen and the cupboards and the front, and now, strangely, I am thinking I wish I had thought to hide in the cupboard, because actually that would have been a better spot. Except that's where he's going now. I shift my weight slightly and my foot slips, skirting along the floor.

In the other bedroom, I hear Tattoo freeze. Now he begins to walk back towards the bedroom where we hide.

I turn and look at Isabel. She's staring at me, wide eyed. He is walking across the living room. In my mind, with my back turned, I can see his dark silhouette.

This man is in a different league from Blue and Scrawny.

We are caught if I let him come in, walk all the way over to the vanity and tear it aside. We are trapped. We are doomed. My knees are killing me as I hear him reach the threshold of this room once again.

I have no choice now. I stand up.

All my life I have never been brave. The only time I've been brave have been snippets here and there. Walking down into basements when I thought I heard a noise.

For people like me, so cushioned from danger, most of the bravery of our lives comes in ways that don't get written up in books. It is hours spent in emergency rooms, waiting for people with more talent than you to tell you good news or bad. It is the willingness to quit a job when somebody has asked you to do something unethical. These are the closest to any kind of bravery that I've ever known.

I stand up and take a gamble. I wait for his silhouette to cross through the door. I know that he has to weigh two hundred and fifty pounds, and I know that the window behind him is rotten. I have no idea how to actually do this. But I know I'm going to do what I'm going to do. As soon as I see his silhouette, Isabel senses that I'm going to move, and she tugs at my arm. I rise fast, for me, moving out from behind the vanity. And I spring as quickly as I can. I run straight for his chest. It is a clumsy and oafish move. I am an overweight man, but I am six foot two and two hundred and sixty-five goddamn pounds, a human battering ram, using my weight to carry me forward.

I am running as fast as I can when I hit him, his heavy body smashes sideways, spinning right through the wall. I fall as he flails out, and I hear him cry out. I practically connect with the well pipe on the other side.

There are pictures of people being impaled in old woodcuts of the historic Dracula. The stories go that at the St. Valentine's Day Massacre, Vlad Dracula killed four thousand people and had them impaled on poles while he ate a large meal at an outdoor table he had set outside. I know this because I've read about it since I was a child. Always in those pictures, the victims are impaled through the back, and the great pike comes out through the front of the chest.

Historically this is all nonsense. That is not how Vlad impaled people. Vlad impaled people by sticking a pole up their rectum and killing them very painfully and slowly. The impalement through the back and out through the chest is an invention of woodcutters wishing to shock—but not shock too much.

The way it is done on the woodcuts, though, is very close to what happens to Tattoo.

Except for that it doesn't come all the way through his chest. Instead, the iron pipe has crushed his spine and he writhes on the pipe like a stuck beetle, howling in pain that is made all the worse by the fact that I ball up and pound my fists on his body, pushing him down farther on the pipe. I roll out of the way and watch him wriggle before shock takes him over and he stops moving.

I lay on the ground and then roll and get up, pacing back and forth. Unsure what to do next. Now, for sure, I have just killed a person. I've never killed before in my life. I have written many scenes and envisioned it. I've watched a thousand movies, but I've never actually taken life from somebody who had a mother. Isabel comes to the hole in the wall.

"What did you do?"

I don't have any answer. "We have to get out of here," I say. "It's time. The sun is coming up."

Chapter 22

MOVING OUT THE BROKEN WINDOW, Isabel hisses and begins to stamp her feet, taken over by a disorienting anger. Nor do I want to process it—I'm frightened that if either of us really gives in and has a full-blown freak-out, we're doomed.

"What in the world is going on?" she cries. "This can't happen. Who *is* this?"

"I don't know."

"Who are *you?*" she hisses, her eyes furious as she turns on me. "You're supposed to be just a *writer.* You're not supposed to be somebody that a bunch of—what is this guy? Is he an *assassin?* Is that what he is?"

"Isabel, seriously, we have to go." As she flips out, I'm aware that Scrawny or one of the others could walk up on us at any moment. "I don't *know,*" I say again. "I mean, assassin? Nobody's coming at me to assassinate me. That's crazy. I don't know who he is. I don't ever come to the farm. You *know* that. You live here—I don't."

Just a short while ago—two days ago, I guess, because I'm losing track of time—we were walking around on the dam. She and I we were reliving a date that we had thirty years ago.

She reaches towards the man who has stopped moving. "You really don't know these people?"

Tattoo's muscular body and tactical boots put him in a world I don't navigate.

I say, "Do I look like somebody who would know these guys?"

And then I realize that sounds smug and effete, like I wouldn't hang out with somebody who has a neck tattoo. But no, I don't know anybody who's my height but a thousand times fitter, who would come to my grandmother's farm and try to kill me.

"Look," I say, "those guys, the ones you frightened with your whole Calamity Jane bit, they are *still* back at the ranch house. Okay? They're back at the house. *This* was another guy. We need to get out of here." And then something occurs to me that I have not asked her all night. My own cell is back at the house as well, but… "Do you have a phone?"

"No," she says. "Don't you think I would have mentioned it if I had a *phone?"* She looks around. "Not that there's any reception out here anyway."

"We need to get to town," I say. "We can take the four-wheeler."

"No, no, no," she says. "We won't both fit. Plus those things are slow. I want to take my truck."

"All right," I say.

I look back at Tattoo.

My feet are killing me. I take his boots. And socks. He's a size twelve and a half, which almost fits.

I look around for a moment. Tattoo had a gun. But it's nowhere to be seen, and as I glance at the snarl of weeds just yards from his body, I know that we don't have time to look for it.

We need to make tracks, to get room between ourselves and this farm. We need to get to the police.

When I've got Tattoo's footwear on I go back into the house and I grab a couple of pieces of the door frame that are laying on the floor and come out and hand one to her.

"Come on, hurry. We'll put this under the tires."

We move brazenly now, through the yard, past the tractor barn. My body doesn't feel like I'm in charge of it. My nerves are on fire.

I'm still thinking of the bug-like way that the man whose shoes I'm wearing died. We move around the tractor barn and look towards the house. In the early morning light, I can see movement. Somebody beside the porch. My captors are waiting for me to come back, or waiting for Tattoo, who must have been standing guard all the time they were torturing me, to bring us back.

As soon as I see the silhouette poke out from the front of the ranch house, I say, "We have to hurry."

We start running, not *serpentine* like in the old movies, we just run. My heart skips a beat as I hear rustling in a blackberry bush as we pass. A rabbit springs from the bush, darting across our path. I trip and fall, and scramble up again, finding traction with Tattoo's excellent tactical boots.

Finally we reach Isabel's truck where it still sits in the ditch. Blue's truck, which Scrawny was driving, still sits on top of the ridge. We take the two boards and placed them under the front tires of Isabel's truck. I wedge them in as best I can, kicking at them with the thick boots. The boards are tipping up a little bit in the mud.

"Okay, I'm gonna start it," she says, and I stay by the wheels. She opens and climbs up behind the wheel of the truck. She turns the key.

It revs a couple of times and doesn't start. She curses and pounds her fists and I say *go again.* I'm wishing now that we had taken the four-wheeler after all, but no, this has to work.

She turns the key again and this time the engine rumbles to life. I'm standing in front of the truck, and she starts to move, and I scramble out of the way. "Wait, wait, wait," I say, watching the wheels. "Okay, go." The wheels spin, failing to grab the boards.

"Stop," I call. I turn around, looking for anything I can use. I find a sandstone rock next to the barbed wire we climbed through just a few hours ago and run back.

Off at the house, our activity has been noticed, and there is shouting. Somebody fires a weapon. I don't feel the bullet fly past me, but I know it's close. *Pop, pop.*

I use the stone to hammer the boards in under the wheels. "Try again!"

She moves the truck slowly and the wheels grip the boards. The truck kicks forward and zooms a few yards past me. "Keep moving," I say. "Slow." I run alongside her and open the door and slide in, climbing up to the seat. I slam the door and she picks up speed.

I hear a bullet slam against the back of a pickup truck. She guns the truck up onto the top of the ridge, scraping past Blue and Scrawny's truck, slicing off its right headlight, and then she hangs the left and we're flying for the iron gate.

"Just shoot through it," I say. She barrels the truck through the metal gate, sending it flying open and teetering on its hinges.

Now we are in the road and driving, and I burst out in ecstatic laughter.

I look back, and I can see people running up onto the ridge, Blue and Scrawny, who seems to have survived his collision with the combine. I don't see Ryan.

As we drive, I look around and find her pistol in the floorboards, laying it on the seat. "Got your gun," I say.

She nods, not really listening as she drives in a sort of reverie that I understand completely.

As she drives the mile to the turn onto Highway 56, she seems to get a little calmer. "We'll go to town," she says, like an incantation. "We'll go to town."

"Can we go to your house?" I suddenly think. "Maybe that would be better."

"No, no, no, no," she says. "I don't want them following me there."

We travel past many farms, and we pass the dam that we climbed together on our date. Where Blue said he and his team spotted me.

By the time we pass the convenience store and get to Main Street, it is past sunup.

"What time is it?"

"I don't know," she says, but then we pass a bank building whose clock reads OK SAVINGS AND LOAN and 6:10am.

We pass a number of closed stores, the same antique places and cafes, plus the Internet Café, a library and a 7-11.

I look at it and touch her shoulder. "Are you going to the police?"

"Mm hmm," she said. "Yes."

I am picturing a long morning of explaining everything that has happened. I am picturing my son and daughter, who I nearly missed ever seeing again.

"I want…"

We have stopped at a light on the empty Main Street and she looks at me. "What?"

128

"I want to call my family," I say. "Before whatever is going to happen to me happens." What I mean is that there is a dead person I will have to answer for.

"What are you saying?" she says, idling. The light has turned green, but I have my hand raised, and she waits. We are the only vehicle on the street.

"7-11," I say. "They're open. I'll go in and get a phone. I can call them. You go to the police."

She cranes her neck to look at the 7-11. Indeed, there are lights on and people inside. The place is open twenty-four hours a day.

"It's just that if I go to the police right now," I say, "and I tell them about the big guy…"

"Okay," she says. She has gotten very calm. "Okay, here's what we're going to do. You go into the T Mobile place. Get yourself a phone, so you can call your family. And I'll go to the police station, it's just at the end of the block. And I'll tell them what's going on. And we'll be back to pick you up. Okay?"

I nod.

"I'll be right back," she says. "I'll get someone to go back with us."

At 6:15, I get out a few doors down from the 7-11 and look back into her truck. "It's gonna be fine," I say. "We made it."

Chapter 23

AS I STAND IN FRONT of the 7-11 on Main Street, I catch my reflection in the glass, and several things occur to me.

I am not at my best. I am wearing a battered grey Simple Minds T-shirt that I have had since the mid-90s, a pair of warm-up pants, and a pair of tactical boots, which, though stolen off a dead man and spattered with mud, are the most presentable thing about my ensemble. I am streaked with mud from head to toe, and my gray-blond hair is wild and dirty, and caked on my right side with blood from an aching knife wound to my ear.

But at any minute I expect to be arrested for murder. I do need to call home, but this will not be the way to do it.

As I stand in front of the 7-11 and look in, I know that I cannot go in there. If I go in there right now, I know what will happen. I can see inside. There are two employees behind the counter. Both of them in their twenties. One a heavyset young man in a 7-11 shirt, the other a woman with short blond hair. They will call the police before they speak to me.

The idea was that I would go in ask them to sell me a new phone, which is already going to be tricky, because I do not have my wallet.

This is so much not going to work that I'm shocked that Isabel, who must not be thinking clearly either, went along with it.

But then I put myself in Isabel's shoes, driving a man she barely knows after a harrowing night of mayhem. If I were her, I wouldn't even come back. Maybe she will, maybe she won't.

I move away from the front of the 7-11 and go to a railing along the sidewalk. All up and down Main Street, most everywhere that is not permanently closed is not open yet.

A little ways up is the Internet Café. The idea makes my stomach rumble. I would kill for a cup of coffee. But again, I have no money, and I look like a man who has spent the night trying not to be slaughtered. But I can set that aside—what I need is to get a message home. Walking along Main Street, I get to the end of the block and stand near the entrance of the café.

Nearby, set back in a large lot all its own, is the Hollow Hill Public Library. It is not gigantic, but it is *new*. New brick, nice concrete, clearly paid for through some bond or other tax action that gave the county seat a good library.

I look homeless at the very least, but homeless people use the library all the time. But it's far too early for it to be open. The Internet Café is the answer. Through the tinted glass of the café I can see a counter up front, tables, and then rows of computers towards the back.

Nearby me on the street, a woman is getting out of her car. She goes around to the back seat to wrestle a baby out of a child seat.

When the woman sees me loitering by the cafe, she visibly bristles. I look like a person that she cannot trust. I look like a person who has not slept and has no money, which in this town is one of the most dangerous kinds of person there is. I decide to start moving.

I open the glass door and move in, walking fast, because I've found that if you walk fast, people notice you less than if you wander around like you're not sure if you're allowed to be here. What I need to project is the kind of privileged I'm-allowed-anywhere air that makes guys like me both ubiquitous and invisible.

There are about ten people in a café set up for three times that, and most of them are folks in casual clothes at tables, having Danishes and reading the news on their iPads. What I want are the monitors and computers in back, which are arrayed on two long tables near a glass wall. Because most people bring their own device and it's less fun to set a little saucer in front of a keyboard, this section is practically empty, with a couple of people at one computer towards the end. I ignore them and move to the other end and sit down in front of one of the computers.

I have two goals.

I am going to contact my son and daughter.

And then I am going to look up the man who cut my ear.

Taking my seat, the crusty sweatpants flaking off bits of mud, I move the mouse and the screen comes alive. A floating dialogue box asks me for a credit card, for which I can look at the Internet for the grand sum of three dollars for every fifteen minutes. Three dollars that I, a man with advanced degrees that I don't even use, do not have.

My heart only sinks halfway because I expected this. I was hoping that they'd have free access—like a library would, if I had a library card, which I don't—but I knew it was a longshot.

I look back over my shoulder. The guy at the counter, a young, serious man who reminds me of my son, glances at me after serving a cappuccino. Then he looks away.

He is probably calculating. Whether I'm dangerous. Whether the other guests are going to complain. Whether I'm going to approach the counter and ask for a handout. That could go several ways, too, because some of these places have a policy that says, give the homeless guy a Danish. And some of them have a policy that says, call the police.

Okay. So it will be harder. I am pretty certain that I can't ask the guy for free Internet access. My best hope is that he quits worrying about me. The guy has not looked back and not picked up a phone, and now as a pair of teenage girls come in, he turns his attention to them.

And then, the pair who were at the computer at the end of the table—an older, dark-skinned man with a farmer's clothes, and a younger man I take to be his son, both scoot back from their chairs. I shoot a glance towards them, momentarily fantasizing that they are deciding to confront me—for what, who knows—but no. They are simply done with the computer.

As they start to walk away, I look at their computer.

An internet browser is still open.

I see the two teenage girls leaving the counter and decide I had better move in case this corner will be the one they want. It isn't—they turn towards a table—but I move like overweight lightening getting to the corner table.

A Chrome browser is open to Monster, a job hunt site. In a little box in the upper corner, I see a countdown:

04:56 minutes remaining.

Okay. I need to quit wasting time because Internet access is gold now.

I enter *gmail.com* into the address bar and log in, fussing a bit to remember my password. When I get my email inbox open, I have too many messages to count. Because I am a human writer, I experience a moment's habitual need to click on a couple subject lines that just might be about writing work. One is from my apparently once-and-future agent (FOLLOWING UP) and another is from something called PublishingCoolNews with the subject line INTERVIEW—FEARLESS?

It's remarkable. My agent wants me to write a new *Dream Tasker* book, but I have heard the title *Fearless* more in the last two weeks than in the last two presidencies.

I send a note to my daughter and son. After debating and restarting a few times, I settle on:

At the farm, checking in. Had some break-ins. Whole big thing. If I call you in an emergency, our lawyer is Tony Salvaggio.

I end it with "Love you!"

What else could I say?

I don't have much time. If Isabel is going to come back, she's going to be looking for me at the 7-11. I have taken too much time already. In fact I have:

02:56 minutes remaining.

I leave email logged in and open a second tab and enter Google. I pull out the slip of paper to remember the spelling and then type:

BRIAN MCMURTRY.

There are thousands of Brian McMurtry's in the world, so next I try Brian McMurtry, Oklahoma. Still too many search results, none of which are useful to me. There is a Brian McMurtry who writes a lot of articles about land use at the University of Oklahoma, and I'm pretty sure that he is not my guy.

I try Brian McMurtry, consultant.

The result astounds me.

There is an entry for a web page for Brian McMurtry, Consultant. The first one that I click on is the staff page of a whole consulting agency, Stonewater Enterprises, with boastful little biographies of the star employees.

Brian McMurtry has a Level Three Security Clearance with the Department of Defense, and I'm not the kind of person who has any idea what that is, but it sounds impressive. He did two tours in Desert Storm, and then several tours elsewhere. He is a general troubleshooter. He is listed as a team leader. He is available for corporate work.

I frown. This does not quite match the Brian McMurtry that I've been thinking about, with the thick accent and the knife, but when I scroll down to the picture, it is indeed the man that I've come to know as Blue.

He is wearing khakis and a polo shirt, and he's smiling broadly with a team behind him on a cruise, which must be… a Christmas party? If I choose to, I can click on a number of glowing recommendations. Brian McMurtry is indeed a consultant.

But what he is doing at my farm is beyond my imagination.

I try to think back through it. Brian, Scrawny, and Ryan showed up at 3:45 in the morning and began to torture me until I got away. Yet another man, Tattoo, was waiting outside to give chase. And as it happens, I have killed him.

I go back to the Christmas party. Brian is raising a toast. Gathered around the silver-topped bar are nine or ten other fine folks, all in blazers that are athletically cut to show off their impressive physiques, the women in long, black dresses that show off powerful latissimus dorsi and quadriceps.

Standing about seven feet from McMurtry in a tan jacket is the man I know as Tattoo. He is not identified.

55 seconds left.

I spend some more time looking and I don't find anything else, other than a LinkedIn page for Brian McMurtry that I just have time to open up. Scanning down the page I see much the same information that I have already found, and possibly more that LinkedIn will not show unless I log in. But I am not about to log into LinkedIn. Because one thing I know is that if somebody looks at his LinkedIn page, he will get a notification, and he will know that I've been looking. And if Brian right now is at *my* computer, he will know that that has happened.

20 seconds.

I have to go. I've taken too long. I shut the tab and see my email is still open.

I can't help myself. I click on the two book emails. My agent is just re-iterating the same stuff and wants to see what I come up with.

The online magazine thing is from a writer called Jazz who writes in a blaze of emojis and exclamation points. He or she is doing a puff piece about Jerry Bale and the possible relaunch of *Dream Tasker*, they're super excited and want an interview, but as mentioned in their subject line:

I'm also totally intrigued by the story that ran a few years ago, about the conflict between you and the business guy in charge of Fearless. Now that so much time has passed, would you care to reminisce? We'd love details!

I shake my head, closing the emails. I have visited enough ghosts. And anyway, I'm out of time, says the computer.

LOGGING YOU OUT. THANK YOU.

I turn back to thoughts of McMurtry as I stand up.

Several things occur to me. First, they're probably long gone. For whatever reason, they probably wanted my laptop. I *do* need to talk to the police. The greatest likelihood is that my nightmare night was a massive mistake.

And that's the other thing that's occurred to me is that Isabel is *also* probably long gone. If I were her, I would leave Mike Dotson far behind.

I'm going to go back out on the street and think for a bit and then figure out a way to get back to the farm. I put the rental slip back into the pocket of my warmup pants next to Isabel's lease.

Before exiting, I go to the bathroom.

My ear is a mess. And it takes me a while to clean the blood off of it. I run some water through my hair. I take off my shirt and give myself what they used to call a whore's bath, using paper towels to wash under my arms and my face. I use as much soap as I can get out of the dispenser.

I go back out I have a feeling that, once Isabel doesn't show, I'm going to come back and use the computer again if I can figure out how. But I need to pace and think.

I go past the counter desk and I nod at the guy, who waves at me as though he is dismayed that I have come into his life.

Out the glass door and into the street. I am very nearly at the end of the block, where I was dropped off.

If Isabel does not come back, how will I get myself back to the farm? Or do I even want to?

Whatever happens, I will need money, I think, pacing on the asphalt. The cold rain has started again, and I step under the awning of a closed hardware store.

I could wait for the library to open, then go into the library and probably find a way to access the Internet there. Then I could contact my kids and have one of them wire me some money to the bank down the street. They could easily issue me enough money so that I could rent a car, and drive home, or back to the farm.

I pace back and forth. Will somebody rent me a car if I don't have an ID? Maybe, maybe, it's a possibility. I'm well-spoken, and I can point to pictures of myself online. I could get my daughter to call and say that my wallet was stolen. And I do have Isabel's lease, which has the address of the farm, not that I can prove I am DOTSON.

But these challenges actually make me feel good, because they the sort of problem I know how to solve. I'm in exactly the same position that one of my kids would be in if one of them were overseas, in Rome or whatever, and lost their purse or wallet. But I'm in a *better* situation, because I know the language, and I'm a citizen here, which although this is not my state, it is at least my *country*.

I stop and look into the glass of the closed hardware store. Suddenly, there is a flickering of police lights and I shrink. I'm about to get arrested for vagrancy.

I look down the street. My body floods with relief. Isabel's pickup truck is coming up fast, and behind it is a police car.

Chapter 24

ISABEL SLOWS ENOUGH FOR ME to slide into her truck, and it almost feels like home, like we've been doing this for years. As we follow Main and leave the stores behind, I realize that my emotions are snapping me back and forth in awareness of what time even means. It's as though I've known her for years, instead of for about sixteen hours across thirty.

"You cleaned up," she says, and I nod, looking back at the police SUV behind us, following at a distance.

"He's following you, like escorting you, right, and not just trying to pull you over?"

She smirks, turning onto the small road that will take us to the turn onto 56 at the convenience store. "He's escorting us. His name is Paul Taylor."

I look back again at the shape of lone figure behind the darkened windshield. I can make out that he's wearing a hat, which in the forty-eight-degree weather is a good idea. "I guess he drew the short straw. How did it go?"

She exhales through pursed lips. "I've had better mornings. I went into the police station and at first, I had no idea what to do. So I went to the guy at the reception desk and told them I had an emergency. And I know I look like I've been in an accident." Like me, Isabel is streaked with mud, although she has washed her face just as I did. "But the reception guy called the, what they call the duty sergeant, and I told them."

"What did you tell them?" I'm trying to figure out where I would start if I were doing this myself.

"I said we had a break-in and you and I had run from your farm, but that the… robbers… were still there."

I am looking at the road, which glistens wet. The freezing rain has abated, but there's a thick mist in the air. We are passing the small houses on the edge of West Hollow Hill, just before it turns to countryside—small, post-war houses with cement porch columns and a lot of mid-century vinyl siding. On small, beige lawns, brightly colored Big Wheels, and plastic toddler slides, turned pale by the beating summer sun, glisten in the wet cold.

"Robbers." I repeat the word. "Yeah, I guess that's what they are. Did you tell them about Tattoo—about the big guy with the tattoos?" I nod my head towards my boots, which were his boots.

I know the law pretty well. I went to law school, even passed the bar exam, though my own laziness and desire for something different from what a law firm could offer kept me from committing to the practice.

I know that if I tell the police that Tattoo was threatening me with a gun, and broke into my house, there is a good chance that in the end I will get by okay. Pretty clear self-defense. But I also know that the police are not your friends. They have their own agendas, their own goals, and sometimes you can get sideways with them. When they see the body, they could believe me and I could be left alone completely, waiting to work out the paperwork later, or I could be arrested on suspicion of murder and held, possibly indefinitely if they futz around and keep postponing my arraignment. I do not want to go to jail.

"Nope," she bites her lip. "I said people broke in and we fought with one of them. I didn't get into a lot of details."

"Okay," I sigh. If I were the police officer behind us, probably I would be deeply suspicious of this vagueness. I would already be thinking that somehow, somewhere along the way, Isabel is not telling the truth. And I would be very worried.

Something strikes me as strange and I look back again. "Wait, they sent just one guy?"

"Yep," she said.

"You told them *robbers* broke in, and they're sending one cop?" I'm not an expert on cop tactics, but usually there would be at least two. "Shouldn't he have a partner? Those guys have guns."

She slaps the steering wheel. "What do you want me to tell you, Mike? We don't have a lot of cops here."

I look back again. I cannot see the eyes of the officer behind the wheel of the SUV, but I'm sure he is watching, wondering how dangerous we, or wherever we're going, will be. I do see a long, thick structure in silhouette behind his head, visible against the road. At least Paul Taylor, Hollow Hill PD, has a shotgun.

"You're gonna make him nervous," she says. "You're making *me* nervous."

"Okay," I say, turning around and facing the road. Then I say, quietly, "thank you." Because I still cannot believe she is in this.

We pass the convenience store and are on our way down 56, just entering the wooded area, soon to pass the dam.

"I'll bet it's the last time you graze on *our* farm," I say. "Oh, my god, I wonder if they've wrecked the ranch house."

She shakes her head.

Instantly I'm thinking again of the fact that my computer and my phone are back there.

I should be glad to be alive. But I'm capable of moving past that and what I'm thinking about is the value that I'm going to lose if the devices are gone, and with them the fifteen thousand or so words that I've already written. Which I would have to write again. And right now, I don't know if I have it in me.

Isabel isn't in my thoughts and thinks I'm just worried about *things*. "What do you want to do? You could come back to *my* place. Or I could take to take you to a hotel if you like. We can deliver Officer Taylor and just keep driving. You don't have to go back to your farm."

Of course it's not my farm, it's my grandmother's, and I'm the one allowing it to be wrecked. Still, either of those alternatives she's presented sound really good. I could be at a pretty decent Day's Inn in Hollow Hill, and I could kick back in a hot tub and watch whatever TV comes across in the room. That sounds *extremely* good. Or I could be with her. Although right now, the chance of getting laid is the farthest thing from my mind.

But no, I left a man impaled on an old well, scrabbling around like a spider. And I left three killers besides him in the ranch house, one of whom I might have severely injured by smashing his head against the side of a combine harvester. It can happen, you know, people in Colorado die of brain injuries all the time where they smack their head skiing, hard enough to knock them for a loop, but then they get up and wander around, and die later in their sleep. Surprise. This is what happened to Natasha Richardson, the actress. By slamming Scrawny's head against a pipe and knocking him out, I may well have committed another murder.

So I need to go back to the farm whether I want to or not.

I rub my hands together. In my T-Shirt the cold is catching up to me, and I'm still not used to the amount of water in the air, which makes the cold penetrate. I adjust her heater.

"How did things go with your phone?" she asks. "Did you get a new one?"

"Oh, I say, No. I—" For a minute, I think about lying and saying that I went into the place, but they wouldn't help me. I don't know why it occurs to me not to tell the truth. But in the end, I can't imagine what the point would be. And I say, "No, I thought about going in. But I didn't. I went to the Internet Café and I sent a note to my kids."

I think about getting into the strange, out-in-the-open professionalism I discovered researching Mr. McMurtry. Near the lake, huge old trees cast shadows on the slick highway. "I'm sorry that this is all happening," I say. "I know. It's not what you signed up for."

She shrugs almost as if to say, *Oh, it's fine. Oh, it's fine that crazy killers came into my life. I was just going to drop off a lease.*

"I understand that, though," she says. "I mean, yeah. I find this whole thing sort of overwhelming. And I am just kind of moving forward one step at a time. Rather than running away."

All of that makes sense to me and sounds remarkably close to what I'm thinking myself. I want to ask Isabel if she considered just going back to her farm instead of going to the police, just abandoning me at the 7-11. That is what a lot of people would have done. Instead I say, "I'm glad you came back."

She says, "Well, you were a pretty good date." I can't help but think this does not speak well of her prospects.

We are passing the dam on the left, where Blue claimed he saw me and

Isabel climbing around.

"But let's start over," Isabel says. "Who do we think those guys are?"

Now that she has asked, I feel compelled to offer up what I've managed to put together. "Okay," I say. "Let's start with the idea, which they told me right up front, that they're consultants and murder is what they do."

"Okay." She says keenly interested. I feel like I'm talking about something that's not happening to me, and it gives me an odd feeling of comfort. Narration allows us to compartmentalize trauma, and I think it's one of the reasons so many people are willing to go on true crime shows and talk about what happened to them. They don't crave the attention. They crave the trappings of narrative.

"So I call him Blue, 'cause we're close like that now? But he's the guy on the rental slip paper from the glove box. His name really is Brian McMurtry. And he told us, he offers this service where people pay for him to take them somewhere and kill somebody with them. Like a safari."

"Jesus," she says. "That sounds like Manson kind of stuff."

I agree. "It *does* sound like Manson kind of stuff. And the other guy, Ryan. He seems like a pretty normal guy. Like he wouldn't even be into all this; he's the client. And the other guy, the scrawny guy, seemed like just a helper. You know they saw us at the dam when we were climbing?"

"Oh, my god," she says.

"But," I say, excited now. "Get this. I don't know how this man-safari fits in, but McMurtry is *not who he says he is.*"

"What?"

"He's a consultant all right, but not some weird rattlesnake-eating guy, he's a defense consultant." I wave my arms incredulously. "I don't know if the Manson thing is a side hustle, but his nine-to-five is doing corporate investigations."

For a moment, Isabel is pale. Then she nods. "That all sounds… I don't understand any of that."

"I know," I say. "If they manage to arrest him, I want to hear all about it."

She rolls her shoulders. We are moving out of the lake area and into the rolling fields. I can feel the closeness of the farm, just about seven miles away now. She exhales, changing the subject.

"Whoo," she says, raising her eyebrows. Her hand drifts from the steering wheel, down to my knee, an intimate gesture, as though we belong together. "I didn't really ask you about your life back in Colorado. Have you been there ever since I knew you as a teenager?"

"Oh no," I say, "I spent most of my life in Texas. My wife and I moved to Colorado a few years before she died."

"And you have kids?"

"Yeah, both grown. But they both live in suburban Denver, not far from me. Close enough that they come over all the time. It's almost like a sitcom. You know? They come around the way people do in TV shows? Where characters who don't live with the main family still come over and talk at all hours?" Life can be like that. Life *is* like that. In Colorado, for me, we are not immune to tragedy, but things are pretty perfect.

"So you wanted to get back into writing?"

I tell her about the shooting in my office, and how my survival and my three weeks off have given me time to try to get back into the writing game, which I feel has always gotten away from me. In that one sense, my *life* seems to have gotten away from me, and I have a chance to maybe get it back.

"I understand." As she says this, we turn onto Dentonville Road. Once again, a mile from the turnoff to the farm. "Can I ask you something before we get there?"

"Sure."

"Are you *really* still going to be able to sit down in that house and write a whole book after all this? You're just gonna sit back down and finish typing?"

I think about it and watching the ground go by, and I know by the grazing field on the left that we are half a mile to the farm. "Yes," I say. "In fact, it's more important than ever. I'm going to finish what I started."

No matter how much the day throws at me, even if I have to re-write the last few days, I am going to finish.

"Okay." She shakes her head, like she doesn't see the point but isn't about to object. We lead our own lives.

Just then she slows, and so does the SUV following us, as we reach the heavily wooded gate of the farmhouse where I killed Tattoo.

142

Chapter 25

IT HAS STARTED TO RAIN again, that frozen rain that seems determined to make my movements as miserable as possible. Rather than going all the way to the gate farther up, the one that leads to the ridge, I nudge Isabel to pull over next to the gate in front of the old farmhouse.

This is overgrown with shrubbery and weeds, so it is difficult to see anything. I have her pull over here for two reasons.

One, as long as we are here, somebody watching from the ranch house will not be able to see us yet. This is our last chance to be close to the farm without being spotted. The police SUV comes to a stop behind us.

"I want to see about the big guy," I say.

I open the door and step out, planting the black tactical boots on the slick asphalt, rain pelting my bare arms and ticky-tacking against off the bed of the truck. I look back towards the SUV.

The police officer, Officer Taylor, is surely looking at me, but I can't make out his face. I can imagine him watching me with a sense of self-pity or even injustice, as though he is being dragged into something that he doesn't want to be a part of. Before walking towards the gate, I turn and walk towards the SUV, my arms held a little away from my body. Even though he is "escorting" us, I don't want him for a moment to think I am reaching into my pockets. It is inconceivable that I could have a gun in these muddy sweatpants that would not be visible, but people get shot, nonetheless.

I reach the door hood and he is a little clearer, now, because although I can't see his face, I can see he's wearing a thick cap, his shoulders enlarged by what must be a very nice jacket.

I am a little surprised that he has even let me approach like this. I would have expected him to get out the moment we stopped, so that he isn't seated. But again, all I know about cops I read about in law school and watched on TV. And further, I am underdressed, shivering, disheveled, bleeding, fat, and old. I do not pose a significant threat to a department store Santa, much less a cop.

I come around the hood and around to the driver's side door of the SUV. As I approach, he rolls down the window.

Paul Taylor looks at me, and indeed his jacket is very warm, with a fur collar that matches the fur on the lining of his hat. I feel a blast of warm air from the SUV. He is cozy. By his chiseled cheekbones he appears quite fit, and from the few crinkles around his eyes and the black hair with bits of gray at his temples, he appears about ten years younger than me.

He looks at me and says, "Yessir?" With a sort of hoot, *yesSIR!* I have heard that before, growing up around the Army.

I almost put my hand on his car windowsill and then think better of it, instead resting it awkwardly on my hip. "Hi. So we didn't… my name's Mike Dotson. This is my grandma's farm." I'm not sure how much Isabel has told him.

"Yessir, how are we doing?"

"Well, I don't know what you know already, but when we were here earlier, there was a guy—" I almost said there was *an old boy,* putting on an Oklahoma accent just for Officer Taylor. But I don't, because I sense that he would be aware of the theatrics and would not appreciate them. Plus, I'm about to point out a dead guy, and that's theatrical enough.

"So I gotta tell you something," I say, leaning down and pointing through the trees. "We ran away from the ranch house. We went into *this* old house." I point in through the weeds and the gate. Leaning forward to look past me, he can see the ruins of the old house, but only barely—as I look, the house is just a few impressions of white paint through the trees. I can make out the dark hole of the porch door, open because Tattoo knocked it off its hinges. But very little else.

He squints as though that will help him see through the foliage. But he nods at me just the same.

"We hid in there. It's my great-grandma's old house." I add this just in case some kind of "castle doctrine," a legal principle that says you can do almost anything to protect your house, will come in handy here. I don't know if Oklahoma has that doctrine at all. "This is before the sun came up. And this... *huge* dude, he came looking for us."

"Okay."

"So he had a gun, and we pushed him through a window," I say.

"You pushed him through a window."

"Yeah."

"He broke in and you pushed him out through a window?"

"Yeah, front window—you can't see it, but it's just to the left of the porch, but... he got stuck on a pipe and that killed him."

Officer Taylor grimaces. Like he's thinking through what to ask next. Like maybe already he's thinking about the castle doctrine, and whether it applies to me. He's probably toggling mental filters over me to decide if I'm one of us, a homeowner, middle-aged white guy, docile, unimportant, but part of the establishment, or am I not, am I threatening, weird, marginalized, scary, less powerful. It all matters, and it can mean life or death.

"Well, that's something," Taylor says.

"Yeah," I agree. "So I want to go look through the gate there, see if he's still there. I thought maybe you'd like to look, too."

Taylor nods and I back up and he gets out. When he stands up, he is a little taller than me, definitely bigger, in the fit way, lean about the waist and wide at the shoulder. We walk to the old fence, trying to find an opening in the creeping green over the gate where we can see clearly through to the house. The best spot is in the center of the gate, where the foliage thins out.

Across the yard, the farmhouse is exactly as I recall. Up on the porch, the door is missing, and the house inside is dark, though I can see the shadow of a stitched sampler on the wall. I know from memory that this sampler says THE HURRIER I GO THE BEHINDER I GET.

Next to the porch, the window is busted out, so destroyed that the wall below the window has ripped away, rotten nails and wood yawning open.

The toothy extrusion of window wood and glass and the wall tell a story of something big coming through a section of the house that is so rotten that it has the integrity of Kleenex.

But.

"So, where is he?" Taylor asks.

Next to the porch and right in front of the broken wall, the pipe well where Tattoo's be on display is bare and exposed. Tattoo is gone.

I don't know what to say. I stare at the well for a minute.

It seems unlikely to me that Tattoo would have been able to lift himself off of the well pipe. Even if by some miracle he were alive and regained consciousness, and I am doubtful that he did, it would be an impossible feat to lift himself off a pike that has impaled him. No, he was dead, and what seems more likely is that my captors came to the main house, found their friend, and removed his body.

That means something important, because either they are hunkered down now with a body, or they have already left this farm.

I say to the officer, "I don't see him."

Taylor nods, because it's the most logical thing for him to hear from me.

"He was there, though," I say. I cannot help thinking how much I sound like a crazy person. And my voice is shaking, because it is so cold, with the sleet coming down.

Taylor notices my discomfort and says, "Do you have anything to wear over that T shirt?"

"I don't," I say. "Everything's back at the other house, the ranch house." I nod northward, as though he can see through the trees, to where the ridge and then the house are.

"Well, why don't we go there, sir," he says, "let's see what we got going on."

This is a nice bit of good-old-boy bonhomie, and it has the effect of making me feel like he's got this thing under control already.

I thought for a moment he was going to offer me a jacket or something, and I'm not even sure, but I think I'm relieved that he didn't. There seems something more respectful in the fact that he *doesn't* offer me something. He's not thinking of me like an escaped patient from a mental hospital or a homeless person. He's thinking of me like somebody who's going to get a better shirt as soon as we get to the house.

We split up and I get back into Isabel's truck while Taylor returns to his SUV.

Isabel's truck is still running, and the blasting warm air is a relief. She starts to move, and the SUV follows, and we run our tiny convoy about three hundred yards north on Dentonville Road, and then come to a stop again briefly at the next gate, the one everyone uses.

It is still open wide and partly in the road because Isabel and I bashed through it earlier, and no one has closed it. We stop here anyway.

Isabel looks at me nervously.

I look up ahead at the ridge. Earlier, the ridge was blocked, because Scrawny and Blue's pickup was there. The one where I found the card that said McMurtry, but now the ridge is empty. I can see the ranch house among the trees in the distance, but no vehicles are in sight because we are looking at the back of the house.

"You sure you want to go in?" I ask. "I could walk, or maybe ride with the cop. It's my farm. You don't have to."

She starts to drive. We pass the gate and wild blackberry bushes and pass one of the big tractor barns and an old hay barn, about to turn right on the ridge. I wonder if anybody could be hiding in any of these buildings, ready to take a sniper shot at us.

We move up onto the ridge, heading north past more blackberry bushes, the big ranch house coming up on our left. The house looks completely normal, though slightly dilapidated, with its peeling red paint, its bare back deck and metal steps. At the end of the fenced-in field where the house sits, there is a small tractor barn, but even my Toyota Matrix crossover SUV would not fit in there. Otherwise, the rear of the house is bare, guarded on the south end by amazing snarls of blackberry bushes and trees encroaching on the old, dead Ford Ranger.

The invaders' vehicles have to be around front if they are here at all.

We see all of this as we slip and slide along the ridge, for a good quarter mile before we reach the house gate, which is also still laying open. We drive over the barbed wire and slowly cross the gate, and now, a few feet at a time, the front of the house and the porch come into view.

I had hoped in this moment that the accoutrements of my captors would have all pulled the same disappearing act as Tattoo's body, but now those hopes are dashed. Under pelting freezing rain, I see the Matrix, and next to it the pickup truck driven by Scrawny and rented by someone named McMurtry, who keeps it very clean.

We stop a little way from the porch.

Normally in a deal like this, at least as I know from television shows and episodes of *Cops*, if somebody rolls up on a house like this, it's very common for the owner to hear them from a good distance away. They might come out onto the front porch and wave or something. Or start shooting. But nobody comes out.

I feel exposed, suddenly aware of how vulnerable we are. These guys have guns and they're crazy, and they still *have not left*.

But even though that should be my foremost thought, mostly I feel a sense of violation.

This is my *grandmother's* house. And in essence, right now, it is *my* house. And it's as though *I'm* visiting it, and whoever possesses it right now is not coming out to greet us.

From inside Isabel's glove box in front of me, a cell phone rings, its chirpy trill filling the cab.

Isabel looks at me, her eyes wide. "Oh my god, shit," she says.

"Is that a cell phone?"

"Yes." She bites her lip in frustration.

"I thought you didn't have your phone." If we had a phone, we could have called somebody early in the morning. If we had reception. But *still*.

"I know, I'm sorry, I'm *sorry*," she says. She reaches across me and pops open the glove box, pulling out a pink iPhone. She looks at it. "It's Officer Taylor."

Taylor is calling Isabel from the SUV behind us.

She presses the green button and the speaker button and lays the phone on her dash. I hear Officer Taylor's voice, tinny and higher pitched, bounce through the pickup cab.

"Ma'am, you want me to go up?"

Isabel looks at me as she talks. "It's not my house."

"I'll go with you," I say.

I open the passenger-side door and step out, the tactical boots squishing against the mud. Officer Taylor gets out and moves towards the porch.

With the cold wind whipping against my arms and the frozen rain falling, I stop him before he reaches the wide front steps. I remind him and myself to take the western side of the steps, because the algae never leaves, even when frozen. He follows my advice and steps gingerly up the western side, planting his feet firmly, because even the good side is slick.

We reach the porch and Taylor approaches the storm door with the Home Depot etched glass door behind it. He starts to open the storm door, but it is latched. Which returns my sense of violation, that someone has had the temerity to lock my grandmother's storm door against me.

Taylor turns to me. "Why don't you take a step back."

I move back to the top of the steps at the edge of the porch.

Taylor knocks on the storm door rapidly. *Bam, bam, bam,* and then looks at me, waiting. And then steps back a moment to get a fuller look at the door.

Suddenly the Home Depot door opens behind the storm door. But I can't see anything on the other side. A person reaches their arm through and unlocks the storm door.

"Careful," I say, like I'm going to be a big help here.

Taylor looks at me with a smile. "No problem."

Taylor opens the storm door and steps through, letting it fall closed. Then he pulls the front door shut behind him as he enters the house.

Silence.

So now the police officer is inside. I don't hear any talking. Seconds, half a minute go by.

I don't like this at all.

I start to walk down the steps, almost losing my footing, then reach the bottom to slog through the grass back to Isabel's truck. As I reach the hood, she looks at me out the driver's side window with a shrug, her hands saying, *what's going on?*

I shake my head, *I don't know.*

Behind me, I hear a creaking sound. I turn to see front door and the storm door open one after the other. I barely have a moment to register that Blue has emerged and raised a rifle.

The man called Brian McMurtry holds a rifle very like the one my friend had when he did his massacre at Blaze Satellite. Blue fires, the sound of the shot cracking across the frozen plains. And in the cold, I hear Isabel sucking air, a weird *chuk* sound, and I turn to see her.

She jerks, spasming, and collapses forward into her steering wheel, her body drooping sideways and out of sight. I have just a moment to see into the driver's side window. Isabel is sprawled in the cab of the truck with blood all over her neck and shoulders.

Just a glimpse, and then I think *run*, but somebody has me by my arms and is dragging me backwards towards the house.

Chapter 26

MY FEET IN TATTOO'S STOLEN tactical boots are bouncing on the soggy ground and I see the barbed wire of the fences enclosing the yard shrinking as someone pulls me away from the truck.

No.

I'm not going to be taken into the house. I am looking at the truck and thinking of the smear of blood, and Isabel's lifeless body laying across it. I've spent all of my life being a victim, and I'm not going to do it anymore. As I am dragged, distances warp, and I am thinking of my own defeat. I am seeing everything that is mine, running away.

It is Halloween, 1978, and I am in the Central Texas town of Killeen, where I live with my parents, a nurse and a soldier.

This bedroom community of Fort Hood is the kind of place where, as you went about your day at school, the thunderous sound of mortar shelling, which was constant at the base, would cause the windows to rattle all day long. It played upon the senses until you didn't notice it anymore.

On Halloween Night, I am seven years old and I go trick or treating. My costume is that of a hunchback. My father has helped me stuff pillowcases under the shoulder of a large coat. And we've used oatmeal and bits of cereal to create a scarred face, and my yellow hair is teased, with black circles around my eyes.

I go out trick or treating alone.

Understand, the 70's were a different time. Back then it was very common for kids to go trick or treating by themselves. Things that we would do by ourselves then, no parent would allow their child to do today. And that's not because the parents in the 1970s were wrong; I actually think it's quite the opposite. I liked that better, a world where parents would just kick you out in the morning and tell you to be back at dusk.

At seven years old, I would go to the grocery store two miles away and get a newspaper and bring it back for my father. I would wander the neighborhood collecting soda bottles in a wagon and take them to the grocery store to collect the returnable deposits. You could do anything by yourself back then.

I say all of this to mean I very much enjoyed that world, even though what happened to me on Halloween is one of my worst memories, and the one that has locked me in a place of victimhood ever since. And I know, because I am not young, that if this is one of my worst memories, then I've been lucky enough not to have a lot of very bad memories, save a few doozies such as the death of my wife.

I go out trick or treating as the hunchback and it's dark. And after crisscrossing up and down the neighborhood, I have a pillowcase full of candy.

Just as would happen later, when I am struck by Sandy and his gang of middle-grade thugs, I make a bad transition very fast. One moment, I'm in a sea of small witches and warlocks, Batmen and Wonder Women, most of those in plastic masks held with rubber bands and vinyl store-bought costumes.

At seven I am already taller than most kids, and where height makes some people confident, for me it is a burden of gravity and exposure. I am a lurching, hulking hunchback in the sea of normality.

And suddenly, I am alone, the sidewalk between me and the nearest kids on either side of the street empty for half a block.

And then running up behind me, a squad of kids. Three, maybe four. It's dark and I see glimpses of curly brown hair, but no faces I can remember as they surround me. Although I am a monstrous seven-year-old, they are bigger than I am, and I am overweight and slow.

They start to push me, chattering amongst themselves. Throwing me off balance.

I feel the candy-filled pillowcase come out of my hand with a tug, and they're laughing and talking to each other. One of them is narrating, telling himself and the others what he's doing, which years later I will know is a way that we distance ourselves from our own actions.

Laughing, one of them says, "Okay, run."

They do, moving away fast, putting dark residential sidewalk between us. I start running after them, working as hard as I can. We're running down the sidewalk catching up to the other trick-or-treaters, vampires and fairies getting in the way as I run after these kids.

Somehow, pushing past a Batman, I close the gap. I have been running nearly three-quarters of a block, and I'm tired.

One of them looks back and hisses incredulously, "Oh, shit, he's still coming."

They pick up speed, finding another gear that I don't have.

I can't run anymore, and I stop, panting, and my eyes fill with ashamed tears.

It's not like the loss of the candy was important, not really. There's always more sugar. But what struck me at that moment and forever is: *why?*

Why do they insist on being so awful?

I walk back home, and my mother is in the house with a girlfriend from the hospital, playing cards and drinking wine. My mom helps me out of my costume, we watch *Saturday Night Live*, and Candice Bergen is on with a funny sketch about dangerous toys.

I had no Halloween candy haul at all that year, other than what my mom was giving out, which wasn't as special because I hadn't gone looking for it.

I'm now 50 years old. And I still can't understand why people insist on being cruel, though I have come to treat cruelty more like the weather. Cruelty just *is*.

Cruelty *is,* and to survive, we find the people that we love, and we fight it.

We board a ship. That ship is our lives. And some of us man the wheel and some of us man the riggings, and we take turns and we go into the storm and the ship is tossed around against the sea.

That's all we can do. We gather our people around us and fight against the storm. And if we are lucky, in the end, we make our way back to shore.

But most of the time, most of life, is the storm.

I have to do something to stop being dragged into that house. The hand on my right shoulder is powerful, and I can tell it's Blue, with Scrawny on the other side. But again, I have weight. I don't have the strength to fight these men off, but I can fall. I drop, lurching forward, and by some miracle I catch the men by surprise. As I feel them loosen their grip on my shoulders, my tactical boots dig in and I rip free, rolling.

I scramble to my feet, seeing them both for just a moment, but I am running. I don't know where to go. I run away from the porch and the trucks, boots expertly gripping the sludge as I turn the corner. Now on the side of the house, I have only a moment. I could run for the ridge, but I would be exposed until I reached the system of buildings around the farmhouse, and they are not going to allow me to get lost in there again.

I breathe hard, blasts of condensation bursting from my mouth in the freezing rain. Next to my feet I see the crisscross latticework that closes off the pier-and-beam foundation of the ranch house. There is about two feet of crawl space under the house. The purpose of the latticework, which is made of thin, rotting wood, is to keep out stray animals.

That is what I am right now: a stray animal.

I drop to my knees and don't even bother taking the time to rip away the latticework. I push on it with my fingers and it bends under, and I crawl like a soldier in the movies, the wood pressing and breaking. Chunks of wood gouge my shoulders as I move under, the wet ground giving way to moist, cold earth.

I crawl without looking back, my elbows jamming into the mud, until I stop and look around, breathing hard.

I am looking at about fifteen hundred square feet of earth. I hear Scrawny and Blue shouting outside, running along the sides of the house. I look back and see their feet pass the battered section of lattice that I have pushed through.

The cold earth is lousy with grimy bits of sheetrock, and stones. I catch my elbow on a nail sticking out of a discarded board, drawing no blood but sending a slicing pain that reminds me to be more careful.

I stop near the center, near a system of plastic pipes that I know to be the underside of the central bathroom off the master bedroom.

I don't know where I'm going. I'm just trying to get as far as I can from the edge, but that done, I have nowhere else to escape to.

I look out to the daylight and see the men continue to circle outside. I wonder where Officer Taylor is.

By now I know enough to know that he is probably already dead. They have probably cut his throat the way they were planning to cut off my eyelid.

There is no reason I can imagine why these men will have stuck to their plan as much as they have, and have driven up their costs to include a dead cop, but that is something I can figure out later, if I am not dead.

Right now, all I can do is survive from moment to moment.

Looking back whence I came, I see a pair of blue-jeaned legs stop near the hole in the latticework. This makes sense because the hole is giant, and only the general dilapidation made them overlook it before. If I am them, I'm thinking there is really only one place I could have gone.

I look up above me at the underside of the house. I'm a little bit east of the bathroom pipes, so I'm under the master bedroom. I look westward and see another mushroom patch of pipes, which has to be all the pipes underneath the kitchen.

For a moment I think that maybe I could punch my way up into the kitchen or up into the bathroom, using the lesser integrity of the wood there to allow me to break it. But the feat would be beyond me, probably beyond The Rock. This house is dilapidated, but unlike the farmhouse, it is not rotten to the core.

Like a stray dog who has run under the house, I'm trapped here.

A shot rings out. I gasp, looking back to see Blue with his rifle.

"Hey boy," he calls. And then he whistles because he also instantly gathered the same image that I have.

I find myself shaking in fear as he fires again, the bullet flying wild. And again.

He is firing evenly along the ground. The bullets embed themselves in the earth somewhere, and I see splotches of mud fly up about a yard from my head.

This isn't going to work.

"Mike," Blue calls. "Come on out, man."

I feel a movement in the earth next to me and look down and see a rat snake slowly moving.

This is not a baby like the ones I got into at the farmhouse—it is nearly three feet long, sliding past me, uninterested in the world of men. I shrink back with an instinctive cry.

The snake's body is hypnotizing as it moves: it thins out and bunches up, rattling bits of sheetrock as it slides over and under.

It is fascinating to me that something so harmless can cause me such horrible feelings of fear and loathing.

"You still with me, boy?" Blue calls. "You better come out."

I don't answer.

"Or we're gonna start just shooting all through here, and then that's it. That's gonna be it for you."

He fires again and this time the bullet destroys a piece of sheet rock near my foot. They see me just fine.

I cannot escape. The rat snake moves blithely by.

Distantly I hear a ringing, a memory of a child's toy, something my daughter had. A cowboy calling out because he has a surprise visitor. *There's a snake in my boot.*

Although this is not something I have ever done, I grab the snake by its neck, just below the head. It whips and squirms in my hand, its little eyes indignant. *I ain't gonna hurtcha, mister*, I imagine it saying. *I'm a rat snake.*

Another bullet rings out and I scream, "Okay, okay, okay!"

But the as the snake squirms in my hand and I can barely believe what I'm doing, I bring the snake down to my leg and I push it into the top of my right boot.

Chapter 27

THE SNAKE SLITHERS IN MY boot as I begin to crawl towards the edge, but I am past any feeling of revulsion now. I have to find my way out of this, or I'm going to die. But right now they have demanded that I come out. And so now that's what I'm doing.

Crawling over the detritus of the underside of a house, I'm thinking now that if I had been smart, if I had been wise, I could have just stayed in the Internet Café, or hung around the library. I could have spent the day reading Ray Bradbury short story collections or looking up old newspaper articles on microfiche.

When I was a kid, that was the kind of thing that writers did—writers in the movies, anyway. At some point in the middle of the story, a beautiful or attractive character who was a writer would go into town. If it were a movie, maybe they'd put on a pair of glasses that made them look studious. And they'd spend the afternoon looking at microfiche, microscopic cards of plastic film that stored entire newspapers from the past. I used to use these, scrolling through the cards with a machine that magnified the tiny film on a large projector screen. I could be doing that right now. I could have done all of that, and instead I have carried myself right back into the hands of my captors.

I make my way back to the edge of the house, and I have to yank the rotten latticework aside to get it out of the way. No sooner does one of my arms get close enough but Blue and Scrawny reach in, tugging my arms and, as they drag me out, tugging my shoulders. I have seen this before, on TV when Moammar Qadhafi was dragged out of his hole in Libya, later to be slaughtered.

They pull me out and into freezing rain. I feel the snake again squirm against my right foot. If I don't find a way to use it, it's going to keep me company when I die.

They half drag me, half force-walk me around the corner of the house and stop in front of the steps. They are about to take the east side and for a moment I think maybe they'll slip, but Scrawny has learned his lesson and he corrects us, moving us all over to the west side. Moving up the steps, they do not loosen their grip on my arms under my shoulders, as though I'm liable to give them any kind of trouble at all when I plainly am not.

The storm door is closed, but Scrawny, on my right, reaches with his right hand and opens it. Next Blue turns the knob of the front door with his left hand, kicking the door to swing it open. As Scrawny holds the storm door open, they push me inside, still holding to my shoulders. They move together, shutting the doors behind them.

Once more I am inside the house.

The wooden chair that I was tied to before is still in its place in the middle of the living room, next to the coffee table.

To my right, on the dining room table, my laptop is still open, exactly as I left it when I wrote the last words of the chapter I was working on when I went to bed last night.

And standing there, not far from the dining table, near the refrigerator, setting down a cup of coffee, is Officer Taylor. He is still in his heavy jacket, but now starts slipping it off. He does not look at all alarmed, and he definitely does not look as though he has been cut in the throat.

Somehow, Paul Taylor is one of them. Now the police officer nods to the guys as he puts his jacket on the chair. Underneath, he is wearing pale blue shirtsleeves, and he rolls each one up.

I don't understand this at all. How could Isabel have managed to go to the police and wind up with this guy, who is so crooked that he has joined my captors. Unless for whatever reason, *everybody* in this town is interested in whatever they want from me. How can so many people be interested in killing the writer who came, as far as I know, unannounced, to this town? Blue and Scrawny sit me down in the chair.

Officer Taylor comes over and takes my arms and puts them through the back of the chair and clasps my wrists together in a pair of restraints. The restraints are those new plastic zip-tie jobs that work faster than handcuffs, though the plastic carves into my wrists instantly. Still, it is a better class of restraint. The guys are moving up in the world.

"Well!" Blue says, as he comes back around in front of me. "This has been a heck of a morning."

Is it really the same morning? Incredibly, it is. I look at a digital clock atop the TV and it says 7:45 am.

I gesture toward the police officer with my head, addressing Blue. "Who is he? Is he even really a cop?"

Blue raises his eyebrows. "I don't even see how it matters."

"Of course I'm a real cop," Officer Taylor says.

I look at Taylor. My wrists are hurting so much that I shift, trying to make it stop. I wince and say, "So you're a crooked cop, are you?"

Taylor says, "I don't know about *crooked*. This is a little consulting."

Jesus. Everyone loves using that word. Suddenly I remember what my shock and panic has caused me not to reckon with. Isabel, her neck blasted in her truck. Someone I knew when I was sixteen and dragged into my life.

"But you…" I sigh. "You shot Isabel. I can't believe you'd just kill someone like that." I look back at Blue. "You said you take people on… safaris—she wasn't a part of that. What could be worth that?"

"I don't see how it matters much to you," Blue says, "You ain't from around here. At least she was."

"Jesus, man, you ain't from around here either," I scoff, the pain in my wrists making me giddy. "You're a fucking consultant from San Davis, California. What is this, a working vacation?"

Blue stops. Runs his fingers through his hair, pursing his lips. He is processing what I just said. Trying to decide if he wants to ask me about it, how I know what I know. He wants to know desperately. But he also knows it's a distraction, and if he answers me, he will be giving me some rein of the conversation.

"What! Do you! Want!" I scream.

Blue seems to relax, as though he's filing away a topic that he will no doubt return to, of how I know he is an import of sorts, a consultant who is more than he says. "Yeah," he answers, looking at Scrawny, who has taken a position next to the couch. "Well, about that."

"Come on," I say. "You said earlier that you were offering Ryan a chance to get his balls back, a chance to kill somebody. But that doesn't seem to be what you're doing *now*. Is it?" I look at Scrawny and Taylor. "Unless getting Ryan's balls back is an *extremely expensive proposition,* and it involves even having this *cop* on hand to make sure that it goes okay and brings me back if I get away. Are you still killing me for Ryan's manhood or is there something else?"

"Let me ask you something," Blue says. "What would you say if you had a chance to get away?"

I just stare. The lawyer-who-never-practiced part of me wants to say *Objection: nonresponsive.* Because he's answering my question with a question. But the thing he said gets my attention and my mind is in a tug-of-war. This sounds like a trap, and I should know better than to take it. I'm not going to answer the truth, which is that if I had a chance, a chance to get away, I would absolutely be interested. And of course, I am now looking for any chance to get away, all the time. Because these guys aren't a bunch of part-time thrill killers. They're dangerous people. And Blue is offering the possibility that they can be reasonable.

"I'm going to ask you for a name," Blue says, "and you're going to tell it to me"

The question he is going to ask me drops into my mind like sack of sand, *whump.* I know the question and yet it doesn't seem possible. I have to dredge my voice up wearily, because I'm not sure I have the answer. And the implications of the repetition of this question are beginning to scare me. "What name?"

"Your editor…"

"Oh, you've got to be kidding…"

Blue rolls his eyes as he shifts from foot to foot in front of me. "Your editor. When you wrote *Fearless* #3, your editor wanted the girlfriend

160

character to be named a certain name."

"I don't understand." I shake my head, incredulously. "I really don't." Somehow, this has come up numerous times over the last week. *Interview*, I think, the subject line of the email I saw just this morning. Even the reporter from the online magazine wanted to ask about this.

"What was the name?" Blue asks. "Because you changed it."

"Yeah," I say. "I changed it because I wasn't gonna let the editor just decide to smear some ex-girlfriend. Plus it was *my* book. If there was going to be a name..."

"This is what'll get you out of here, Mike." Blue says. "I don't care about the why. What was the name?"

"I don't *know* what the name was," I say. I search my mind. I remember phone calls, emails. My agent saying he's hearing bad things about my relationship with the editor. "Just, I don't know. Alexis. V... something. I don't remember, honestly."

"Well, you should tell us what that name was."

I scoff, "Jesus! I just said I don't remember. Who the fuck cares, it was *twenty-five years ago!"*

Blue smacks me across the face. The chair rocks back and I slam down on my arms. I can't believe they don't break, and the pain makes me howl. The snake in my boot moves around my feet, cozy and warm and unconcerned. I am in so much pain that I start wheezing. "It doesn't matter," I rasp. "I can't believe something so ridiculous... has come up."

As I blink, I see someone moving next to the closet by the bathroom. Fidgeting nervously and looking like he is stuck at the worst networking event ever, Ryan stares back. Seeing the guy I still want to call Costco, I shout, "Oh, is he still here?"

Taylor grabs the back of the chair and lifts me, planting me firmly as tears sting my eyes and I huff, "It doesn't matter."

And part of me now thinks that this is a dream, an absurd dream. Maybe I'm still back in the Blaze Satellite headquarters building. And Glenn is killing people because his career has been ruined by his girlfriend, and I've been shot. That makes sense. As I'm dying, this is my dream. And because for some reason I'm pretty damn self-destructive, my dream is nearly as bad as bleeding out during a workplace shooting.

"Who the fuck cares what the name was?" I say again, looking down at my muddy sweatpants. "It doesn't even matter."

I hear Blue inhale angrily. He is fed up. He gets down on his knees and comes toward me and raises a fist. He is about to punch me in the face. As he does this, I'm thinking: he is out of control now. And just as surely as the thin bones in my nose are going to lacerate and probably break his hand, I know that he is going to kill me. He has won. I gasp.

"That's enough," a voice says. Blue stops and looks past me, toward the kitchen.

I strained to move my head, trying to see who is coming in the room. But I already know. It is Isabel, her white shirt stained with fake blood, a look of angry concentration on her very alive face.

"We're running out of time," she says. "Mike, we need the name."

Chapter 28

MY MIND REELS AS I stare, mouth agape, at this strange revenant.

For a moment Isabel's voice still rings in the air like a shot. Other than that, all I can hear is the sound of winter. There is a cold wind blowing outside, and the house is so drafty that it echoes through the walls.

But I'm not feeling the cold at all now. I'm dumbfounded.

Isabel is involved with the men. I don't understand how this could be possible. I watch her as she takes a handkerchief from her jeans pocket, rubbing stray bits of glop from her face. She walks around so I can see her without straining.

"This was supposed to be easy," she says. "But you haven't given it to us, and we're running out of time."

I struggle to make sense of what she's saying. "I'm just here to write a book, I don't understand."

As I talk, I run over it again in mind. I came here to write a book because I have three weeks off. I went to see Isabel. We spent the morning together. Isabel, who I went out with some thirty years ago. After our morning date, and I went back to the farmhouse, and I started to write. Then early this morning, the break-in, and Isabel came and rescued me.

They've certainly made clear what it is that they want to know. They want to know a name that somebody tried to make me put into a manuscript back when I was a regular writer.

Already, certain pieces of the morning are coming into a new light for me. Isabel, casually pressing me for this name. Isabel easily agreeing to go get the police herself. I wonder, if I hadn't suggested it myself, whether she would have found a way to maneuver me to letting her find Paul Taylor, with whom she is already in cahoots. That must have been a stroke of luck for her.

Isabel, freaking out after I killed Tattoo. Was that freak-out real? Was she knocked off her game, then?

So much doesn't make sense to me. How did all of this come together?

And why they would be running out of time?

But I don't remember the name. Or *do I?* I've tried to think about it. The first name that came to my mind was Alexis V something. Maybe Vogler. Vogler sounds right.

Except that Chris Vogler is the name of the guy who wrote *The Writer's Journey*, which I listened to on the way across Kansas, the place where people in my position don't survive. I am so sure that is the name, but I am just as sure that I am misremembering because of Chris Vogler's audiobook.

I'm thinking back on it now. I'm thinking back on being a twenty-something wunderkind writing a series of adventure novels during and after law school, and that stupid request, *change the name of the girlfriend of the main character to whatever it was*, this name that a dumbass executive wanted.

And like I told Isabel, I fought them all the way. Nobody has mentioned it to me since. Although that is also about the time that my career came to an end.

"Okay," I say, looking at Isabel. "I get it, I get it, I get that I have no idea who you are. But I'm telling you…"

"Who I am doesn't matter."

"… I'm telling you, I don't know this name you're looking for."

Inside, what I really don't understand is something that I can't even quite articulate. How did *she* put this together? How did she decide? How did she figure out a way to get close to me? Why would a girl I went out with in the 80s be the one to join a bunch of *consultants* when I came to the farm on a lark?

"What do you mean you're running out of time?" I ask. But a curious thing is happening. Since getting back this morning, now that suddenly I am faced with a group of professionals with a goal in mind, I am not quite as terrified. I'm still scared, but I'm *interested*. A puzzle has been presented to me, and it is fascinating. "What do you mean, *out of time?*"

She looks at Blue and sits on the edge of the sofa, her knees together. She is physically a different person now, poised and icy. She seems to contemplate what to say next, and her eyes flick back and forth. Retroactively I recognize this, because it is a flicker I have seen before when she is faced with choices and has to decide what to say. One of them happened when her cell phone went off in the glove compartment, while she had told me that she had forgotten her cell phone. I now realize I watched her decide to go with a simple answer, that she'd forgotten. And she turned whatever anxiety she felt in that moment into physicality, rolling her eyes and wringing her hands. She is able to grab her emotions and channel them.

And all the while she was probably already preparing for a question I did not even think to ask: if she had forgotten that her cell phone was in the glove compartment, why did Officer Taylor have her number to call her on it? She probably had two or three answers lined up that would make some sense in the moment.

Because all of this has been about keeping me in the moment. The key to this morning, in these people's endeavor to get a name that I do not remember, was not the torture. The key was in Isabel's interrogation of me in the barn after the torture had softened me up. Except for that along the way, I got lucky, and killed Tattoo, and she had to roll to backup plans.

All of this is coming into focus as she decides how she is going to answer. Finally she speaks.

"Do you know what *hashing* is, Mike?"

I confess that I do not. My wrists are killing me and that's taking up a fair amount of my brain, but, "No, I don't know what *hashing* is."

"Hashing," she says, leaning forward, her fingers interlaced, "is a process where any important information is turned into something else, usually by an algorithm. It's a process that is typically done by companies looking to send out a lot of data, some of which they'd like to… make a *hash* of. So your phone number will become another, fake phone number. And so on."

"I have no idea…"

"But it doesn't have to be by algorithm, there might be any reason why an organization or a person would replace an important piece of data. All kinds."

165

"Oh," I say. As though I'm following. "Well, look, see, it was a Hispanic character so I thought it needed a Hispanic name, and whatever they were asking for sounded stupid. That was it. There wasn't really any—"

"There is, in Lucerne, Switzerland, a safe deposit box."

Of all of the things I expected to hear about, a safe deposit in Switzerland has to be dead last.

She goes on. Her voice is smooth and clear, like she is giving me instructions on how to jump out of an airplane, and it is very important that I listen to every word.

"Except as requested by the account holder himself, that safe deposit box can only be opened with a passcode. At six o'clock PM today, Swiss time, as is customary for the bank that holds it, when the account holder has been dead for three weeks..." Here she holds up her thumb and two fingers, "... this box is going to be superheated and its contents destroyed-- *unless* somebody can come forward with the passcode.

"The contents of this box were entrusted to the account holder, but security demanded that those who held equal interest would have access to the passcode, which would be hidden in a way that would be known *only* to the account holder, and revealed in his will upon the account holder's death. Three weeks—*three weeks*—ago, we learned in the account holder's *will*, just where the passcode was to be found. Unfortunately, it took us two weeks to realize that the passcode had been *hashed*... by you.

"That passcode is the name that you were given twenty-five years ago." She leans back. "I don't care why you did it, Mike. I don't *care* about this *stupid* victory over some dead executive. I don't care if we're interrupting your *writer's retreat*. We need. The fucking. Name."

I take all of this in. She has explained what she is looking for remarkably well. "What's in the safe deposit box?"

"It doesn't matter." She shakes her head, as if reasoning with a child. "What matters is that you need to tell us that name."

I am thinking: were you this crazy when we went out in the 80s? But I say, "I don't remember."

Blue smashes me across the side of the head with his open hand. My glasses fly off, bouncing off the TV next to the couch. I rock in the chair and

166

then Taylor grabs it and plants it again. My skin is raw, and my face is in pain from having been hit so many times in the last seven hours. They are all blurs now. "I don't know," I say. "I have no idea. If I knew I would *tell* you. I'm just here to write a book."

But she's already said that this line of response is totally irrelevant to them. What they want is my information, information that I wasn't even aware that I have.

Blue raises a blurry hand to strike me again and I say, "Wait, wait, wait, I might… give me my glasses."

Isabel nods and Taylor goes to get the glasses. He picks them up and puts them on my face. Isabel has risen and is standing directly at the other end of the coffee table from me, next to the fireplace.

"I think, I *think* I might still have it. I might have it on my computer."

She crosses her arms. "What do you mean you might still have it? It's twenty-five years ago. And it wasn't in the book in the end. Why would you have it on *that* computer?" Meaning my laptop.

"I keep *everything,*" I say. And it's true. Every book I ever wrote, even short stories and works I have started and abandoned. Everything always goes into an archive folder with subfolders and subfolders. Beyond that, every time I upgrade my computer, the archive folder gets copied and copied and copied. I keep multiple versions of the same book, multiple drafts. The reality is, if that name is in one of the early drafts of *Fearless* #3—and there's every reason to believe that it is, because that's how I remember it—then there's a very good chance that it is somewhere on my computer.

"I keep everything," I say again, "it's *on* there." I gesture with my head which is still pounding from Blue's last strike. "I can find it for you."

"Will you need to go online?" Blue asks, I remember now that his real name—I guess *Blue* is my *hash* of it-- is Brian McMurtry, and he is a security consultant. His accent also has smoothed out, not nearly so Hee-Haw as it was when he was pretending to be a thrill-killer. He turns to Isabel. "If he gets to go online, he might be able to send an emergency…"

"I get it," Isabel says. "Do you?"

"Need to go online?" I answer this as though now we are a bunch of co-workers planning a marketing event. "No… I probably should use an online backup, but this stuff is all on the hard drive."

Although if I were *thinking* more clearly, I would be lying to them already. And I would say something about needing to access it all on my Google Drive.

But it wouldn't matter because there is no internet in this house anyway. There is no Wi Fi. I'm not going to be able to access Google Drive or any internet drive in any way.

"I keep everything. It's all on my hard drive."

Isabel is looking at the clock. It is 9:03 in the morning. I ask, "What's that in Swiss time?"

"4:03 in the afternoon," she says. She has until six in safe-deposit-box land, giving Isabel less than two hours to complete her task by sending a name I cannot remember across the world.

And unfortunately, I'm not *completely* certain that I'm going to find what I'm looking for. Because I make mistakes. I clear out duplicates. I cannot guarantee that I have been telling her or myself the truth about keeping everything. I *try*.

"Well, I need to get onto my computer," I say.

Isabel nods and Taylor wastes no time. He comes over and uses a wire cutter to the remove the zip-ties from my hands. He grabs my shoulder, but I get up on my own, shaking him off. I'm tired of being manhandled.

I turn around, walking towards the kitchen with Blue and Taylor close by. As we pass the doorway into the bedroom, I see Ryan, peeking out, like he's waiting for us to be finished.

This pudgy man from Tulsa who I first thought of as *Costco* looks ill, like he is no part of this at all.

It is just one more piece that I need to put into place. What is he *doing* here? There is nothing about him that says dangerous security consultant. The ones who do fit that description, Blue and Scrawny, Taylor, and of late, Isabel, walk with me over to the dining table.

Taylor pulls out the chair for me, the one where he has draped his jacket, while Blue and Scrawny sit me in the chair in front of my computer.

The screen of the Dell XPS laptop is dark, and I tap the space bar to wake it up.

Blue does not have a gun showing, but I know that he has his rifle nearby, and probably a pistol as well. Isabel does have a gun, though she has not pulled it out.

I narrate to them what I'm doing, because that is how we make distance ourselves from our lives.

"I have to log into my computer." Floating before me, on a PC that is actually only used by me, are three icons, one for myself and each of my two children. They don't even need to come over and use my computer, but I created logins for them just the same, a small way of pretending that they have not grown up and moved away.

"We'll pick me," I narrate. I click it and am asked for my password. I try to type the series of random numbers and I fumble it. It makes me wait 15 seconds before trying again. My captors are getting impatient and I say, "I'm sorry, I just I, I'm just I..." I can't even find the right word. I am nervous.

I try to enter my password again, and I am in. I am confronted by my desktop, which to my shame displays a high-definition image of the 1966 Batmobile.

"Now... I have to think about it. File manager." I open up the system of folders, and now I'm clicking. I go into a folder marked WRITING ARCHIVE.

I click on it and I say, "Check this out, I'm moving backwards through my career."

There are archives within archives, and I am hunting. Every time I switched computers, I made subtle, inadvertent changes in how I labeled the folders. But I do find something called ARCHIVE BACKUP C.

It is in this one that I find Microsoft Word files going back to the 90s. I locate a folder called *Fearless_3."*

Inside there are multiple folders, including one called DELIVER, which was my label for folders where I'd place the final version that would go to print, and then yet another folder called ARCHIVE, and under that a folder called DRAFTS. And under that, folders with the names of months.

"Now I gotta just look because I have no idea," I say. I click open several before I finally find a word document that looks good: FEARLESS_3_ DRAFT_2.

The consultants are watching this intently. I open up a Word document, which takes extra time to convert itself to the most recent version of the same word processor. When the document finally opens, I see words that my fingers typed twenty years ago, and I that I can actually almost remember typing.

What I don't know is how to search for something when I don't know the name. If I did, I could have just searched the whole computer.

I am a little stunned when I scroll down and pass the name Rosario Hinojosa, the name I finally used, which means the answer is not in this draft. But it doesn't matter.

"Okay," I say. "I know we're talking about the name of the girlfriend. I remember she shows up in like Chapter two or three. So, let's scroll to chapter two." My audience is leaning over.

And that's when I reach down into my boot and I bring out a three-foot-long rat snake.

As I run for my life, I remember the name.

Chapter 29

HERE IS HOW I LOST my career.

In 1996, I was twenty-five years old, and I'd sold three books, a trilogy called *Dream Tasker.* I hadn't made a lot of money on the series, though two books had already come out.

The important thing to remember about novels is that you might work on a book for a month, or six months, or six years, but in the world of traditional publishing, you'll get paid based on what the publisher thinks that they're going to make off of the work.

The publisher doesn't buy a book forever. They buy the license to publish it for royalties. This makes selling a book roughly equivalent to selling the rights to drill for oil on your land. Somebody comes on your land and says, *I'd like to drill for oil here, put up an oil well and pump oil out of the ground and sell it. Would you give me the rights to do that?*

We live in a world where you answer: *Sure.* And then when the publisher is selling the oil, you get what are called royalties. Maybe ten percent royalties, in which case for every dollar that that driller makes selling the oil from your land, they'll give you ten cents. But since it might take a while for that to matter to you, if the oil guy thinks he's going to sell a lot of oil, he'll pay you a bunch of royalties in advance. That's what it's called: an advance on royalties.

So if the driller thinks that they're going to make millions of dollars, and therefore pay you hundreds of thousands of dollars, they might be willing to give you some of that money upfront, say, fifty thousand dollars.

A book is like an oil well. The publisher is the driller, and he offers an advance. But with books, it's often nothing.

I sold my first three books for an advance of sixteen thousand dollars. I was in college at the time. And on a scholarship, so I didn't need tuition money, but I knew that there was no way that I was going to be able to live on the kind of money that books would bring in. What I didn't know was that there were other ways of working as a writer, so instead I went to law school.

When I was a first-year law student, the only good thing to come out of my studies happened in the library. That is where I met my wife, Silke Baumann, a first-year from Upstate New York. And we hit it off because she would often study late at the library right when I was doing my hours for a work-study job at the computer room.

I was a terrible law student. Most of the time, when I was doing my work-study for, I think, eight dollars an hour, I would use most of that time to work on writing one of the novels that I had sold. I would finish a book once per year for every year that I was in law school.

And those three novels that I wrote early on were the most original work that I ever did, a wild combination of fantasy and science fiction and spy thriller. I gladly cribbed from every inspiration I could think of, making take-over-the-world stories with whole subplots gleaned from *The Tell-Tale Heart* and *Macbeth*. And the third, when I was sort of scrambling for ideas, was a strange plot where Jupiter Chris was moving through a sort of retelling of *The House of Seven Gables*.

But I have to be honest: at that point, my heart wasn't really in it. Although I was able to sell all three of those books to a midlist fantasy publishing house, which meant that I was a professional writer for sure, I wasn't the kind of writer who would get any respect, not with my numbers, anyway.

I never was very good at playing the game exactly right. Ideally, I should have been going to a lot of conferences and shows and doing what I could to grow my career. But at the same time, I always wanted to be the careful one. So some shows I couldn't go to, because I was studying the law, while some classes I couldn't keep up with, because I wasn't studying enough, because I was also trying to write books.

In my third year of law school, just as I was completing my third *Dream*

Tasker book, I landed my first tie-in novel. This was the first of the *Fearless* books, which were adventures based on a TV series from White Pinnacle Studios about a bunch of high school escape artists possessing all kinds of esoteric secrets and getting into high-velocity tales of international intrigue.

I would like to say that the reason White Pinnacle picked me to do those books was because I wrote adventures that were very similar to what they needed—not the fantasy stuff, but a lot of the more elaborate escapes and twists. But actually, the reason is that I found them first. I approached the producers of *Fearless*, calling the production studio from my apartment near the law school.

I told the woman who picked up the phone at the production office that I was Mike Dotson, and I was a writer of fantasies, and I'd read on the internet that there was rumor that they were going to be doing novels based on the *Fearless* series.

The remarkable thing here is that I actually said that I had read this on the *internet*. And there hardly *was* any internet at that time, aside from a few chat rooms on AOL, and a few special interest groups on early platforms like Delphi. And a few Usenet groups, which were long message boards where people talked about anything at all. I definitely had not heard any such rumor.

But the woman said, "Well, actually we've been thinking about it. So that's interesting. If you'll give us your agent's name, we can be in touch."

And so I gave her my agent's name, and within a couple of weeks, I was signed to write my first tie-in series.

Those novels on average took about three months each to write. And the great thing about writing books is that you have a goal in your life. When you're not writing, the evening comes around, and you're not sure what it is you're supposed to be doing. But if you have a novel to write, then you *know* what you're supposed to be doing at night: writing your novel.

Even on nights when you're not writing on it, the great thing is you can tell yourself, *I'm taking tonight off, but I have a novel to write. So this is a special night.*

I was in the process of writing *Fearless* #3 the spring of 1999. By this time I was out of law school, and Silke and I had gotten married and moved to Fort Worth, Texas.

Notes came back for the book after I finished the first draft. Notes are what we call the feedback the publisher sends you, telling what they'd like to see changed. I invite notes into my work because I think everyone has the best interest of the product at heart. Plus, with tie-in work, the publisher is like a client. It's their baby, in the end.

We think that this particular subplot should be cut.

We think that this character's motivation is too similar to this other book.

What if we got rid of this particular action scene, or what if we made this sequence a little bit more complicated, or less complicated?

But there was one really *weird* one.

The assistant editor who always sent me my notes, a guy in New York named Wayne Chang, sent me a few pages of notes for the first draft, and included in them was:

We would like the name of the love interest, the girlfriend introduced in Chapter Three, to be changed to Alexis Vauxhall.

Now, that was a very weird request. Because I'm eager to please, my first instinct was to say, "Sure, fine."

But the character as written was Mexican-American, with the name Rosario Hinojosa. And I had spent a lot of time putting little bits of Spanish into her dialogue, had her telling bits of her background growing up on the border between Texas and Mexico. So the more I thought about it, the more a name like *Alexis Vauxhall* wasn't going to fit. At least not as well. Sure, Alexis Vauxhall could be Mexican, but I liked the sound of a more obviously Latinx name.

So I sent an email to Wayne: *I'm not sure where this is coming from. But I don't think that Alexis Vauxhall is going to work for that character. Nice name, though, maybe we could use it in the future?*

And I really didn't think anything about it, and I kept using the name Rosario Hinojosa.

So the next round of edits came about six weeks later, because I'd send another draft, and so they sent another list.

We'd like you to change the name of Rosario Hinojosa to Alexis Vauxhall.

I called up White Pinnacle Books, and when Chang answered the phone, I said, "What's the deal with this name? I don't get it, this is, this is weird."

Chang sounded like he was shrugging. "I don't know, man. I wish I could explain it. But, Niles, he really wants the character name."

Niles, mind you, was Niles Peary, a man who wore many expensive hats. He was Executive Vice President at White Pinnacle Books. He was also an executive producer on the *Fearless* TV series. And finally, he owned the relationship between White Pinnacle and a number of other publishers that White Pinnacle distributed, including Bale, the publishers of my *Dream Tasker* series.

"Niles wants it to be Alexis Vauxhall."

"This... I don't understand."

Chang sounded like he had more important fish to fry. "I don't know, but he's taken an interest in this. And when he takes an interest in this, he won't let anything go. I think it's an ex-girlfriend he wants to name it after."

"But she turns out to be the *bad guy*," I said, incredulously. "That's a terrible gift."

So after a few weeks, I sent yet another draft. And it came back again, yet again with the same request.

Please change the name of Rosario Hinojosa to Alexis Vauxhall.

Now my agent was calling. This was getting ridiculous, because if they kept giving me notes, that stalled my ability to get paid for the book, and a big piece of the advance was riding on getting through these changes. Whether or not I would get a $10,000 check depended a lot on whether I was willing to change this character's name.

I said no, but they did it anyway. I got paid and turned my attention to trying to think of my next proposal, which I was stuck on.

Six months went by, and then it came time for the *final* draft, the version that would go to print, which the publisher sent to me one last time.

At that moment, just before it went out, I took that opportunity to change the name back to Rosario Hinojosa and sent it back to them. The book was much farther down the line by now. None of the same people looked at it. About two months after that, the character that Executive Vice President Niles had wanted to be called Alexis Vauxhall reached the bookshelves with the name Rosario Hinojosa.

As it happens, I never sold another book again.

Chapter 30

IT WOULD NOT BE CORRECT to say a rat snake is the one thing they are not expecting. There are probably many things that they are not expecting. They're not expecting that I would suddenly become an action star, because I don't. They're not expecting for me to become brave, because I have not been. But they're definitely not expecting me to suddenly lift a squirming snake by just below its jaw so that it wriggles around, flipping in all directions. To the one, all of them shrink back in revulsion, and I take that moment to escape.

I hear a shot ring out, slamming against the stove as I pass it, but I'm into the laundry room already. My world has narrowed to a tunnel-vision on the back door. I am laying out my path: I'm going to get through the back door, get off the deck, and I'm going to run to the road and I'm going to keep running, and I am not going to trust anyone that I'm not related to.

I focus on the doorknob, grab it, rip the door open, twisting my wide body as much as I can to get through it without sparing a moment. This is my only shot.

I get through, feeling my shirt tear on the metal flange of the doorjamb, and then I'm outside, and I pull the door closed behind me.

My momentum carries me forward as I turn for the metal stairs, and my feet come right out from under me, because even with the grip of the tactical boots, I am not prepared for the slickness of the back deck. I land on my ass and fly, my feet before me, and I sail right off the wood.

My landing is not impressive; I slam down to the wet grass on my ass, sliding and walloping my back against the ground. I let out a massive groan, pain vibrating through my body, but my tunnel vision now is on the road.

I turn over and start crawling, readying my legs to get me up again. But I realize this hasn't gone the way I wanted, I should be out the gate and up on the ridge by now, so I look for a place to hide, because it is a bright, cold morning and they are going to be out and on me at any second.

I'm looking for any kind of cover, and I spot the small tractor barn nearby where my grandfather used to keep a brush hog, a sort of giant lawnmower you attach to a tractor.

That's not bad, but against the fence there's also the giant morass of trees and blackberry bushes with the dead Ford Ranger pickup in the middle of it. I have to decide. The bushes are the direction I want to go, but the tractor barn is better cover. I think. I don't know. As I crawl on the frozen ground, I cannot decide.

The back door opens.

I look back and see Scrawny with a revolver in his hand. He is too careful to be taken out by the deck as I have been, and when he plants his feet, he fires. But his shot goes wild and he angrily decides to give chase. He pumps his arms wildly in anger as he crosses to his right on the deck.

He is at the metal steps and I am crab walking, scrabbling away from him towards the small tractor barn, because that is where I'm pointed. My back is doing arias of pain, but I forget it in an instant.

I see what's going to happen to Scrawny about a millisecond before he does. The metal steps are covered with ice. Scrawny hits the first step and his legs fly out from under him at such a pronounced angle that his whole body goes horizontal in the air. Then his head comes down on the metal. Scrawny twists and gives out a sickening moan as his head lodges between two steps and the rest of his body whipsaws down against the rest.

He goes quiet but not still. All of it's a blur.

I stop, looking back toward the Ranger pickup truck. I start crawling towards it. I couldn't get under it because it has become one with the weeds and the trees. But I can get behind it. Then in an instant when I feel safe, I can head off onto the ridge and just keep running as planned.

None of this seems like it's going to work, but it has to.

When I look back, Scrawny's body is twitching, his arms moving. I think maybe he is reaching for his revolver, which lies in the grass nearby, but there is no way he is conscious.

Then I make a decision. I want his gun.

I begin to crawl and then get up, hunched, running back towards Scrawny.

I'm making a *lot* of decisions right now, and one of them is to let go of flinching. If I'm going to survive, I need to divorce myself from the sensitivities and the sensibilities that have served me for so long.

I am a person who has never thrown a punch in anger, and since my relatively peaceful childhood and before tonight, have rarely received one from another person, who has believed that violence is the last resort of the unimaginative. But I am going to need to divorce my mind from judgments of all these things. I'm going to need to take Scrawny's gun even though his broken body appears to be reaching for it as well. I moved towards the step, looking up at the back door.

Someone is waiting for me because now, finally, they shoot. Looking up, I see Blue—no fool, he is inside the house, door wide open, and using his rifle to try to take me out. He misses, the bullet splattering in the mud next to me. I keep moving towards Scrawny and finally reach the stairs of the back deck, where his gun lies in the grass about two feet under Scrawny's hips.

Scrawny's neck looks like an air conditioning vent tube that has been twisted sideways. I can see bones begging to dig out through his skin. His body appears to be pulsing as though it is controlled by some mechanism that has stopped working properly. He is in shock, and incredibly, his arms are scrambling.

I reach for his revolver. Scrawny's teeth are bared, but they do not snap at me. His eyes are not seeing. He is someone with a mother, and right now I am not feeling sorry.

I pick up the gun. It is a .38 caliber revolver.

I have used this kind of gun exactly once in my life, when I was about twelve years old on the farm. My grandfather took me out to the creek, where the trash dump is, and we used several of his guns to shoot targets. He didn't teach me very much about how to hit a target except when using the .22 rifle.

So I don't remember much.

All I remember about the guns were the safety lessons. *Carry a long gun pointed up at the sky. Every bullet has your name on it. A .22 caliber bullet can fly about two miles, so if you're going to shoot, always have a backstop, like a rise or a hill, or shoot downwards.*

Every lesson was about where the bullet was going to go. But for the life of me—and I have many, many hours of memories of using a long rifle, and for years have lived in the gun-friendly state of Colorado, I have not seen any need to go shooting as an adult. And I cannot remember anything about how to aim a revolver. But I can shoot it.

I'm a big guy, six-foot-two. And though I am out of shape, my arms are large, and the gun is a fairly light hunk of metal. But right now what I want most is not to get shot. Here, hunkered by the stairs, I'm not giving Blue a good vantage point to shoot at me. He's going to wait for me to get back out where I was, if he can't figure a way to sneak up on me.

He'll either come directly out this door, or he or Taylor or Isabel will go out the front door and try to sneak up on me. He or they will flank me. Now I look wildly left and right, looking for the flank, and I know now that for some crazy reason, I am thinking like somebody who is not ready to die.

I hear Blue come through the door. Must be he's sick of waiting, and he's not gonna do any of this flanking shit.

Now is the time, before he can aim, I am betting he will need to lower the gun as he exits. I lean out and I can just see Blue's head and shoulders. I fall back letting my body go to the earth, raising the pistol in both hands. I point and begin to click.

Revolvers are nearly impossible to aim, and the first bullet slams into the back of the house.

The second one hits Blue in his cheek and tears the whole right side of his face off. He goes down like a sack of potatoes and out of sight as I scrabble back under the deck. Incredibly, that is two down. Snatches of a movie I watched with my grandfather, *Sergeant York*, flicker through my mind. As I remember it, York killed a whole bunch of Nazis by waiting them to come down the same corridor, like turkeys in a charnel house. But these guys are not turkeys.

I breathe and crawl back out and begin to run, because I'm not going to wait for Isabel and Taylor to come out. With my eye on the road, my next goal is the old pickup truck.

Chapter 31

THERE ARE ABOUT THIRTY YARDS between me and the old pickup truck. I hear a hustling, rough sound coming from around the side of the house. The sound is unrecognizable to me, but it is extremely clear, because the cold air carries sound perfectly. The only other sound is my own breathing and my steps and the clacking of frozen rain.

I don't look back, but whoever has come out has stopped to see Blue's and Scrawny's bodies. Maybe or maybe not picked up Blue's rifle.

I'm still carrying Scrawny's revolver, though having shot at Blue twice, and Scrawny having shot once, I have no idea if any rounds are left. I don't know if Scrawny took time to reload it before coming out. With six shots, there will be a maximum of three bullets in this gun, and maybe there are none. I can't check until I get somewhere to take cover.

I reach the pickup truck.

The light green 1968 Ford Ranger pickup has faded to a watercolor mint. The truck is parked up against a blackberry bush and a scrub tree, and a barbed wire fence that runs through the blackberries, separating this backyard from my grandparent's old horse pasture. I run towards the front of the truck and crouch down by the front fender, putting the engine between me and the ranch house.

I know that I am the last person to have driven this truck. After I used it, I parked the truck right here, next to the blackberry bush and the tree and barbed wire. I took the keys out. I hung them once against the door. That was easily thirty years ago, and this truck has not moved since.

There are blackberry bushes, thorny and full of sweetness, moving through the cab and crawling through the upholstery. One of the tree's limbs has moved up through the engine block. The truck has settled, so that dirt surrounds the wheels up to the middle bottom of the hubcaps.

And at some point, my grandparents decided that this truck wasn't going anywhere, and started using it to store things that probably also didn't need to go anywhere. So there is a large spool of baling wire. There is an enormous leather-and-metal harness, which probably went around one of the quarter horses when they had horses here, laid in the bed of this truck and exposed to the elements. There is a sheen of frozen water over everything.

The problem is that though I can hunker behind the nose of the truck, there is nowhere to hide in it. There is no *under* this truck. There is no on the other side of this truck, because there is the enormous blackberry bush. The truck may as well be a mound. I can't even get into the cab.

This truck was a bad choice to run to.

I hear the hustling sound again and poke my head out. The sound is rattling of the twist ties, radio, and other gear on the belt of Taylor, who is in his police shirtsleeves and running towards me. He pulls out a taser, which makes sense because Isabel has probably told him that Blue was wrong to try to kill me, and they still need THE NAME.

She has probably told him that what they need is for me to be perhaps wounded but docile, ready to do some more searching on my computer.

He stops and spreads his legs and raises the taser to fire it. I dive for the ground. Two little taser darts fly like a fishing line, unspooling their cords in the air, and land in the earth, sputtering like finger poppers on the Fourth of July.

I stand back up, lifting the revolver, hoping I have more shots. But as I pull the trigger aiming at Taylor, nothing happens. It is empty after all.

Taylor can't believe his luck. I throw the gun at him, an amazing gesture that I learned from two-bit thugs on the *Superman* show that I grew up watching—not the Jesus Superman of the late 70s, but the drill sergeant Superman of the 50s, which was on TV in the 70s.

Taylor reaches for his gun and I run for the house and jag left and head for the little tractor barn. It is bouncing in my vision as I run towards it, and Taylor is shouting at me to *freeze*, using police language because that training is apparently bone deep.

The small tractor barn, which is covered in corrugated tin, is only about eight feet tall and ten feet deep. I reach its double door, which has a latch of wood and a lace for a padlock. But it is not locked. I try to pull the door, fail, remember to move the wooden latch bar, and rip it open. I run inside.

I hear Taylor coming after me. And though I don't see him, he tells me that this time he has his gun, and he means to use it.

"You need to come out," he calls from outside, "or I'm gonna shoot you. I'm not gonna *kill* you, but I'm going to *hurt* you. I'm going to put a bullet right through your *ankle*, and you're going to scream." He's saying all of this fast, an impressive, freewheeling blank verse poem of violent threats.

The door of the tractor barn is thin, and there is a little door that is used to roll propane tanks and other things in and out the side as I look around the room. Too small to crawl through, though maybe I could tear it wider. There is an abundance of crap. Old paint cans. An old tractor wheel. I stop looking for tools to fight him off, because what I am not going to find is another gun.

The center of the tractor barn is taken up with a sleek, shiny, green late-model riding lawnmower. It must be used by my brother to cut the grass when he comes here with my grandmother. What is amazing to me about this thing is that it is nearly as big and bulky as my great-grandfather's old Farm-All in the tractor barn among the old buildings.

Taylor has stopped chattering. He clearly wants me to come out rather than have to come inside, because he is afraid that if he comes inside, I'm going to whack him over the head with something, which I absolutely will do.

But I need to get out of here. Because if I wait, he's going to get brave, and he's going to come in, and then he's going to shoot me in the head. Because even if he *says* he's going to shoot me in the ankle, I have a feeling that fear will catch up to him, and my chances are not good.

I get on the riding lawn mower and look for the start. I don't know the first thing about riding one of these, although a terrible memory flashes in my mind.

When I was very young, probably about ten, my grandfather, a giant and joyous man, let me use the riding lawn mower. I was cutting the grass—my grandfather called it *brush hogging*—while he did other chores on the farm, and at one point he came out to sit by a tree.

I was riding across the yard and had finished my mowing, and somehow, I lost control of the tractor. It was so long ago that I have no memory of how. Maybe my shoelaces got jammed in the brakes and the gas. But I realized I was out of control and I panicked. And my grandfather realized that I was coming right for him.

I see him now in my memory, becoming aware that I am going to run him over. He scrambles fast just as I manage to yank the lawn mower out of the way. It is a near miss that I have not thought about until this moment, a point where I could easily have killed him. And I don't remember him ever mentioning it again.

The riding lawn mower, I find, can't be started without a key. I look around, hoping to see a tractor key on a post, but no such luck.

I do see a pair of needle-nose pliers, and I take a chance and grab them. As Taylor yells once again towards me, I jam the needle nose pliers into the key slot, and twist.

The riding lawn mower rumbles and roars to life. Then I do something that I'm going to think about every day for the rest of my life.

I put the tractor in DRIVE, hit the gas, and slam forward out the double doors of the little tractor barn.

Taylor doesn't even have time to turn around. He folds backwards like a balloon man in front of a used car lot, and I brush hog him like an old cornfield.

I am going to think about it for the rest of my life because it is the coolest thing I have ever done.

Chapter 32

I REALIZE NOW THAT I'VE been looking towards the front of the brush hog and not paying any attention to the house. I jerk my head towards the back deck and door, because I would be a clean shot for anybody who came looking for me. But nobody comes running out. The turkey shoot has ended.

I swing my leg over to slide off the tractor and just then two vehicles come roaring around the front of the house. Both trucks: Isabel's and Blue's. Unless there are any other consultants in hiding, Ryan must be driving Blue's vehicle.

At first, I think they're going to come for me, but no: both are zooming away, as if in a race. Isabel's truck pulls ahead and whips through the gate with Ryan close behind. Both roar up the ridge.

With the blenderized remains of Taylor just next to me and the bodies of Scrawny and Blue nearby, I watch as the two trucks drive fast but not too fast along the ridge, and a quarter mile away they take the left and head out to the gate, and right on the road.

There is a strange comedy in watching them run away.

I am flabbergasted that Isabel would give up. It must be close to nine-forty-five now, giving her a little over an hour to complete her assignment.

And then I realize: she must have taken my computer.

I get off the little tractor and start to walk.

I don't want to go up the middle steps that killed Scrawny, first because they are a nightmare, but also because he is blocking the way.

I go around the front of the house, up the front steps on the west side, and in through the storm door and front door, which both still lay open. All told, the wreckage of last night has not made much of a difference in the appearance of the living room.

I slowly spin around, taking in the atmosphere of the house. It is cold and quiet.

I cannot believe that I am at last alone, save for the bodies on the back lawn. It feels like I've been dealing with these people for days. I don't know what I'm supposed to do right now.

I shake off the strangeness of my sudden solitude and walk over to the dining table. My computer, incredibly, is still there. It is possible that Isabel in her haste has forgotten it. Draped across the chair is Taylor's thick police jacket.

What to do. I believe what I'm supposed to do is call the police, or just dial 911, if I could get cell phone reception. All of this is a jumble in my head.

To call 911, I would need my cell phone, and having found the computer safe and sound, I hurry back to the laundry room.

The back door is open, and the back deck is awash in blood, Blue's body out of sight except the lower part of his leg.

I bend down by the washing machine and reach back, feeling around the linoleum tile, my fingers scraping grime and dust.

I find my cell phone. I have no bars.

All I really wanted to do was come here and write a book. None of the past day has made any sense at all. Scratch that: none of my trip, from the moment I met Isabel. As I move silently, unsure of where to go next in this house, I feel the ruffle of the envelope in my pocket. I take it out, looking at the address and the name DOTSON.

I walk back with my phone and currently useless phone next to my laptop, and absently right the ceramic rooster I knocked over last night. I lay the envelope on the table and stretch. My shoulders and arms and back feel like one long, mottled bruise.

I turn around and find a utensil drawer, find a steak knife, and return to the table. I tip the knife into the seam of the envelope and slice it open with the serrated edge of the knife.

Inside the envelope is a thick fold of seven or eight pages. I open them.

They are blank.

Who is Isabel Hardy? I have a mind to find out.

My foot bumps against something else and I look down to see, in a jumble next to the chair, the Members Only jacket that Ryan was wearing last night when he said that he was hot. I pick it up and feel the uneven weight because there's something in the pocket. At first, I think it might be another revolver. But no, it's a billfold.

Opening it up, I see a driver's license in a little plastic window with the name Ryan Jenkins and an address in Broken Arrow, a suburb of Tulsa.

I want to find out about Isabel Hardy, but I have a better idea right now, because I have Ryan's wallet.

I need to change clothes. I'd like to take a shower, but right now, I want answers. I take off the size twelve-and-a-half tactical boots that I've been wearing for God knows how many hours and stretch my feet for a moment before putting on a pair of my own hiking boots, size thirteens. I wiggle my toes with satisfaction.

I don't bother to change my Simple Minds T Shirt. I throw on Taylor's nice, warm police jacket. I go back and lock the back door, and then grab my keys from a weirdly shaped ceramic mug that says YOU SAID YOU WANTED HALF A CUP OF COFFEE, and head out the front door, locking it behind me.

I go out to the Matrix. There's ice on the windshield again, and it takes me a moment to scrape it off. Then at the last minute, I go back in and grab the computer. I'm not going to be separated from it.

I bring it back down the steps, lay it in the back seat and take off.

Google Maps tells me that it will be forty minutes to get to Ryan's house. As I drive over the barbed wire, leaving at least two dead bodies in my wake, and up onto the ridge, I feel like I am stoned in some way. My body is vibrating, and my breath is just a little shallow.

I open the window to let the cold air in. As I drive out onto Dentonville Road, leaving the gate open, I turn on the radio. There's nothing that I would really want to hear.

I'm hoping for something that brings back the Oklahoma of my childhood, riding around with my grandfather listening to Porter Wagner and

Lefty Frizzell. But you don't bring back the past by turning on the radio. I hear lot of new country that I don't recognize, and on the other stations, new pop that of *course* I don't recognize. I live largely in the past.

Rather than finding an oldies station, I settle on an NPR affiliate out of Tulsa, which is the direction I'm headed to confront a man who for some reason spent the night with a bunch of people who tried to kill me.

Broken Arrow, Oklahoma is a tidy and unassuming, safe little bedroom community. It is mostly single-family homes, the usual nicely kept single-story houses with clean front yards and SUVs and small, late model vehicles in the driveway. It is not the home of the rich, but decidedly not the home of the poor. It is the perfect place for someone who is probably a middle manager at an advertising agency or a defense contractor. It has not changed in half a century, but it continues to look the kind of beautiful that suburbia was created to enjoy.

Google Maps on my phone tells me how to get to Ryan's house. I take turn after turn into his neighborhood, which is demarcated by a tombstone-like hunk of polished cement and brick in the middle of an entry street: FOREST BROOK ESTATES. Sounds nice.

I follow the turns into this honeycomb of houses as though I'm going to be dropping off a UPS package. Ryan lives on a street called Rusdell, and soon I find myself calmly driving my little Matrix down Rusdell Street. At 10:27 in the morning, I pull to the curb a few houses down from Ryan's. I get out, grabbing Ryan's jacket and draping it over my arm.

Then I reach back in and lock my own wallet into the glove compartment. I walk a few steps toward the curb, my hand feeling the handle of the revolver, which I have put into the pocket of Taylor's police jacket. It is still empty.

I pass a pale, white brick house, a red brick house that looks almost just like it, and finally stand before Ryan's house, which is another house of red brick, with Ivy growing prettily all around the door, which is yet another etched-glass Home Depot special behind yet another storm door.

Blue's rental truck is sitting in the driveway, its undersides spattered with mud. I walk up the driveway, pass the truck, and turn onto the little sidewalk that approaches the door.

I put my hand on the hammered-copper handle of the storm door and start to pull, and then stop. I realize that I'm not sure what to say to whoever comes to the door.

I hear voices inside and I crouch a little, shifting so I can see through the clear parts of the frosted pattern. I can see down the entryway of the house where tile becomes carpet, through a corner of the living room, and into the kitchen. Ryan is seated at a late breakfast.

He is facing me but looking down, staring at a cup of coffee and a bowl of cereal. Ryan, who just a short while ago I saw standing uncomfortably next to the closet in the ranch house, is now showered and wearing an X-MEN T shirt and boxer shorts.

There's a woman with a shrub-like brown mom cut puttering around him, bringing him a glass of orange juice. Ryan speaks and I can't hear it at all. Although maybe I hear a murmur. *Working all night.* That's what I hear him say. Which is funny, because if you'd actually been working all night, it seems unlikely that you would finally sit down and then make sure and use the phrase, because it's obvious that you've been working all night.

The woman repeats whatever he says, and she kisses Ryan on the head, and he glumly pokes at his cereal.

I'm wondering how he's going to explain the fact that he came home in a pickup that is not his. Less than twelve hours ago, this man was holding a knife to my throat. Whether he had the guts to use it or not.

I stand and watch through the glass. Ryan brings his hands to his coffee cup. Runs his fingers around the brim. Doesn't lift it.

I am pretty certain that Ryan was as flabbergasted at the turn that the day has taken as I am, which does not absolve him.

What would it take, I wonder? To do something you'd only ever read about, to decide to become a killer, and then find out you *weren't really a killer*.

Was that something that I might do? I think not.

But then, I did, after all, run a brush hog over Mr. Taylor. Ryan circles the mouth of the cup again with shaking fingers. His wife is oblivious to his nerves. We see what we want to see.

I have Ryan's wallet in the other pocket of my jacket. Opposite the revolver. And I wonder for a moment if I should just set the wallet down on the mat I am standing on (the mat says AS FOR ME AND MY HOUSE WE

WILL SERVE THE LORD) and walk away.

But no, I want to talk to the man I first labeled Costco.

With a little bit of mischief, I wait for Ryan to finally bring the coffee cup up towards his lips, and I rap on the door with my knuckles. *Bam bam bam.*

Ryan starts, his coffee sloshing on Cyclops and Wolverine, and looks out towards the door. His eyes must focus then because I watch his blood run cold. His wife looks towards the door, her hands on her hips. Who could that possibly be?

Ryan says something. His hand pads the air as he rises uncertainly, as if to say, I got it.

He comes towards the door.

What he undoubtedly sees behind the glass, because I doubt he has realized it is me, is a police jacket. I can't see *his* face very well because I've stood up straight and he is now a shadow behind the frosted glass.

But I know that he is trying to decide what to do. Whether he should decline to answer the door or shout for me to go away. But because he is a certain kind of man, I also know that he will be uncomfortable shouting for this stranger to go away, because he rarely shouts, and this will only rouse more attention from his wife—and if there are kids in the house, from them as well. He will not want questions from the household, will not want his nighttime fantasies visited upon those he loves best.

He wants to figure out a way to make this strange police officer's questions go away as quickly as possible. I know all of this because as I said, he is like family.

He gets closer and looks through the glass. I'm standing a couple of feet away and he looks straight at me. Only now does recognition dawn on him. He yanks his head back as if bitten. He looks back, and his wife is not watching. He said he would handle it and she has wandered off.

He doesn't know what to do now. I decide to help him along and raise my hand to knock again, and he opens the door. We are now separated by the glass of a storm door.

Ryan is looking down.

David Mamet has this comment in *The Spanish Prisoner*, where Steve Martin's character says, somebody who owes you something morally, but not legally, will begin to act cruelly towards you. To suppress their guilt.

And I expect something like that. I expect that if Ryan can summon the nerve, he will be insulting, and call me a liar before I even say a word.

But he surprises me. He looks like a dog who has been kicked.

"What is it?"

"Hi, Ryan. You remember me? Mike? From Hollow Hill?"

He looks up, biting his lip.

"Ryan Jenkins, that's your name?"

"Yes," he says. "How did you know my name... how did you..."

"Why don't we talk?" I say brightly.

"Honey?" his wife calls. She has appeared from somewhere and is in the kitchen, calling curiously towards him.

Ryan looks back, "Oh, they're just... asking some questions about something that happened at work. No worries."

For a guy who has been kicked around a lot, he lies pretty quickly and well. He looks back at me with a new smarm as though he has regained some of his confidence. It's time to get rid of me. I'm alive, right? No harm, no foul. "Look," he says.

"In case you're wondering," I say, "I have your wallet. And a gun."

He says, "Why don't we go sit in the backyard?"

Chapter 33

RYAN SAYS A FEW WORDS to his wife, and he comes out and joins me on the front walk. I hand him his jacket and he takes it, and as he shuts the storm door, he says "I thought you were a cop with that jacket you got." Amazing. He is making small talk. He leads me around the garage past Blue's truck, and around the corner.

At the side of the house there's a tall wood privacy fence with one of those metal latches that you press down on, and various balls and chains move to make the gate slide open. It's a nice gate.

We enter his back yard. I'm expecting to see a swimming pool, and in fact Ryan sort of has one. There's an above ground swimming pool, but a nice one, very large, with some sturdy wooden decking all around it. Between this and the house is a deck with large umbrellas. The pool is covered over for the winter.

And of course it is still quite cold. Luckily Ryan has the jacket I have given him, his own Member's Only jacket I found back on the ranch house floor.

Now we sit on a little bench, next to the back door. And he reaches into a cooler and asks me if I would like something, a beer or a coke.

I say no. He doesn't get anything for himself, but he does reach under the bench and retrieve a pack of Marlboros. He lights one, his hands shaking. After he takes a puff on the cigarette, I realize he is waiting for me to talk. I thumb my phone in my pocket, wondering if my reception here close to town is as good as it was on the highway.

"Ryan, how involved were you in all of this?"

"Oh," he shakes his head. "I mean, man, I have no idea what all that was about. Really." He spreads his hands.

"What do you mean?" I ask. "You were there."

"Okay. Okay," he says, placating. "What you heard was what it was supposed to be. A couple of months ago, I was on one of the Reddit boards that I read. One of the black pill sites."

A *black pill* site is a message board dedicated to a peculiar view of the world, that it is not only different from what we think it is, but more meaningless. That's remarkably similar to my own worldview, except something—empathy, I think—sends me in a different direction. He's mumbling these things as though it's all very understandable. And maybe we're just friends and he's filling me in on a project that went wrong.

"Anyway," I say, "these guys presented themselves as consultants to get your balls back, if I recall the term."

He chuckles at this. Like the joke's on him and not me.

"How much did they charge?"

"Eighteen thousand dollars," he says.

I am awestruck. First off, that somebody like this guy has eighteen thousand dollars laying around that he can sink into a secret project that will involve committing several felonies. But second, I am amazed that eighteen thousand dollars is all it takes to get somebody to kill somebody. It's both too much and too little. And that's how Blue's setup begins to make sense.

"That was the way it was presented," he says. "So, you know, I clear out an old 401K, and I contact these guys. It's a safari. So we do this thing, I set up an excuse of working all night. They have to pick me up twice, once for what they call reconnaissance, and once for real. These guys pick me up at the mall in the morning and we go out there."

Amazing. They picked him up—in Blue's rented truck—at the mall. He could get an Orange Julius and then go kill someone.

"So these guys," he continues, "when I meet them, they're smooth, but they're just a couple good old boys. They drive like they kind of know where they're going, and they say they have a prospect that's coming to town and they want to check it out. So we go out to the dam and they have a bag of trash, and we get out.

"You're up on the dam. With the woman. They look up and they're casual, but they say, that's the guy. New in town. Though clearly, I'm thinking, you seem to have a wife or girlfriend."

I am listening to him narrate my date, which of course Isabel led me to just for this rendezvous.

"So now they bring me back to Tulsa, to work. And after hours I drive to the mall again, and they pick me up again, and this time we go waaaay out to BFE."

BFE would be my farm.

"And now, man. Now it's real." He is lost in the moment. "I've never done anything like this, I've never even been arrested. And they prod me along and break into this house.

"And here's the thing. I was terrified. But at least I knew what was going on. What was going on was that I had already made the biggest fucking mistake of my *life.*" He practically has tears in his eyes. "Look. I've never done anything like this. It was a mistake."

"Yeah," I say, "but…"

"But it was a mistake that made sense to me until that woman broke in. And at that point, *nothing* after that made sense, because now… all the sudden they wanted *information* from you."

"Yes, they did," I say. "A name."

"Yeah. This fucking name. And then they're ignoring me, man. I'm stuck. I'm a *prisoner.*"

"Did you ask them to take you home?"

"I couldn't ask them to do *anything*," he says. "At this point, I'm as much of a prisoner as you were."

I stop for a moment and wonder if in fact that's true. If somehow, in all of this, Ryan—who paid some guys that he met through Reddit eighteen thousand dollars to find somebody that he could murder—actually felt through most of this as if he were as much a prisoner as I was. I mean, isn't Ryan the real victim here?

"Ryan, listen," I say. "Here's your wallet." I take it out of my breast pocket and hand it to him. He stuffs it in his jacket pocket, and something strikes him the wrong way. He is wide-eyed, confused by what he feels against his hand.

"Let's go back around front," I say.

He nods and we get up, going to the impressive gate again, and through. He is feeling at his pocket with increasing nervousness.

After the gate, as we reach the side of the house, I say, "I think I'd like to talk to your wife."

He says, "Why would you want to do that?"

"Come on," I say, stopping. "Why would I want to do that? You guys tried to *kill* me. But what I really want to know, is your story *true?* Are you really such a, such a *loser*, that you had no idea what these guys were up to?"

"I didn't," he says, hunching his shoulders and pacing. He throws down his cigarette. "I swear."

"Because what, you thought you were just gonna murder someone and that was it?" I walk with him around to the driveway, and now I am walking fast, turning left towards the front door. I see a shadow of his wife at the door, as though she is pacing, wondering what is keeping hubby.

"Why shouldn't I ask her?"

And he says, with utmost sincerity, "Because I don't want my *life* messed up. You're gonna mess up my life, man, and you're *fine."*

"Ryan! You were on a black pill site that told you it would be a good idea for you to find somebody and kill them to get your *balls* back," I say. "I think that might be *interesting* to your spouse."

The door opens, and his wife, who has grown curious because I've started to talk louder, says "Honey?"

"Ma'am, I think you should know…" I say.

Ryan flushes and sputters, and then he does exactly what I think he will do. He pulls Scrawny's empty revolver out and points it at me. "This guy's crazy, stop, stop, freeze."

There is a whoop in the street. And as Jared pulls the trigger uselessly, three Tulsa police cars tear into view. One of them comes screeching to a halt in front the house, and then the other two. There are lights flashing, brightly bouncing off the asphalt.

They are here because I called 911 as soon as Ryan came out, and the operators there have been listening to this man confess to—at the very least—attempted murder. Truth is, what he *said* didn't have to matter. Even if you call 911 and stay silent, cops will come. They're nobody's friend, but this part is their job.

As cops pour out of their cars, Ryan still has the gun pointed at me as the police officers scream for him to get on the ground. His wife starts screaming as Ryan spins, stunned, dropping the gun. Which is good for him, because he doesn't want to get shot, and good for me, because pistols, even cop pistols, are hard to aim.

As they swarm him, I am backing up, backing up, into the driveway, and then around the house, and then I turn around.

I run through the awesome gate and past the above-ground swimming pool and climb the back fence. This is not easy for me because I am old and heavy, and the wooden gate sways under me, but I make it over. I fall and get up in someone else's back yard. This one has a chain-link fence, and now I walk, almost nonchalantly, through this back yard. Maybe someone sees me, but it is cold and rainy, and no one is looking outside.

The gate out of this back yard is not locked, and I step through and alongside a house and into the next residential street.

I walk down the block and take a right, and then another right, and with a glorious blaze of police lights farther up the block, I find my Matrix and get in.

It will take some time for the police to catch up to me, and right now I don't want to talk to them.

But I have another problem. When I get into the Matrix, my computer is gone.

Chapter 34

I AM NOT AT ALL cold even though it's freezing outside, because I have the policeman's jacket still and I've been running.

I left my laptop computer on the passenger side. That it is no longer there is not that surprising, but I feel extremely stupid. I left the car unlocked. I have fifteen thousand words that are now irretrievably lost.

I stare into space, trying to take in the gravity of what has happened. How could I be such an idiot. If I were in *downtown* Tulsa, and I went inside a Hilton or something, and I left a computer on the passenger side seat, I would not be at all surprised to get back in the car and find out that it's not there.

But here, that's not the case. I'm in the middle of a suburb, a bedroom community. It is late morning on a Monday, and it's very cold outside, and it just seems unlikely that someone would have broken into my car.

And just when I'm thinking I have discovered suburban thievery, I see a folded piece of paper on my dash.

I stare. In the distance, the police lights are still flashing, and though I can't tell for sure, I think the group of men moving to the street are escorting Ryan into the back of a police car.

I reach out and pick up the folded paper as though it were toxic. I open it up and find a neat scrawl in blue pen.

MEET ME AT THE DAM.

Chapter 35

I DRIVE BY THE POLICE cars and their flashing lights in front of Ryan's house. I am not sure if he is now in one of the cars or inside his house, because police are milling around. I drive slow so that my boring little crossover SUV will attract no attention.

I head back out onto the freeway. It takes me 30 minutes to make my way back to Hollow Hill, back through the new restaurants, back down the old closed up Main Street, past the dilapidated hardware stores, past the grocery stores and the 7-11 and then the last, big convenience store just when it all turns to country, and onto the road out to the WPA dam.

I look at the clock. It is 11:30 when I reach the turn-off for the dam.

As on our date, the dam is frozen and damp. I park and look up.

Isabel is waiting for me on one of the giant stones of the dam on the left side. She's not standing, not pacing, just seated on one of the stones, which I think must be freezing her ass.

And she has my computer on her lap.

She has either discovered the name she needed from the computer, searching it on her own, or she has not. I cannot imagine why she would want me here. Maybe she's here just to push me off the dam. It's impossible to tell. But I want to know.

I begin the arduous climb up the path next to the stones. At one point I have to put my hand on the ground and it's muddy and cold.

When I reach her, she doesn't get up. She just looks up at me with the computer on her knees.

I say, "You have the computer, so what do you need me for?"

She pulls her phone out of her pants pocket and looks at it. "It doesn't really matter now," she says.

"Everybody keeps saying things like that. I went to see Ryan at his house. Do you know he paid eighteen thousand dollars to have an opportunity to kill somebody? That doesn't seem like nearly enough, but it seems like a lot more than he has laying around. And yet he said the same thing: it doesn't matter now. No harm, no foul."

Isabel shrugs.

"I think his story is true, though," I say. "I don't think he actually had any idea what you guys were up to."

She nods. For a moment she is the flirtatious, fifty-ish woman I climbed up here with before.

"So explain it to me," I say.

"I needed you to get me the name," she says. "It was as simple as that. I needed the passcode. That was my assignment."

"Okay," I say. "But if you needed me to give you the name to open the safe deposit box, why didn't you just ask?" I do not mention that I know the name now. I'm afraid it will get her excited, and she is holding fifteen thousand words I cannot afford to lose.

"We couldn't take the chance that you wouldn't give it to us," she said.

"How did you know that I was going to be back at the farm?"

"Oh," she says, as though this detail had escaped her. "We knew because you told the *world*. We knew you had the passcode, and there was that picture of you, after the shooting in Denver. And then there was your quote to a reporter. You said you were going to take three weeks to write. We were moving pretty fast. We had to. We got into your life, read interviews you've done—you're a pretty chatty Cathy when you add it all up. From what I read, I knew that if you were going to try to write a book, chances were, you were going to be going to your old farm."

"I don't get it, though," I say. "Were there a bunch of you all over the place, how did you get this assignment? Blue—sorry, McMurtry comes in from California, but what, you just were *here*, and I fell into your lap?"

199

She looks at me with genuine astonishment. "Oh my God," she says. "What?"

"You haven't worked out… that I'm not Isabel Hardy?"

I sway in place.

Because of course she isn't. Isabel Hardy was a girl I went out with once or twice in the 80s. This woman learned something about me, probably from a story I told a reporter at some time, and the rest fell into place.

"All I had to do was convince you that I had been here all along," she said. "We have these situations all the time. There are countless people paying eighteen thousand dollars to kill somebody. It's a fake business we run. And we take those opportunities to get the information we need. Because the people that we bring on their safaris, they're in the wind afterwards.

"Anyway, it doesn't matter now, because the deadline has passed," she says.

I say, "the funny thing is I remembered the name."

She inhales through her nose. She is having a very bad assignment. Things are tough for consultants.

She pulls out a gun and aims it at me.

Chapter 36

I DON'T KNOW WHAT KIND of gun it is, but it looks a lot nicer than the .38 revolver that I stole and gave to Ryan. It looks like the kind of gun that people used to use in black and white serials that I've seen on TV. One of those smooth things. Really other than the stuff my grandfather taught me, I don't know shit about guns. But she's pointing it at me, and I have a good feeling that that's enough to know.

She says, "There may still be... a chance. If I call now. I can get lucky. Tell me the name."

"I'll tell you what," I say, my hands raised. "Give me the computer, and I will. Really. I don't give a shit about your safe deposit box. I'll trade, gladly." And I mean it. If I lose those words, I may never start again.

She is thinking, watching time tick away. She is thinking someone in Switzerland, some officious banker in a black suit, is maybe already removing the safe deposit box and carrying it wherever he carries the boxes that are going to be scorched. And that means that like a call from the governor during a condemned man's trip to the gas chamber, she may be able to get there in time.

She reaches out with the computer. Makes sense. She still has the gun. It's her best move.

I take the computer from her. As soon as it is in my hand, I swipe it hard, down on her gun hand. The laptop weighs about seven pounds and it knocks her arm wild.

And by some miracle, the gun doesn't go off before she drops it, but it doesn't matter.

Because I slip and fall backwards, and now I am moving through space.

I tumble over the side of the dam, falling five or six feet, landing with a heavy thud on the slab below. My head misses the stone I land on, whipping my neck back over the side and giving me a wrenching pain, but at least I do not crack my skull.

I groan, the laptop in my right hand on my stomach.

Isabel jumps down and lands next to me, grabbing me up and slamming me back against the next stone. This time my head smacks against granite.

"Tell me."

"David Copperfield," I wheeze. "Fuck you."

She whacks me across the face, hard, and I see the world swim. I drop, sliding down. And then I grab onto her ankle.

For a moment, as she topples, I think what we must look like, two middle-aged people wrestling on the heavy stones of this dam as cold mist surrounds us. She lands on the edge of the stone, nearly going over the side.

Before she finds her balance, I whack her across the face with the edge of the laptop. She falls back and over into nothingness.

She doesn't fall down to the next stone along the side. She goes over the edge, plummeting some twenty feet. I watch over the side with a wave of guilt as her head smacks against a stone on the way down. And then her body lands on frozen water at the bottom of the dam. She lies next to a carving in the stone that says WPA - Works Progress Administration.

"Alexis Vauxhall, as it turns out," I say.

There is no other sound except wind whistling around the dam.

There is me, a middle-aged man with his laptop computer, and a dead woman at the bottom of the dam.

I get up, wincing, and move off the stones and onto the sludgy path. I climb about twenty more feet to the top of the dam and look out across the lake, which is liquid but cold.

It is nearly noon. I breathe, feeling pain throughout my body, and watch birds flying on the lake.

I turn around and slowly make my way down the path with my laptop computer. The body of Isabel—or whoever she is—lies on the ice. By all rights, I should not be alive.

There is somewhere I want to go.

I get back into the Matrix. I leave the window down, feeling the cold air on my face as I drive back to Isabel's farm.

This is where I came to see her yesterday morning, and I run over it again in my head.

As I park in front of the Hardy's farmhouse, which is very much like the ruined farmhouse on my own farm, with its wide front porch and amber glowing lights inside.

Past the house are other small buildings, all the accoutrements of a farm, a tractor barn and a smaller tractor barn. Past that I see grain silos and other equipment and buildings. Just like on my farm.

I stop the car and stare for a moment at the porch, where yesterday, I came to see Isabel. Or whoever.

I replay the scene in my head. Because I am the guy who saw her name on a check.

And so, following the name on the check to the address on the check, I came to this house and Isabel came to the door. Isabel, a woman I now know to be a contractor from somewhere else.

She is not Isabel, the farm girl who was interested in marketing that I went out with one summer when I was a teenager.

I get out. I shut off the Matrix. Close the door, put the key in my pocket and walk towards the porch.

I am keenly aware that I have left my computer once more on the front seat of the Matrix. And even as I walk away from it, I think maybe I should go back and hide it in case anybody in this house is watching.

But it's too late now, and anyway, I don't think anyone's here. I think her crew is scattered around my farm like busted equipment, like houses left to rot.

I get to the porch and look at the little bench we sat on with its attractive, new heat lamps. There are a few dregs of snapped beans, though because Isabel is a neat person, she took most of it away. So the bowls, of course, are gone. But this is where I sat and there is where she sat, and we became a couple snapping beans.

I turn back towards the front door. Look through the storm door. And the glass door. I open the storm door. Look through. I can't see anything. There is a curtain in the way. And through the cracks in the curtain, all I can make out is an armchair and some light.

I step back, closing the storm door, and go over to one of the two large windows, one to the right of the door and one to the left one near the bench, where we were snapping beans. I look through the left window and into the living room. I see a couch and an easy chair and a coffee table and TV on a stand against the wall, all visible through the crack in the curtains.

Walking to the right side of the porch, I see another chair, and a desk and a dining room table. Everything is off; everything is clean, but somehow, none of this looks right. There is nothing on the dining table. There was nothing on the coffee table.

I go back to the door. There is no doorbell. I open the storm door, and I rap on the window, very fast. *Bam bam bam.*

It is the middle of the day, so if anybody is here, they will not be particularly disturbed by somebody knocking on the door. Although out here, because it takes extra effort to get to anybody's door, I would probably not be particularly welcome.

If Isabel lived here alone, there will be no one. And of course she doesn't live here. I'm really just trying to find out who in Hell's house this is. I'm trying to put the story completely together. Nobody comes to the door.

That's good enough, I think. I look over down the front steps and see a paver stone. I go down, pick it up, go back up, and open the storm door again. I heave the paver stone through the huge oval window in the door. The glass shatters and falls, tumbling on the floor beyond.

I reach through and unlock the door. In a movie this is the moment when anybody waiting will chop my fingers off, because I am very vulnerable right now, but that doesn't happen.

I open the door and go inside.

The living room is exactly how I could see from the window. But I can see beyond that into other rooms, into the kitchen and into a bedroom.

And as I step a few feet into the hall, there is a bathroom on my left.

Everything is dark.

I flip on the lights.

Everything is dusty.

Nobody has been in this house for decades.

Slowly I turn around, looking at this... *set*. It was intended only to be seen by me through the window of the door. Nobody has been using this house.

I'm trying to think of how Isabel, new Isabel, played it. She gets a call, and the call says, by noon on Monday, you must have this name. The only person who can give you this name is a man named Mike Dotson. Find him. The rest, she told me.

She looks at materials I've been quoted in and finds that I've referred to spending the summer here in 1988. She finds reference to Isabel Hardy, whose parents had a farm, and finds a place where I made a reference to this in a short story I wrote when I was still writing short stories.

Then it's easy. She will pose as a girl that I went out with once, and she will take it for granted that neither of us will be expected to remember any of it very well. That will be her story.

She gets to Oklahoma. She puts her team in place. And she sets the trap. She leaves a check for me.

She assumes that I will come looking for her. I can only imagine that if I did *not* come looking for her, she would have played it a different way. But of course, I am predictable, and I come looking for her right away. We sit and we snap beans—even though of course it is the winter, and because I don't live in the country, and because I am so intrigued with this woman from my past, I am not thinking of the fact that snapping beans is a preposterous activity for the winter. But it's a nice date. It feels like a Hallmark movie. It's a good detail.

We sit. And then we go on the real date. Whenever we talk about the past, she lets me lead. As for her, she merely adds details, which I readily agree with. She is taking my story and running with it. Isabel is doing exactly what psychics do on stage every day, she is building a history, taking cues from me. She has become this Isabel character that neither of us really remembers.

There probably *is* a real Isabel out there, if she's still alive, but she is irrelevant to this case, because New Isabel is on a deadline so short that she will be in the wind by the time anyone notices.

All her story has to do is hold together for these few hours. Once she has created herself as an old girlfriend, possibly a new love, the next chapter in her play is a doozy, a risky one.

She rescues me from the bad guys who have broken into the house. And then as we hide, she tries to get the information from me. It should work. I am soft and fifty, a gentle giant, and I should open up like a melon.

But of course, it all goes wrong when I get too lucky and kill Tattoo. They are running out of time.

And unfortunately for them, I win.

I leave this soulless house and go out to the porch, leaving the front door open. It doesn't matter. This house will fall apart.

I get back in the Matrix and head back to the farm. It is another two miles to Dentonville Road, and then I take a right, driving towards the farm.

If there are no police waiting for me, I will have to call them. I'm hoping that I can answer their questions within a few hours.

And after that, I have a book to finish.

I roll the window up and turn on NPR.

Epilogue

THE NARROW AND CRAMPED AMERICAN Airlines MD80 airplane sets down at DFW Airport at eight o'clock in the morning, earlier than I'm used to getting up, much less getting to work. But adrenaline is keeping me bright and awake. I am doing something now that I have not done in many years.

The moment the plane parks at the gate, everyone aboard immediately gets up. I have a window seat and as long as you don't have to pee, it's a perfect little cocoon. I lean into the window and pull out my phone. I text my daughter and son that I have landed safely. Then I scroll through my phone for several minutes, circling around the work before the work, as is my habit. Finally I bring up a set of notes that I have saved and refer to them once more. Because when I tell the story aloud at a podium, I want to get it right.

It has been almost one year since the shooting at Blaze Satellite Television, making it also exactly one year since my writing retreat.

I scroll through the script, occasionally editing a word here or there.

When the crowd on the plane is thinned out, I grab my bag from the overhead compartment and head out to the gate. In the old days, someone meeting you at the airport could meet you at the gate, but those days are gone like trick-or-treating alone.

There's a security exit close in front of me, and when I emerge on the other side, I see the couple I'm supposed to meet. Standing next to a baggage claim sign is a pair of earnest-looking young people, a young man and a young woman with similar spiky cuts, though hers is a candy-apple red, while his is a yellow even yellower than my own when I was his age. They are both wearing multicolored T-Shirts with anime characters I don't recognize. The girl is holding up a sign that says DOTSON.

When I give a look of recognition and raise my hand slightly, they wave urgently, and I approach. They are bursting with energy and look to be each about nineteen years old.

"I'm Maisie Dix," the girl says. Her hair is so lacquered that it moves like a helmet as she talks. "I'm an associate, Guest Relations." I love how she talks with her hands, which is something I associate a lot with my son. "And this is Tom, also Guest Relations, and he'll be driving." Tom is already nodding, super stoked, which is nice if a little strange, because I'm not used to people gushing. "Welcome to PopFest!" they say in unison. I am feeling energized by their enthusiasm.

Tom and Maisie chatter excitedly as they lead me away out to the sidewalk and the crosswalk to the parking garages. DFW Airport is an airport that is particularly built for a state that is in love with cars. In other cities, you park wherever they want you to park and then you have to go to a great deal of trouble to find the gate you're looking for. DFW is the opposite; if you know what gate you're going to, you can always park right by it.

So as soon as we are through the door, it is a quick walk under a shade of the multi-story passenger pickup building, into their car. In the parking garage, the shade is cool, but not cold. Even in February, as with Oklahoma, the weather varies, and we are in a warm snap. Though as with Oklahoma, there is more water in the air than I am used to, and the humidity causes me to sweat.

As we walk, Maisy looks at me as though she is afraid that I'm going to have a heart attack. But I wave her off and thank her again for picking me up. Tom takes my bag and stows it.

"So, oh my god," she says as we reach a shiny green Toyota RAV4 crossover SUV. As Tom opens the door, Maisie chatters on. "I just finished reading *Dream Tasker 50* and I just cannot stop talking about it."

"So true," Tom says with a smile. "She literally cannot stop talking about it."

As I get in the back seat, Tom gets behind the wheel and Maisie gets in the front passenger side. Tom pulls out from the parking spot and Maisie turns around, leaning her arm on the seat, chattering again. We reach Airport Freeway, a twenty-five-minute drive to the hotel in downtown Dallas. I look at the gridlock of cars and am amazed that as bad as traffic was when I lived here decades ago, it has only gotten worse.

When I look out from the freeway, I can see stores and restaurants and apartment buildings. And for a moment I have X-Ray vision and I can see the rolling hills beneath. And they're very like the shallow, rolling hills on the plains of Oklahoma. And because I can see through all of this modernity, I am at peace.

"So, okay," Maisie says, her hands swinging wildly. "How long did it take you to write it?"

I think about the writing of it, have been thinking about it a lot. *Dream Tasker 50* begins with the exact line that I wrote when I started outlining: *Our Jupiter is fifty.* The book itself came faster than anything that I have ever written before.

I haven't answered yet and she says, "I *know* you're supposed to talk about all of this in your acceptance speech, but still, I heard someone say it was three *weeks.*"

She is right. It took me three weeks to write the first draft, minus the day or so that I had to deal with the *consultants* who tried to kill me. In the end I found the story and divided up the time. "For the rough draft," I clarify. "Just the rough draft."

The story of *Dream Tasker 50* jogs back and forth between two narratives: Jupiter Chris's new adventure, where he is called out of retirement to deal with a biological weapon that is going to be inserted into vaccines around the world, taking advantage of people's fear of vaccines while also creating massive casualties; and a storyline in the past, about Jupiter Chris, younger than we usually see him, eight or ten years old, in moments that form him. By the time I was twelve years old, I was already me, more than I ever cared to admit. We are made what we are, and we are made early.

Dream Tasker 50 came out under the Jerry Bane Commemorative imprint and was rushed to market. So it came out faster than the usual eighteen months that it takes for a book to get from draft to shelves, even if the book is under contract.

By the time it came out, a lot of people were already talking about it, partly because there was a little bit of marketing around the commemorations of the books championed by my deceased editor, Jerry Bane. But mainly they were talking because of newspaper publicity, or what would probably be called "earned media" by Isabel, the real Isabel, the one who was interested in marketing. Earned media means exposure that one does not pay for but *earns*; they *work* for it.

I did indeed work for this media, though the publicity was an accident. I wrote a few cryptic comments on my Facebook page. And that turned into a blog post.

But then my blog post inspired someone else's amazed *Slate* article, and that turned into a flabbergasted *Times* article. And suddenly, I was on NPR.

So several times, I have told this story of how a middle-aged author who has not published a book since the Clinton administration, who had three weeks off from work because of a shooting in Denver, was attacked and tortured by criminals while on a writing retreat in Oklahoma—and manage to effect his escape. The story always ends with how it ended: I still had a book to write.

This writing part is what Maisie wants to ask about, which tells me something. If I tell you I survived a break in with a bunch of thrill-killers and used the rest of my vacation to finish a draft on my book, and your next question is about the book, you are a writer.

A lot of people ask me about Isabel. Not the New Isabel whose body was retrieved from the dam and whose bonus for accessing the safe deposit box must have gone uncollected. But the original Isabel. The answer is common and sad. Isabel Hardy died of breast cancer at the age of 43, seven years before I met New Isabel.

I have not yet chosen to tell the story of what happened in Oklahoma except in interviews. And tonight I will touch on it because it is expected.

I will retell the story during my acceptance speech of the Book of the Year Award from the Dallas PopFest, which I suspect they have given me because I used to spend a lot of time in the Dallas/Fort Worth area, and because I am willing to show up.

With the help of NPR and all that, the book *is* a best-seller, but I do not expect it to win any prizes, except among very excited genre fans, like my new friends, Maisie and Tom.

I will tell the story of the break-in. But to be honest, that will only take a small part of the program, because what I'm really interested in sharing is exactly what Maisie asks me for. She bites her lip and she says, "So, how do you do it? Like if I want to write a book, how do I organize it??

"There are a lot of ways," I say. And I start to tell her several of them as Tom drives us towards the glistening towers of Dallas.

If you liked *18 Miles From Town*, you might also enjoy reading the following titles available on Amazon from Castle Bridge Media:

Austinites *By In Churl Yo*

Bloodsucker City *By Jim Towns*

THE CASTLE OF HORROR ANTHOLOGY SERIES
Castle Of Horror Anthology Volume 1
Castle of Horror Anthology Volume 2: Holiday Horrors
Castle of Horror Anthology Volume 3: Scary Summer Stories
Castle of Horror Anthology Volume 4: Women Running From Houses
Castle of Horror Anthology Volume 5: Thinly Veiled: The 70s
Castle of Horror Anthology Volume 6: Femme Fatales
Edited By Jason Henderson (Vol. 6 Edited by P.J. Hoover)

Castle of Horror Podcast Book of Great Horror:
Our Favorites, Top Tens, and Bizarre Pleasures
Edited By Jason Henderson

FuturePast Sci-Fi Anthology
Edited by In Churl Yo

Isonation *By In Churl Yo*

THE PATH
Book 1: The Blue-Spangled Blue *By David Bowles*
Book 2: The Deepest Green *By David Bowles*

Surf Mystic: Night of the Book Man *By Peyton Douglas*

Nightwalkers: Gothic Horror Movies *By Bruce Lanier Wright*

Please remember to leave us your reviews on Amazon and Goodreads!

CASTLE BRIDGE MEDIA
DENVER, COLORADO, USA

THANK YOU FOR SUPPORTING INDEPENDENT PUBLISHERS AND AUTHORS!

castlebridgemedia.com

Made in the USA
Columbia, SC
08 December 2021

50722239R00117